Demon's Fire

Lee Cockburn

Clink
Street

London | New York

Published by Clink Street Publishing 2019

ISBN:
978-1-913136-69-7 - paperback
978-1-913136-70-3 - ebook

Chapter 1
Revenge

Wisps of deadly smoke swept silently under the door, through the tiny cracks, some so small it seemed impossible, but the ever-creeping death would not be stopped. The cruel acrid heated gases moved silently through the night, hunting, searching, stalking its prey, getting hotter and hotter. He went around locking all the exit doors, sealing the building squirting accelerant as he went; he made sure the fire would take hold quickly and effectively, closing off every entrance, delaying the fire service from stopping the blaze. His eyes narrowed, his face twisted and contorted with the most hideous, sinister smirk as he moved silently in the night, fully aware of what he was doing and the damage he would cause. He believed there would be millions of pounds worth of drugs within, owned by Burnett. His mind soured by revenge, blinded by sadness and fuelled by his inner rage, his motivation was to light up this building and if Burnett's men were inside, then so be it.

Sorina Costea, a Romanian national, tossed and turned in her makeshift camp bed, as she did every night, restless in her prison, her living hell that was now her pitiful life. Her body ached. She was sore in unimaginable places from the many men that had taken and abused her, both physically and sexually on a daily basis. All the women were taken to that special place every day, that horrible place, vile and depraved, to be sex slaves to men. None of the men were kind, most were brutal, forcing them to do what she believed to be unnatural things, sometimes with such force and masochistic pleasure, her mind became confused at how many men there had been. She and the others were forced to offer themselves to countless men over and over, day after day, on a relentless and cruel schedule.

Her guards would also rape her, along with the other more attractive women and teenage girls. The physical scars and pain she felt, were nothing compared to her heartache. It superseded everything, so much so it seemed to block out much of the physical pain. Ever since they had wrenched her little boy Nicu from her arms, some months before, she could no longer feel their intrusion into her body. He was five years old with dark hair and beautiful brown eyes, a picture of perfection and innocence. When they took him, their eyes were cold as ice, cruel, dark and unfeeling, as they told her that he would fetch a very high price from a certain type of buyer. Her eyes had never been dry since that day. Her heart and mind yearned for her treasured son, something that had brought her many beatings, as it was putting some of the punters off, although many others revelled in her tearful sadness, enjoying the extra emotion as they stole her physical attributes for their selfish pleasure.

Unaware that she was crying out loud, one of the other women turned and hissed at her to be quiet; she was in the camp bed next to Sorina, only two feet away, as were the numerous others that were crammed into the lower basement of the textile warehouse, innocuous in the centre of the Sighthill industrial estate in Edinburgh, an unseen prison for so many, hidden in plain sight, amid the well-used daily thoroughfare.

The stench in the room was overpowering for those who entered, so many people in such a confined space, two toilets and two sinks for them all to share, in a small room at the back of their prison. Those who had children when they arrived, no longer had them. Some were lied to as to where they had been taken, others were not so lucky, the harsh reality of the fate of their children was revealed to them with evil delight, their most precious gift either sold to rich families, or worse, paedophile rings. Some were used for begging and the rest for other cruel purposes.

"Sorry, I didn't realise," Sorina said sincerely, not wanting to disturb the others who were also totally exhausted. Most of them were either drugged or sedated to dampen down their spirit, lessening their will and ability to fight or escape.

Sighing, she laid her head back down on the stained pillow. Sorina was not sedated and was now fully alert. She had learnt the art of secreting pills in her mouth and spitting them out once her captor had gone, also injecting the needle right through her muscle, pushing it so far that it popped out of her skin at the other side, avoiding becoming addicted like the others, but she knew only too well that she still had to appear heavily under the influence, because if they caught her once, that would be it. They would do the injecting for her, forcefully, and they wouldn't be careful.

Her nose twitched as she caught the first worrying scent in the air. There was a slight hint of smoke in the room, just enough to be noticed over all of the other unpleasant odours. Her eyes opened wide into a panicked stare. Her heart started to race as she jumped up from her cot, blinking heavily in the dark to try and see. The room they were packed into was nearly pitch black, never lit fully, another unpleasant and spirit crushing measure, sensory deprivation.

Even though, she could barely see, her nose was not wrong. There was now a heavier and more obvious smell of smoke and it was getting worse. She began to feel panic. She already knew they were locked in, with heavy-duty doors, all kept locked morning, noon and night to prevent their escape.

Sorina's scream was loud and filled with terror. Some of the other women jumped up, those that were able, others barely moved, so drugged that their reactions were gone. Sorina ran around the room trying desperately to wake those still sleeping, not wanting any harm to come to those she now called her friends. Others who were not so selfless, chose to run straight for the only door, the one that they were shoved back through every day, after being prostituted for hours. The first of the women to the door tripped up slamming her face with force as she fell heavily against the solid steel. Those running blindly behind fell down awkwardly on top of her. She felt her breath being forced from her lungs, winding her and trapping her where she lay, unable to shout or draw breath. The weight of the others was oppressive and she was unable to move, unable to expand her chest and breathe in the vital air she now so desperately needed. Others continued to follow in the darkness, unsteady on their feet, desperately trying to reach the door in an attempt to escape. The door was locked tight, secured with a heavy-duty solid steel bar on both sides. More women also tripped, landing clumsily on top of the growing pile of bodies that struggled in front of them, hidden by the darkness, crushing those beneath and causing those that could breathe to scream out in panicked terror, their lungs now starting to burn, their breathing coming in desperate lung damaging gasps.

The two men who had been assigned to guard the women were both on fire where they sat, their flesh sizzling. Neither had moved. They sat motionless on the comfortable seats in the room nearest to the entrance of where the women were imprisoned. The face of the guard nearest to the seat of the fire had begun to melt, plasma weeping out of bubbling blisters, his skin shrinking as it burned. He did not move or cry out because the bullet to his head had killed him instantly, brain matter spraying out grotesquely on the wall behind him. Both had been assassinated where they sat, cold blooded murder. *No great loss,* the shooter thought. He imagined their roles in Burnett's business, overly enthusiastic   with the women Burnett supplied, rapists, brutal enforcers.   Any cruel role Burnett demanded, they would take on. For all he knew, they could have had a part in the murders that ruined his life.

The smoke was now pouring under the door and there was no way of getting to it to block the gap. The heat was intensifying. Sorina's eyes were wide open, bloodshot with the lack of air. She knew she would not survive much longer.

The woman, who had rushed to the door first, now realised her haste to escape without helping the others would be her demise, her cyanosed lips and nose signs that she was no longer getting oxygen. Her eyes gave their last terrified and desperate stare before they closed forever. There was now a ferocity in the heat and smoke building up near to the roof, curling, circling and searching the room to fill every space available, its intensity growing, relentless in its progress, thick and black as it curled round out of control and filled every pocket of air. The smoke danced merrily across the room twisting upwards like the crests of waves, then swirling downwards as there was nowhere else for it to go, every inch above full to capacity.

Sorina watched the others trying to flee like moths to a flame, their lemming-like behaviour, sad to see, but her voice was drowned out as she tried to warn them. Their bloodcurdling screams made her voice inaudible. She listened in horror at their futile attempts to escape. A couple of the girls had scrabbled over the women on the floor and were right up at the top of the pile of bodies next to the door, banging loudly, screaming for help, foolishly standing upright, heads high. Their lungs filled quickly with the noxious fumes, their bruised knuckles blistering from the heat of the metal door. Screams quickly fell silent. Those who managed to get up from the mass of bodies soon fell back down to the ground as they too were overcome by the smoke.

***

His gut twisted as he remembered hearing the sound of a faint tapping at the other side of the door as he ran from where he had shot the men. *Holy shit,* he thought as his mind raced. *There was someone trapped in there. I thought it was the lab!* He hoped it was people working for Burnett. The fire was now too intense and there was no way he could go back to check if anyone was inside.

***

9

Sorina held her top to her mouth, holding her breath as she ran blindly to the back of the room. She was now alone in the dark in the small toilet area. She knew there was a drain there, not very big, but she thought it might be big enough for her to squeeze into. Her petite frame, from her lack of appetite over the last weeks, might now serve her well. Using a stiletto heel she prised up the drain cover and yanked with all of her strength to pull it off, the smell from within putrid, but to stay where she was and not try to escape was certain death. Giving herself a shake, she prepared herself for the uncertainty she faced, terrified of dying as she was not ready to die. She squeezed her elbows in tight against her chest and wriggled into the drain, head first, her movements slow and snake-like as her limbs were rendered useless, pinned closely to her sides. She had to use her toes to slowly push herself though the tight and restricting gap, gravity helping her descent. She was barely able to breath in the tight space. She was terrified of what she was fleeing from, but the perilous predicament she was now presented with made her panic. She tried to gasp for air in fear and terror. Her lungs barely expanded. She was losing control. Claustrophobia gripped her with the hands of the Grim Reaper. She shut her eyes and felt her ribs being tightly crushed as she tried to move her arms just a little. She thought that her life would end right there. She was waiting for the inevitable when she started to slide slowly forwards, gravity taking control, her weight and position allowing the grotesque slime coating in the pipe to help her on her way. Her speed gathered and she was unable to control her descent until she landed heavily on her elbows and face on the concrete floor in the centre of the sewer below. She was submerged in a foot of stinking water. The disgusting stench was overwhelming and repellent but laced with the much-needed hint of life-giving air. This allowed her to finally take a deep breath, one that she had begun to believe she would never take again.

Another woman had followed Sorina into the toilet area and had watched as her feet disappeared into the tiny gap. The room was now filled with heavy thick acrid smoke, which was getting lower and lower. Claustrophobia made her hesitate before attempting to follow in Sorina's path. She wasn't large in any way, but she was slightly larger than Sorina around the hips, catastrophically so. Her head and shoulders managed to enter the drain. She shuffled forward like a caterpillar, until her hips stopped her progress. She could no longer move forward and was now unable to move backwards either. She was stuck, wedged in and unable to move either way. Another of the women now followed. She was gasping for air, coughing and choking on the smoke, her eyes and nose streaming, covered in black soot like deposits. She tripped on the legs protruding from the drain like fence posts. Seeing her chance to escape, she started to push the woman in the drain viciously downwards, then pulled at her even more violently upwards, in an attempt to get her out of the way, an overwhelming will to save herself taking over, crushing any other normal caring human emotion. She was so desperate that she would do anything to live, but all her cruel and violent effort was wasted. The smoke that filled the room was now heavy with intense heat and flammable gases, which ignited in a flashover with such ferocity that there wasn't an inch of the prison left unburned. The women, the mattresses, their few belongings, all went up in flames as the fire burned out of control devouring everything within. Those that were still alive ran around aimlessly like headless chickens, their bodies engulfed with flames, their skin melting as they moved freakishly around the room, screaming, tripping and falling with the vigour and force of the fire. They only ran a few agonising steps each before they fell, their nerves dead to any sensation. They would never move again as they joined those who had already fallen.

***

Dressed in black from head to toe, a balaclava covering his face, he made his way swiftly down towards the tram line that ran parallel with the industrial estate. Once into the Gyle area, he popped with ease a window of the first decent motor he came across, his skills honed from his youth. He also started the car with very little effort and drove at speed towards the bypass that surrounded Edinburgh, only removing his headwear once he was out of view of the prying CCTV cameras in the area. He drove to the place where he planned to dump the vehicle and find another. His veins coursed with adrenaline, visible in his neck. His head felt like it was going to explode, the realisation of what he had just done hitting home. He continued to wonder who could have been in the warehouse. He did not know how Nelson Burnett, head of the city's organised crime group, would respond, but he knew that this would certainly get his attention and that his own life was now in mortal danger. He would be hunted by many, and he would suffer badly if he was ever caught, but he smiled all the same.

Only now did he think of the scale of what he had done to get his revenge, the carnage and value of damage he had caused and what the fall out would be throughout the city. Others would try to move in on Burnett's turf and there would be much violence and death required to restore the equilibrium, but he couldn't allow this to deter him. The adrenaline subsided, and he thought back to the two men he had shot at the warehouse and where they had been sitting. *Why had the door been barricaded from the outside?* He thought it strange that the bar could be lifted easily, giving no security for what was kept inside. Anyone would be able to gain entry if required. His heart sank. He felt nauseous as he thought back to Nelson's other trade, brothels and prostitution. There was always a constant supply of girls. He shook his head and tried to convince himself that all that was inside that building was drugs, and that the tapping he had heard was that of a few more scumbags that had got what was coming to them, but still his heart felt heavy. Burnett never revealed where he kept his girls, and he certainly didn't trust them to live freely. *What if?* A tear appeared in the corner of his eye as he remembered his beautiful wife and unborn child and what had happened to them. He vomited uncontrollably, his heart sore at the thought that he might have inflicted the same terror on some other innocents.

***

Sorina knew she had to move quickly to avoid being injured if there was an explosion above her. The four-storey building could come down on top of her.

The warehouse was now fully ablaze, lighting up the sky with an orange glow as the sirens rang out in the night.

Chapter 2
Unexpected Guest

Hours earlier, Kay sat motionless as the doorbell rang. It was very late and she felt sick at the thought of someone visiting her at this late hour without prior warning. She hoped that if she just sat there they would give up and go away, but her skin felt like it had pins and needles all over it . The bell rang again, and then again a short while after, a little impatiently and with purpose. She got up slowly and moved to the curtains, fearful of who might be there, the demons within making her skin crawl. Images of John Brennan's evil face flashed vividly in her mind, imagining that he was still alive and coming to get her.

"Shit, I thought I was over this. I'm better now. Just take a bloody look out of the window, woman!" she said aloud, trying to convince herself everything would be alright as she forced herself to pluck up the courage to actually look.

Eventually she peered out, her presence still hidden from the caller, although the lights in the living room were visible from outside, which the person standing there would have noticed. Kay sighed with relief as she looked at the slight figure that stood on the doorstep, recognising it straight away. Although relieved that there was no physical threat, she was still apprehensive about the reason for her caller's late visit. The visitor looked up at the window as Kay was still looking out, making her physically jump backwards, thinking that she had been seen watching. Her heart was still hammering inside her ribcage, but she moved towards the door and after a slight pause and a chance to gather herself, she opened it wide. They both stood there just looking at one another, neither speaking at first.

"Fran, come in! Are you alright?" Kay finally said in a semi-friendly voice, a little bewildered at the visit and a little angry too at how she had been made to feel.

Kay liked Fran. She was funny, kind, a hard-working detective and a valued member of the team in the Major Investigation Unit at Fettes, where they both worked, Kay as a civilian member of staff. Unfortunately, Fran was beautiful too and the last time Kay had seen her, she was up close and personal with Taylor and it was clear Taylor liked her too, probably a little too much.

"Thanks, Kay. I'm really sorry that it's so late, and I'm sorry if I scared you," Fran said with remorseful eyes. "I needed to speak to you, to explain things. I haven't been able to sleep at all since you came back to the office,"

"What do you mean? What do you need to say, Fran, that's so important to have to say it now? Could it not have waited till morning?" Kay was feeling a little sick at what she knew already.

Fran looked up at her from the couch, her eyes honest and genuinely sad, Kay sitting opposite her, looking straight at her with expectant eyes.

"I'm really sorry, Kay. I never meant to hurt you."

"Sorry for what, Fran? What have you got to be sorry about?" Kay said, opening the way to let Fran feel like she could speak truthfully without consequence.

"I know you saw us, Taylor and I, the other day in the office. I know you did. I saw your reaction, I watched your face. I would have reacted too had the roles been reversed and I now know how you feel."

"Saw what?" Kay lied, wanting her to continue.

"Come on, Kay! You saw that there were feelings there between us, subtle, but I know you saw it. Taylor saw you too and she changed towards me instantly. I love her Kay. I know

16

you don't want to hear that, but I do and I know you love her too. We've been together since a short while after you let her go. I'm sorry, I really am. She's lovely, lovely in many ways, intoxicating, addictive. You'll understand that. She makes me feel alive, alive in ways you probably know too well. She's got something that makes you go a little crazy and also feel a little vulnerable because of the way she is."

Kay looked straight at her. "Why are you here though? You don't need to explain anything to me. I let her go; she is a free agent, free to move on. You've got nothing to feel guilty about. I regret letting her go, I will admit that now, but I was damaged beyond repair back then, or so I thought, but here I am and I'm doing alright now, I think." She smiled sadly.

"I'm here, because she loves you. You, Kay! Not me, although I do think she has feelings for me too, but since she saw you the other day, she's barely noticed me. Her mind is somewhere else, and I assume it's with you Kay."

"That's not all though, is it Fran? What else are you here to tell me? What's really wrong?"

Fran sat silently for a moment, then looked into Kay's trusting eyes. They stared at her a little puzzled.

"What Fran? It can't be that bad, can it?" Kay's stomach was now twisting in knots and she felt sick.

"Before that night Kay, the night that Brennan did what he did to all of us... I'm really sorry, I was selfish and I wanted her, I'd had a bit to drink and ever since that night..."

"What night would that be?" Kay said sitting forward, her eyes demanding the truth.

"The night that I seduced Taylor, in the hotel," Fran said, her head lowered, eyes to the floor.

Kay sat there, her eyes watering. The words she heard had numbed her heart and cut her a little, but they did not surprise her as she thought back to the days when the team were away hunting for the serial killer Brennan. Taylor hadn't been in touch for a couple of days and Kay had felt it then and now remembered it vividly, the obvious lack of contact.

"I just came to say sorry. I'm so sorry Kay, I was selfish. I felt sick when I heard how badly injured you were, knowing what I'd done."

"And now, your guilt hasn't stopped you now though has it?" Kay said with a little venom in her words, her hurt escaping.

"Kay, you broke her heart. She was lost without you. Taylor is Taylor, I gave her very little option to refuse that night, but she didn't invite me in after our encounter. When you left and ended it with her, she didn't come to me straight away, but when she did, I was selfishly glad, glad because of how she makes me feel."

Fran apologised again, a weight off her shoulders. She got up to leave. Kay stood up too and walked over to her, opening her arms, a forgiving offer of a hug. Fran started to cry, her head awash with mixed emotions, guilt, sadness, terror from the night that they had all been brutally assaulted and sexually violated by John Brennan, and deep loss, because she knew that Taylor's heart lay with Kay and, now that Kay was back, she had lost Taylor for good.

Fran moved towards Kay and accepted her genuine embrace. They cried together. There was so much emotion to let go of, they needed to let out their suppressed feelings and sadness. Then they started to laugh at each other, at the state they were in, and moved away from each other, feeling a little awkward.

"Thank you, Kay. I mean it, I really am sorry. I just thought she was really nice, I didn't actually think it would happen. Circumstance, opportunity, heightened emotion, stress, and pure lust - a million excuses, none of them justified enough to hurt you like that though."

Fran kissed Kay on the cheek with genuine affection. They had a bond, they all did, including Taylor.

"Sorry for giving you a fright and for keeping you up so late, sorry for everything. I'll see you at work next week then. You've been missed, Kay, I mean that," she said with her familiar kind smile.

Chapter 3
Gruesome Discovery

The fire service roared up the deserted street that lead towards the textiles warehouse, the smoke thick and menacing. The flames were now rising up to the third floor, licking the sides and crawling up the walls like ivy hugging close. They curled over the edge of the roof, their orange glow now lighting up the night. Smoke billowed high into the night in plumes of black, rising like a volcanic ash cloud high into the sky. Police officers from Wester Hailes and Corstorphine stations were now in attendance, setting up cordons at what they thought was a safe distance, checking other businesses for security workers or night shift crews, in an attempt to evacuate them in case there were any explosions to come. Their radios shone like fireflies in the night and the airwaves were alight with frenzied radio chatter.

The fire officers were kitting up with breathing apparatus, as the watch manager shouted to the crew manager, "Are there any confirmed persons within? I'm not sending my troops in there if there's no confirmation of life in danger! Speak to the cops, find out who owns this unit, who the key holder is. Is there security 24/7? We need to know who could have been in there, not that I think anyone would survive this anyway. Who is the police incident officer for the cops? We need to get our heads together on this one."

Officers called up to the area control room, but there were no numbers stored on the database. There was not much information on the warehouse at all. Even the local officers didn't know anything about the building. They'd never been to any calls there. It just seemed to tick along under the radar, nobody realising that that was the plan.

The first two firefighters, wearing the full breathing apparatus and heat resistant suits, moved into position, heaving their hose and reels closer towards the building. As they approached with relative caution, there was an almighty explosion above them. It came from inside the third floor and shattered all of the windows, glass spraying violently towards the firefighters, their helmets and visors taking the brunt of the flying glass fragments.

"Withdraw, pull back, get under cover! I thought the bloody gas supply was isolated. Is it?" The watch manager yelled at the officer responsible for the task.

"Yes, ma'am. I made sure it was and I double-checked it. There must have been something else in there. It definitely wasn't the gas that caused that. What's bloody stored in this building?"

Some of the unprotected officers within the cordons started to feel unwell from the fumes coming from the building after the explosion. They were noxious and filled with strong smelling, damaging chemicals.

"We need a CBRN (chemical, biological, radiological and nuclear) team down here, a full specialist HAZMAT (hazardous materials) fire crew, with the SORT (specialist, operations response team) Paramedics as well! Get some ambulances down here too, and decontamination tents, please, asap. We'll need CID and the Major Investigation Team too. There's more to this than we thought. More response officers are needed. Check city wide, and let's get this cordon another 200 metres back. It's too dangerous here!" The officer on scene reeled off instructions into her radio, already knowing that something big was happening.

New crews were arriving from Crewe Road, Meadowbank and Tollcross stations, as the Sighthill crew, who were first on the scene, were already committed and having little effect on the blaze. Even with fire officers up on the high ladder with high velocity hoses, their efforts barely changing anything as the fire had intensified after the explosion.

The cops on the cordon moved back further. Those affected by the fumes were on their way to be checked out by the arriving ambulances. One said, "Can you smell that?"

"Smell what, the chemicals?" his colleague replied.

"No, the other smell. The one like barbecued pork, the putrid unforgettable smell of burnt flesh, that one."

"Your fucking kidding me! I can't smell anything. I think my nostrils have been melted."

"I can smell it, no doubt about it. I'll let the firies know. They've all got masks on, but I think there were people in that building - whether any are still alive is another thing."

The watch commander received the message regarding the smell coming from the warehouse and, with the new information at hand, reassessed her action plan. The danger to her officers was still too high, considering the ferocity of the fire, and it was highly unlikely that anyone inside would not have perished. There was no way anyone could survive the fumes and heat and she had to take cognisance of that.

She put her radio to her now curled up lips and sighed heavily as she relayed her message, "We need more sets here, now! We believe there might be persons trapped within the building. We need as many units as we can get here. This fire is completely out of control!"

The reply came quickly, "They're already coming from all over the city, ETA two minutes."

Taylor's radio shone into action back at MIT at Fettes. The inferno was now looking more like a criminal act than a spontaneous fire.

"Marcus, are you good to go? Get a couple of the others too, I think we'll need as many as we can get down there. Where's Fran? I've not seen her for ages."

"She nipped out boss. I said I'd cover her for a bit. Sorry, Taylor, it was dead in here. She said she had to sort something out. Will I call her?"

"Yes, bloody call her! Tell her to go straight to the scene and wait at the RVP," Taylor said with anger in her tone, although neither Fran nor Marcus could have known that this would happen.

Just as Taylor swung on her coat, Fran slipped into the office, her phone ringing in her hand.

"I'm here, sorry. I didn't mean to take so long. What's happening, where are we heading to?"

"Next time you are out of the bloody office, I need to know where you are and why. I'm responsible for your welfare as long as you're on the work's clock. Get your stuff together, we'll see you in the carpark in five." Taylor's tone was commanding and clearly filled with annoyance.

Taylor Nicks, the Sergeant in the Major Investigation team, was up to ninety. She had been for the last week or so, ever since she found out that Kay had returned to the office. She had been distant to everyone, making minimal conversation, barely functioning and only when necessary. Taylor seemed to be somewhere else all the time. However, the minute she had asserted her authority over her colleague and lover Fran, she regretted it, her tone and animosity completely unnecessary and misplaced. She wanted to blame Fran for everything, everything that had gone wrong with her and Kay but, deep down, she knew it was her own fault and hers alone.

Marcus's big expressive eyes bored into her, taken aback at the way she had spoken to Fran, which he thought was totally out of order.

She looked back at him defensively, "What? I need to know what's going on, a little courtesy at least."

"It's not the subject boss, it's the way you spoke to her. Was there any need for that?"

"Don't, Marcus, I don't need this shit right now." She sighed heavily as she spoke with sadness in her eyes, her heart torn between two lovers. She felt she had to try and distance herself from Fran because her emotions were all over the place, and she didn't know what to do.

Fran felt physically sick. Tears ran down her face when she thought of how much her life had changed in only a week.

Taylor's heart had been ripped away from her at just the sight of Kay, Kay still that majestic figure. Everything about her was beautiful. She was smart, intelligent and clearly still in love with Taylor. Fran's heart was heavy following her meeting with Kay, one that could only lead to more heartache between her and Taylor. She realised Taylor would be angry but didn't know what consequence and damage she may have caused by easing her own conscience. How would it affect Taylor's chances with Kay, which she honestly had not meant to jeopardise?

The three police officers suffering breathing difficulties were now on their way to the Royal Infirmary, where staff had already set up a quarantine room with no vents to avoid any possible CBRN related contamination, a multitude of pollutants from the drug lab sealed in safely in the adapted treatment room.

Multiple fire crews were now at the scene. Gallons of water per second were being pumped under high pressure directly at the fire. Progress was very slow, but at least their efforts were now making a difference. It had been at least fifteen minutes since the last explosion, which was good news.

***

Sorina noticed the increase in water coming from the drain, fifty metres from where she was now sitting, having dropped down from it just half an hour ago. She started to feel unwell as she had struck her head hard on the concrete when she landed. She had also inhaled a lot of smoke and now there were new noxious smells coming up from the water. Her head flopped forward, striking the ground heavily once again, her cheek splashing in the water. Her eyes rolled back in her head as she finally lost consciousness.

***

As Taylor and the others arrived on scene, all of them looked out at the sight before them. It was total mayhem, the rendezvous point stretching back hundreds of metres, the response vehicles parked nose to tail on every section of spare road. Marcus had to drive a fair way past to park their car. All four of the Major Investigation Team stared at the carnage before their eyes.

They walked quickly to the outer cordon, only to be told they couldn't go any further by the probationary constable on point. Initially miffed at this Taylor was about to argue her case until the young cop explained, almost verbatim, the dangers pointed out to him by the fire service, and the absolute order that nobody was to get through, unless they were wearing full protective equipment. Taylor, smiled at this. He was right and she would just have to wait. She trudged back to the car and put the heating back on.

***

Nelson Burnett picked up his phone and read the text, "You fuck with me, then I'll fuck with you, this is just the start, oh and sorry for your loss."

***

Craig McNare's fingers were trembling when he typed, the stench of accelerant emanating up from his clothing. He swigged heavily on a bottle of vodka, a sinister look etched on his face, tinged with sadness as his mind floated back to her unanswered screams.

***

Burnett ground his teeth together, making a grotesque noise. He hated anyone that got in his way. He didn't know who had sent the message, which added to his rage. What did it even mean? News of the fire hadn't reached him yet. He threw the phone against the wall, smashing it into pieces, already thinking of what he would do to the person that had sent the text.

***

Morning came, gently lighting up the sky. Taylor was still sitting sulking in the front of the car, Fran and another detective in the rear, Marcus dozing with his head against the window, drool dribbling from his mouth. The sight of him was enough to make Taylor smile, a first for the night, bursting out into an infectious chuckle. The others looked at Marcus too and they joined in, cameras capturing the moment to share at every opportunity with everyone, as often as possible. This was a welcome relief to the intense mood in the car, although everyone felt wrecked after spending the evening squashed in there.

Taylor got out of the car and stretched her long athletic frame, her blouse pulling tightly around her breasts, her jacket pulling tightly round her shoulders, straining at the seams, ironing out the crushed material after their less than five-star evening. Taylor could sense Fran watching her but did not look round. She wanted to but couldn't. She strode purposefully back up to the cordon where the cop on duty was nearly frozen to the spot. She remembered these days, shitty cordon details all night, freezing your tits off and bursting for a piss with no one coming to your rescue. She gave him a genuine smile and the young officer almost sprang to attention.

"How are things going? The fire looks like it's pretty much out now. Can you call your supervisor and see if I can speak to the watch commander. I think we need a multi-agency meeting or something, to see what's happening next."

"No problems, Sergeant. I'll see what the state of play is. I take it you will be waiting here."

"Yep, I will be," she said with a frustrated tone because she had already been put in her place about the importance of the cordons.

The watch commander came over, her face covered in sweat and black residue from a night in close proximity to a raging fire. She held out her hand to shake Taylor's and started to speak. She had a broad Borders accent, a weatherbeaten face and a very strong grip. Taylor visibly winced as her knuckles were crushed by the firm hand shake and she thought she saw a twinkle in the commander's face, fully aware of what she had just done to Taylor's hand. There had always been a little rivalry between the services, but it was all good-natured fun.

"That's the fire out, but it will still take a while to cool the embers down, enough to stop it reigniting anyway. We are venting it now and the HAZMAT team are in there, trying to ascertain what might have been in there and what caused the explosions."

"Has there been any confirmation of persons within. I got the update last night that somebody thought there might be?"

"Nothing obvious visually, but there's so much debris from the upper floors and, from the floor plans of the building, it appears that there might have been a basement, which hasn't been checked yet for obvious reasons. There's a definite whiff of something though, so we'll let you know."

"Can I bring my team closer and set up a forward command point closer to the scene? Will that be okay?"

"No!" the watch commander said abruptly in her gruffest voice as she watched Taylor's face crumple a little with disappointment.

A moment later a big smile came over the commander's face. "Just kidding, of course you can, but I'll show you where is safe, alright!" she said with a beaming jovial face. She loved a practical joke now and again. It always seemed to lighten up the darkest moments, and she knew this incident still had something more sinister to reveal.

Taylor couldn't help but smile back. She thought the commander was serious and had been about to have a word with her. Instantly, there was an acceptance of one another and a mutual respect for the roles that each of them performed.

Taylor said in a more serious tone, "We'll have to take primacy of the scene now though, because it's quite clear that some sort of crime has taken place here. It's just the seriousness of it that has yet to be revealed."

"No problem. I'll let you know when it's safe to enter. You can bring your lot right up to where our appliances are. The troops know the score, but there will have been a lot of evidence already destroyed."

"Thanks, I'll go and get the others up here." Taylor smiled as she went.

The commander contacted the firefighters and asked about their progress. Their reply was promising and they told her they had cleared a pathway to a set of stairs leading down from the ground floor to what they believed to be the entrance to the basement.

"Let me know what you find down there, everything, even things that you don't think are significant. I mean it, nothing you think that is of interest will be a problem. Understood?"

"Understood ma'am, every minute detail."

They moved steadily down the stairs leading to the basement. All wore breathing apparatus, just in case pockets of gas and noxious fumes were present, which could be deadly if inhaled.

The lead officer stopped and looked down at a charred corpse next to the burnt-out frame of a chair. The body was gnarled and curled into a grotesque and unnatural position, some limbs fractured with the heat of the fire, muscles pulled tight and dried out clinging to the skeleton, the sex unidentifiable, although by looking at what was left of it, the size of the skeletal frame, it was most likely that of a male. Another corpse lay in a similar state and position on the couch frame next to it.

They went past the burnt bodies, being careful not to disrupt too much, one of the officers mentioning the very static seated position that one of the corpses was still in, showing no signs of attempting to escape the fire. The officer peered through his visor and noticed that it looked like there was a hole in the front of the skull, and on looking at the back saw a bigger jagged hole. The same injuries were mirrored on the other body.

The radio crackled loudly and the watch commander pressed the talk button. "Go ahead."

"We've got two bodies here, charred remains, unrecognisable, still firmly seated at the outside of the door to the basement and, from just looking with the naked eye, they have small holes in the front of their heads, and their skulls are blown off at the rear. I think they are gunshot wounds, boss!"

"Received! I'll let the detectives know. Is it safe to continue?" the commander asked.

"Yes, yes, safe to continue, but we have a pretty solid door here. It has been badly charred, but still looks like it will take some heavy-duty equipment to force open. It's melted shut! There's also a heavy-duty metal bar keeping the door shut from this side, someone didn't want something to get out of that room."

"If you have the Mode of Entry kit with you, please proceed with caution, and thanks for the update, maybe see if there are welders available too?"

"Yes ma'am, copy that. We have the bosh and the hydraulic ram with us. That might not do it. I'll keep you updated."

The sound was deafening as the twenty-six kilogram bosh came crashing against the door, over and over, with the muscular firefighter putting all his weight into it, the hydraulic ram also pushing at full capacity against the door and frame. There was so much combined pressure applied to the door with the equipment that this caused the frame and brickwork surrounding it to crumble away, causing the door to give, but it only just leant inwards a little. It didn't fall down fully, suspended in mid fall, as there was an obstacle on the other side. The front two firefighters heaved the industrial strength door back towards them. It weighed an absolute ton and, as they did so, it revealed a horrific scene, beyond anything any of them had ever seen before, and they'd seen a lot. A mound of badly charred and contorted bodies confronted them, their mouths agape in terror from the agonising deaths they must have suffered. The bodies were grotesque in their positioning, eyes and facial features melted away with the intense heat they had endured. Their very own body fat would have fuelled the fire for hours as they physically melted away, hours after the furnishings of the room had already burnt out and extinguished. The lifeless corpses stared up at the firefighters, their eye sockets giving the impression of a wide-eyed stare of desperation, an expression of unbridled horror, burnt with such ferocity that it captured the atrocity, the terror and agony suffered by each one, their struggle to survive futile.

The first officer looked at the corpses with sadness as he started to try and count the bodies he could see and decipher individually. He looked further into the room and saw all the mangled bed frames, spanning the length of the room, twisted by the intensity of the fire. They stretched along the basement, packed in tight in the dark and suffocating prison. The firefighters had to squeeze past the piled up corpses, trying not to stand on them as they entered the room to search for more. It didn't take long to find another, then another, contorted and twisted, along with the bed frames they were now encased in, showing that some hadn't even tried to escape, or couldn't.

Finally, they reached the end of the long dormitory, where there was a small room. The first officer rolled his eyes back in his head at another vile and distressing scene, the tiny room revealing another story of a desperate effort to live. The next firefighter in, Lana, stood still and just stared. She had hoped that there wouldn't be any more bodies, but there before them were another three and a half, half because one corpse had only their legs and part of their hips visible. The legs were protruding like a charred tree standing straight up from the drain and three more people appeared to be clutching her legs. The sight was hideous, even for the long serving officers. This was a site of mass devastation and sadness, a picture of depraved cruelty, and mass murder if the fire had been started deliberately, and all of the signs they had seen so far were pointing to foul play.

Taylor let the radio drop down from her mouth as she turned to the others, her eyes wide and her face revealing that the news received was not good.

"Multiple bodies have been found down in the basement. All appear to have been imprisoned there, and there are two bodies at the door, probably guards. It looks like they have had bullets put through their skulls!"

Fran and Marcus looked stunned. Edinburgh had gone off the rails in the last year but this was pure madness. Mass murder was a step into another league.

So many things had happened of late, multiple murders, so much misery caused, injured colleagues, lost love, all revolving around the many tragedies the team had to investigate, their own lives having to go on with the pain and adversity surrounding them all.

Chapter 4
New Beginning

Michelle Smith looked into her mirror. She had only been home from her shift at the Public Protection Unit for an hour. It had been a long day, with much more to come. She would be very much involved in the enquiry into the deaths of the women at the warehouse. It was assumed they had been trafficked into the country. She gave a heavy sigh, for the sadness she felt for the women, but she had to pick herself up and try and forget work and enjoy her own life.

She started getting ready for her date, the first date with Pete Ewar from the Roads Policing Unit. They had only known each other a couple of months since his near-fatal road collision when their paths had first crossed. It was life or death for Pete at the time, as he had suffered major injuries, a cracked skull, his pelvis broken in two places and all three bones in his right leg fractured. He had also suffered numerous facial lacerations, internal injuries and various other wounds all over his body. Michelle and her work partner were one of the first sets to assist on that day, the day of that fateful pursuit. The scene she had come across still haunted her on a daily basis. She saw that the roads policing vehicle had been rammed on the driver's side, Pete's side. The other vehicle had obviously been travelling at speed when it struck the traffic car, so when she got there all she saw was his piercing blue eyes, Pete's eyes staring through curtains of streaming blood. He looked straight into hers, pleading for her so save him. He was barely able to lift his broken arm in an attempt to get her to come to him, but she was already there, on her knees, her scarf off and being used to stop the blood pulsing out from the deep gash in his head, her soft words of comfort flowing naturally from her lips as she looked down at her injured colleague, wondering if it was possible for him to survive this. She had held his hand and stayed with him as the fire service cut him free from the vehicle. The paramedics had worked tirelessly to stabilise him at the scene. Time had seemed to stand still as his life hung in the balance. Pete had gripped her hand as if his life depended on it, the grip weakening as his life faded.

She finished off with her make-up, her blue eyes gleaming with the enhanced effect the make-up gave them. Her lips glistened as she gave her last pout in the mirror, her brown shoulder length hair straightened to perfection. She was finally ready. Her heart fluttered with excited anticipation.

Pete also looked at himself in the mirror, a look he had once thought he would never be able to take again. He had trimmed his stubble perfectly and put on his favourite scent, Acqua Di Gio. His hair was neat and the product held it perfectly in place. His shirt was fitted, black and tight in the right places. Black skinny jeans hugged his trim legs, and his shoes were immaculate as if he was going on parade, a habit he had maintained since his days at police college. He was really nervous. He almost felt like his jeans were holding him together. Pins and plates in his legs kept his bones in place, although months of rehabilitation had enhanced his muscle tone again. He wondered if he could still manage to function as a man and this really worried him. His pelvis had been very badly damaged. His heart was pounding at the thought of failure or something going wrong. He had been staying with his parents since the accident as he needed them to help look after him. Michelle had been coming in to see him daily and offer support where needed, keeping his spirits up with her positive attitude and her lust for life. They had grown close to one another, nothing sexual for obvious reasons, not that both of them hadn't thought about it and they joked about how great they would both be.

Pete arrived promptly at Michelle's gate, his heart fluttering, but there was also fear. He had a bouquet of hand-selected flowers in one hand and a bottle of fine wine in the other, trembling as he gripped them. He reached up and rang the doorbell and waited patiently for Michelle to come to the door, time standing still as he waited but, when the door opened, the wait was worth it. Michelle looked stunning. Her dress was fitted and pleasantly revealing, classy and figure-hugging where it would be gazed upon with desire, and that he certainly did. His eyes were transfixed on her. She was beautiful, stunning in fact, something she had hidden well with the jeans and jumpers that she always wore when she came to see him. Michelle would have been happy to take things further before this, but Pete being a proud guy wanted to wait, needed to wait until his injuries had healed a little more so that he could be confident his body was working properly once again. He didn't want to let her down and feel like a failure. Michelle looked at him. He too looked immaculate, his regained strength more apparent in what he wore, and he was very handsome.

She invited him in, noticing that he winced as he lifted his leg up to climb the stairs. He saw her expression change, her eyes fixed on him, worry etched on her face. She motioned towards him to offer her arm to help him, but he gestured he was okay. Michelle cared for him a lot and did not want him to feel that she felt sorry for him. All she wanted to do was let him know that she was there for him.

He straightened up and went inside, following her through to the kitchen. He wanted her, he wanted her so much. The months of waiting had created a desire that the next short while would feel like an age. His desire was barely containable, but he had waited this long.

Michelle turned with a glass of bubbly for each of them and handed it to him. She let him take one drink before she kissed him, full on the lips. Her kisses were filled with pent-up uncontrollable desire. Unlike Pete, she was not prepared to wait and had no intention of making polite small talk. They had talked enough and waited so long, that's all they had done since the day they had met. Pete responded with more open-mouthed kisses, tongues joined in a lust filled dance, both moving in perfect harmony. Her hands searched his body, touching, feeling, stroking him all over. She wanted him to make love to her. His hand wrapped around her. She felt his desire as she pulled up close to him. He started to unbutton her beautiful dress to take it off, which he thought was a pity because she looked great in it. He kissed her shoulders as he pulled the dress gently down, his thumb pulling at her bra, exposing her breast. His mouth engulfed her, her nipples both taut and excited at his touch and the firm pull from his mouth. His other hand had slipped up her dress and was gently stroking over her underwear, his fingers gently pushing under the silky material, instantly causing Michelle to moan as his fingers brushed against her, her clitoris standing up to meet his touch. He pushed gently and firmly into her, causing her to draw a breath in sharply as she pushed back needily towards his fingers, wanting them inside her, wanting him to push them deep up into her, and her wish was his command as his fingers slipped inside her. She gripped his head tightly as her tongue devoured his and their kisses were set alight. His skilled hands brought her to a thundering climax. She moaned with desire as he continued to stroke her. She grappled at his jeans, wanting him inside her. She knew he was avoiding it. He swallowed hard and stopped what he was doing to lift her onto the counter. She helped him get out of his jeans, her eyes meeting his, giving him that look, the one he knew so well, the one she had given him through his time in rehab, the one that meant that she knew he would be able to do it. They smiled at each other as he entered her. This time it wasn't his fingers. His pleasure pulsed through his veins as he made love to her, his pent-up tension and apprehension of failure now gone. His body was clearly working. She gripped his shoulders, then tightly onto his taut buttocks, as he rocked her whole body with his feverish lovemaking. His release was with an extreme rush of euphoric pleasure, his orgasm twisting deep inside him. Michelle too was close to coming again and he saw that. He smiled at her as he dropped to his knees to pleasure her with his mouth. She gripped his hair making sure he didn't stop, his fingers again pushing deep inside her, as his tongue swirled over her, taking her to another long-awaited pulsating orgasm, both of them savouring the pleasure of one another. He stood up and leant against her naked body. She held him as they kissed each other deeply. Pete looked into her eyes and said, "Thank you, thank you for everything you've done for me. I truly believe that without you I wouldn't be here today." He hesitated. Then said, "I love you, I have done for quite a while now, but I didn't want to hold you back if I couldn't recover." His eyes were filled with genuine emotion and gratitude for the loyalty she had shown over the past months.

Michelle looked at him. "After that, I think we've saved each other," she said. "And I'll certainly be having more of that. I love you too. I don't think I could be without you now, I wouldn't want to be." Her smile lit up the room, beaming from ear to ear.

She turned round on the shiny kitchen counter, her lithe torso twisting round to pick up his glass. His eyes followed her. He looked at her breasts with pleasure as she turned round, his hand instinctively reaching up to touch them and she smiled as she handed him his champagne, liking his continued desire to caress her. One hand gently cupped her breast and the other a glass of champagne and this time she allowed him to finish his drink, pouring him another glass without interruption. He sipped his drink between kisses and sensual touches. Then he lifted her gently down from the counter. The night was young and they had a lot of catching up to do.

Chapter 5
Head Count

The body count was finalised at twenty-five. The pathologist had been there throughout the whole arduous task of separating the grotesque mass of entangled bodies. The MIT, CID, SEB and the mortuary assistants had all worked tirelessly over several days, taking meticulous care to avoid interfering or obliterating any vital evidence that hadn't been destroyed in the fire. Unfortunately, the transference of burnt and conjoined skin between the twisted and charred corpses was unavoidable, which would cause further issues when they attempted to take DNA and seek the identity of all that had perished within their prison. Taylor surveyed the scene. The claustrophobic room looked like a picture of one of the death chambers from the Holocaust, charred and melted paintwork coating every wall, the tangled mass of metal, melted beyond recognition. The foul stench of burnt flesh and death hung heavily in the air. She looked round for anything that might have been missed. She shivered as she felt the air thick with their fear and the terror they must have gone through, trapped in there while their lungs burned as their futile attempts to escape were halted and they took their last agonising breaths. Taylor shook her head to clear the ugly thoughts. Her mind was already heading down the route of human trafficking. The first corpses had all been identified as female. This must have been their prison, herded in there in the evenings after being forced to work for hours during the day, she surmised. She looked at the twisted metal of the bed frames again, and this time she started to count, twenty-three, twenty-four, twenty-five, twenty-six? Twenty-six beds, twenty-five bodies!

Her mind started racing through the possibilities. She thought to herself for a while as her hand gently rubbed her chin, which she found helped her thought process. *Why the extra bed? I'm sure whoever was running the show would make sure things ran to capacity, greed the main factor. Maybe the extra one was still out; maybe she had died and hadn't been replaced, because death was part and parcel with these women, either suicide to escape the rape and torture or death through an accidental overdose, an escape from their enforced slavery. All worked until their broken bodies ached from the cruel and brutal treatment they received, the perverted violation from some of the punters that they were forced to entertain.* She looked round the room again. *There's no way anyone could have escaped this horrific nightmare, is there?*

The MIT team were back at their cars. They were devouring their lunch, the stench of the charred bodies and the vile sights they had just seen unable to deter them in any way from their ravenous appetites. They were all hardened to the sights and smells they were made to endure on a regular basis, all of them exhausted from the last two days. The search records and crime scene notes were filled with their findings, accuracy a necessity, itemised evidence, drawings, plotted markers of the relevant finds and the photographs of the bodies in situ, their positions when found, samples taken from everywhere and each of the bodies still had to be examined and processed. There was a profound sadness for all involved here. No matter how long they had served, none had witnessed death on this scale before. The loss of life in this manner and the scale of this tragedy took the incident to another level. The fear and suffering of the women trapped here was unimaginable. A quick death must have been a godsend for those who succumbed to the fumes in their cots where they lay, fortunate enough to be oblivious to what was happening to the others, their screams, sheer terror, their helpless plight. Chatter between the team was not at the usual feverish humour-filled pitch. It was subdued with their thoughts of the victims' final torment before death, all they had witnessed in there, the women's mummified facial expressions set on their statuesque faces for eternity.

Taylor eventually emerged from the fire-damaged building, just as one of the firefighters had returned as they too still had samples and investigations to carry out at the scene to prove whether the fire had been set deliberately and where and how it had been done. The firefighter wasn't part of the investigatory team, but she was there to assist in their enquiries. She had been present when they fought the fire that night, and she had been one of the first officers into the room. She was a well-built, toned and muscular woman, but had femininely handsome and attractive features, which Taylor couldn't help but notice. They exchanged pleasant greetings and were passing each other when Taylor recognised her as one of the firefighters from the other night.

"Excuse me. Hi, you were there the other night, weren't you? I'm sure I saw you the night of the fire?" Taylor said.

Lana turned around, and smiled. "Yep, I was there. What a night that was, eh? Very sad, worst I've ever seen, and I've seen quite a bit."

"I'm DS Taylor Nicks from the Major Investigation Team," Taylor said as she politely stretched out her hand and introduced herself.

"Hi, Lana Masters, just a plain old firefighter." Lana shook Taylor's hand with a big infectious smile across her face.

"Never just anything," Taylor replied, smiling back, Lana's smile already catching on.

"Did you see everything in the basement that night, Firefighter Lana Masters?" Taylor asked with a sarcastic tone.

Both laughed, which was a tonic, considering what they were dealing with.

"No, really, was there anything that stood out to you? Anything we are missing? Because I counted the beds today and there were twenty-six and the final body count was twenty-five. I'd hate to think we've missed something, or someone. Is there a chance someone could have gotten out?" Taylor now asked in a more serious tone.

"Well, there were only two sites where bodies were found as you will know. The door was secured to an industrial level, heavy-duty, no escape there. All the bodies were either piled at the door, in their beds or at the drain in the toilet area, but the drain was tiny, really tiny, and there was a pretty small woman jammed in it, blocking it when we got there, with others round about her," Lana said sadly as she recalled the horrifying scene when they entered the prison cell for the first time, a sight she would never forget.

Taylor decided to take another look and asked the Scenes of Crime troops to come with her to measure the drain just to see the exact dimensions of it and if there could be any chance a very small person could get through it.

Lana went with them out of curiosity to see the drain without the corpses piled hideously up on top of it.

When they measured it, the space seemed tiny and it seemed highly unlikely that someone could have a frame small enough to fit through it, but on examining the drain properly, Taylor thought that it wasn't impossible and a sinking feeling came over her.

Taylor got on the radio immediately to contact the local council, the water board and those that dealt with the city's sewers. Her stomach twisted in discomfort, tinged with a little fear that it had taken her this long to notice that there was a possibility that someone may have gotten out of there and could be trapped somewhere, injured or even worse, dead. *Fuck, fuck, fuuuuccckkk!* Her mind swirled with what ifs and thoughts of the poor soul that could be dying somewhere.

Fran watched as Taylor came striding out of the building deep in thought. Lana and the SEB crew were chatting quite the thing, but Taylor was looking a little disturbed, her mind clearly focussed and she looked really tense.

Fran walked towards her and asked if she was okay. Taylor spoke quietly, "The bloody drain in there might be fucking big enough for someone to have gotten out, shit, fuck, piss, god damn sonofabitch. We better not have missed the chance to save someone. They could be a first-hand witness to everything, everyone involved, and there would be a fucking massive enquiry into our fucking oversight. Oversight - bloody disaster more like!"

Fran's face was a picture, her eyes wide and staring, "No fucking way! That drain was tiny, miniscule in fact. I wouldn't get my leg in there and I'm not that big."

"Oh, are you not?" Taylor said with a cheeky grin, finally laughing as she hinted that Fran was bigger than she thought she was.

The ice was finally broken between them, but Taylor knew her head was in a total mess. Her life was totally fucked up. She was torn between her love for Kay and the feelings she had for Fran. If that wasn't enough, she had slept with her boss, DCI Brooke Sommerville, who she still liked too, and she knew it was reciprocated. Plus, she still flirted with other women; she had just enjoyed the company of the firefighter Lana, who she couldn't help notice was very attractive and funny.

They headed to the car chatting, when Fran turned to her with a serious look on her face and said, "Taylor, I've got something to tell you. I'm really sorry. I felt so lost recently since Kay came back, and I might have done something really stupid. I couldn't help it, I felt so guilty and I couldn't work with her knowing what we did."

"What we did, what do you mean, what we did? Fran, who did you speak to and what did you say?"

"What we did behind her back, at the hotel." Fran reminded her.

"Why? Bloody hell, Fran, why would you do that? Why? She didn't need to know that now."

"I needed to, it didn't feel right. I felt that she could see right through me and I wanted to come clean and, anyway, she was really nice about it. She said she felt that you were distant when you got back from the detail and she suspected that something had happened. She also thanked me for being truthful. She didn't even seem that mad at you. She knows you and what you're like and she's not wrong, Taylor, is she? DCI Sommerville for one," Fran said defensively with a hint of self-righteousness, because all she had ever done wrong was fall for Taylor.

This was all Taylor needed, a fraught life at work and even more so at home now. Her momentary lapse of happiness was now gone. She wanted to be mad at Fran, but she knew Fran was hurting and it was all because of her. Fran was her own woman, with her own mind, and if she felt that she needed to get her guilt off her chest, then so be it. Taylor would just have to deal with the consequences with Kay.

They both walked back to the car. Nothing else was said, and the others just watched in silence. They had seen Fran and Taylor's postures as they spoke to each other, straining their ears to hear what was being said, because all cops like a bit of gossip.

Nobody said a word when they got back in the car, and Taylor revved the engine and headed back to the office.

The team had been working out of the local station for two days, using the incident room at Wester Hailes as it was closer to the scene, less busy and convenient for all of the other services to use, so when they returned to their headquarters at Fettes for the first time since the fire, the DCI was standing there to meet them, and she had a look of uneasy apprehension as they all walked in. Taylor appeared moody, the team following in silence, all of them laden down with evidence bags and boxes. Taylor looked at the DCI and then surveyed the office. There she was, back at work, sitting at a desk, her long wavy locks cascading down over her well-formed shoulders, her slim and pronounced features just as Taylor remembered them. Her eyes glistened as she looked up and caught Taylor looking straight at her, her eyes boring into Taylor's, a long deep stare, which seemed to pierce right into her. They looked at each other for what seemed like an age, before Kay finally smiled and turned back to the computer. Taylor's heart fluttered before she felt what seemed like a pain shoot right through it. Everything just seemed to be so messed up.

Chapter 6
Nelson Burnett

"Where the fuck is my drink ya lazy bitch? I've been fuckin' sittin' here waiting for fuckin' ages," Nelson yelled as he ranted at his missus (a very loose term for the way he treated her, more like a sex slave). Irene scurried through from the kitchen with a large whisky in a crystal glass in one hand and a beer in the other, the bruises around her eyes now yellow and brown from the beating she had received from him a couple of days ago, after the fire. She was slight in appearance, her hair peroxide blonde and tied back in a pony-tail. She wore skinny jeans and a loose-fitting cotton top with a push-me-up red bra. Nelson liked red and he hand selected all of her underwear. He sat in the penthouse flat down at Waterfront, his round circular bay windows giving him a clear and wonderful view of the Firth of Forth, stretching all the way over the water to Kirkcaldy and to North Berwick, the Berwick Law visible on a clear day, not that he ever looked out to enjoy it. He only ever looked out to check that no one was coming for him. He had a sprawling black soft leather corner suite with faux fur covering it. Artwork, large canvases of mainly female nudes, hung on the walls. They weren't tasteless but were positioned in such a way that they drew your gaze wherever you were in the room, the nudity forced in your face. Nelson liked to look at them. He liked being watched. He liked women naked. He snatched the glass from Irene's hand, gulping the contents down in a oner and then swigged greedily out of the Peroni bottle before looking up at her.

"Sorry, sorry for the other day, Irene. I wis fuckin' stressed out. Some cunt is tryin' to fuck wi' me and you know what I'm like when I'm angry. I cannae help it, a just lose the fuckin' plot and when you gave me that look, a just lost it and a got the red mist and cannae remember doin' it. I'm sorry."

He reached out and gripped her backside, pulling her towards him. She didn't hate him when he was being nice. He just had a streak to him that scared the shit out of her. He got violent, out of control, when he was angry and he hit out at the nearest person to him, which was usually always her. He was good to her in many other ways. They had been together for over a year and kept her pretty well. She never wanted for anything, payment for her silence and loyalty to him, and payment to turn a blind eye to his business interests.

He pulled her to him and kissed her, his face rough on hers as he hadn't shaved, his breath tinged with whisky. He lifted her top up over her head and pulled at her jeans to reveal her matching red panties. He grabbed at her bra, exposing her ample bosom and sucked hungrily at her nipples, biting down on them, which she really liked. His fingers entered her as he got her ready for him, and she moaned loudly. She hated him and she loved him, a woman caught in the palm of his dangerous hands. He pulled her over onto her knees and pushed his cock up inside her. She winced a little as he was a big man in more than just stature, but his other hand came round the front to rub her pussy as he thrust into her again. She pushed back to take all of him inside her, the way he liked it, and he groaned and started fucking her harder. She screamed out loud with pleasure as his fingers rubbed harshly over her clit, his cock pounding inside her, making her cum so hard that she ejaculated. Her screams of pleasure excited him. He continued to fuck her, harder and harder, slipping into her with ease, her pleasure visible. This made him smile as his pace became almost frantic, his muscular frame tightening up as he too came hard. As he finished, he pulled down hard on her nipple and pulled her hair back, kissing her hungrily on her full lips, his tongue devouring her. She kissed him back, his assault last week fading from her skin and her memory. Although he wasn't a tender man in any way, she did enjoy it when he fucked her.

Chapter 7
Searching

Using every ounce of her failing strength, Sorina climbed up the rusty rungs of the ladder leading up to the circular drain above. She managed to reach it but, as she tried to push up against it, the sheer weight of it didn't budge at all. Her heart sank and she coughed repeatedly, her lungs now filling up with fluid as pneumonia took its grip. Her whole body shook violently. She was dying on her feet, the cold causing her body to shut down. With the last of her strength, she managed to reach up to the drain one last time. She poked her fingers through it, wiggling them and attempting to call out. She managed to hold them up there for less than a minute, but it was enough. A teenager from Edinburgh College, was sitting on the kerb texting her pals. She got a fright when she heard the eerie sounding voice escaping from the drain, causing a shiver to travel up her spine. Looking round in disbelief, she saw tiny fingers poking out from the small holes, fingers that disappeared before she even got up from the step. She looked around for someone to help her, or just to be there with her, as she was totally freaked out by what she thought she had seen and wanted to run away. Her thoughts of running went quickly though, as she heard a shriek from within the drain, and she knew she had to help whoever was down there. She moved forward and leant over the drain, calling down tentatively into it, several times, but there was no response. She wondered if the person was still alive, struggling with the reality of what was happening. Could she have imagined it?

Luckily another student walked by and said, "What're you doing on your knees? Are you alright?"

"I think someone is down there. I heard someone call out and I saw little fingers poking out."

"Aye, right, are you on something?" he said as he looked at her, seeing if she was all right, or drugged up.

She looked back at him, her eyes normal and her expression deadly serious. "I'm sure I did, but she's not answering or speaking anymore."

"Have you called the police yet?"

"Eh, no, not yet, should I?"

"Eh, yeh! If there's a chance there's someone down there," he said with a look on his face that suggested she was stupid.

"Oh, alright, I will then."

Her hands were shaking as she dialled 999.

Simultaneously, a heavy drain cover was being lifted in the Wester Hailes area, only a couple of hundred metres away from where the student was making her call. Council workers specially trained in confined spaces had been requested by police. They entered carefully, making their way down the slippery ladder into what they'd call a crawl space. The air was rancid, but they couldn't smell it as their faces were covered with breathing equipment to protect them from the pockets of noxious gases that build up with everything that ends up in the sewers, the human waste and chemicals, all giving off toxic gases as they mix together. Marcus on the other hand, who was standing at the drain where the men had just entered, whipped his head back quickly as he inhaled a nose full of the putrid smell, a mixture of excrement and something rotting down there, not a good combination. Taylor laughed at him as she had warned him way too late, "Don't get too close Marcus. That rank smell will give you the boak." Her shoulders were already moving up and down with mirth at his expense. Her strong and fearless partner Marcus was retching and salivating at the taste of the foul fumes coming up from the sewer. Fran and the other two detectives there were also taking the piss out of him, all of them unable to join the team going down into the drain as they had not been trained to work in confined spaces or use the equipment. The specialist operations response team also went down, along with trained paramedics wearing full breathing apparatus, hoping to be of use and not just for body recovery.

After Taylor's thoughts that one of the captives had maybe managed to escape, the wheels were put in motion immediately to put a specialist team together to go into the drainage system and search for any possible survivors. She had mixed feelings about the search, sadness about the delay if someone was down there and annoyance that she hadn't noticed the drain at the fire sooner.

They were over 170 metres away from the site of the fire, but the drain they entered was the best, most direct option to take them to an area with enough space to get down. They moved along quickly and efficiently. They were skilled at navigating the network of claustrophobic passages and had to slow down to let the paramedics keep up. Their shouts echoed eerily through the drains, the reverberating sound disturbing if you'd ever watched a horror movie. The walls seemed to close in on them, water slithering down the sides constantly, and the light from their head torches seemed to get swallowed up by the darkness.

Sorina had hurt herself when she fell, her remaining strength used to crawl back to her makeshift bed. Her last effort to be rescued had failed. Her body was still shivering uncontrollably, her breath rapid and shallow, her heart weakening as life ebbed away from her. She had already ripped the majority of her clothes off, the false feeling of warmth a symptom of the hypothermia that was now taking hold of her. Her body was shutting down. She lay on a makeshift pile of discarded items, litter, material, foliage and anything she could get her hands on to keep her off of the cold concrete. She was only meters away from the ladder she had climbed up so many times. Sorina was a resourceful woman, but her efforts had failed. All the makeshift bed had done was string out her insufferable chances of survival a little longer. She was now in an almost euphoric state of delirium, accepting that death was imminent and unavoidable. Her body ached so much that she wanted to die, her will to live gone. She had barely eaten since her little boy Nicu had been ripped from her arms and in her mind her reasons to stay alive were now all gone. Her heart, now so weak, allowed her thoughts to believe that he was no longer alive. She could still hear so vividly his terrified and desperate screams from the day they stole him away, her precious little boy. She had screamed with all of the oxygen she had in her lungs as she begged them not to take him from her, but all that had achieved was to get her beaten, then and every time she asked where they had taken him. Since he had been taken, there had been no news, nothing to give her hope that he might still be alive. Her eyes flickered delicately in response to the rat that was now climbing on her face, its tail lying across her lips as its whiskers brushed her eyelashes. It sniffed at her, aware that she was no longer a danger, and started to nibble at her brow, it too hungry and wanting to survive. The minute a little blood was drawn, several more rats scuttled along the edge of the water in her direction, their claws collecting the sludge and dirt that clung to the surfaces down there, faecal matter, urine, everything that humans threw down the toilet. She barely felt the pain as they started to eat her. She was barely alive, frozen where she lay, unable to respond and protect herself as her brain failed to send signals to her limbs to stop them. A slight sigh escaped her mouth before she fell unconscious. Her shivering stopped.

The man in the lead spoke to his colleague through their comms, "I hope there isn't anyone down here. Can you imagine being in this shithole in the pitch black for days, fucking terrifying."

"It doesn't bare thinking about, his mate replied. "I hope to God their theory was wrong and there was some other reason for the extra bed at the fire. They reckon nobody got out. Keep going, I think the drain they want checked is about fifteen metres up this way, according to these schematic plans. Keep an eye out though. We don't know where they might have gone even if they did manage to escape down here."

They crawled forward carefully. Their large dragon lamp fully illuminated the drain in front of them, but there was nobody there, nothing on the ground as they moved forward until they got directly under the drain coming from the warehouse. They looked up at the tiny space above them and thought escape would have been impossible for anybody other than a small child, their minds were almost made up until they looked at the concrete beneath their feet. In the glistening sludge was a depression shaped in a foetal position, the impression of a small body carved delicately there to see, evidence that someone had indeed, dropped down from the drain. The drain's exit was higher up than the tunnel walls they moved in and the imprint was a grim clue that someone had actually managed to survive the fire and escape. They would most likely be injured from the fall but could have moved off in several different directions. They could have gone for miles if they were able. The search had now grown far more complex and desperate. They were now in a race against time.

The news of the confirmation of an escape was radioed back to Taylor, who was pacing the pavement. The information made her feel sick to the pit of her stomach. There was sadness too for the person who was down there. *Could they still be alive? Fuck, I pray they are.*

The torches lit up the slimy mud in front of them, and their pace quickened at the thought that the imprints would lead them right to their goal. The rescue team just hoped that whoever it was hadn't been able to get too far.

All of the information was being passed back to Taylor, and her heart pounded with hope and anticipation, praying that whoever was down there would survive.

Fran was listening out to the local channel, Wester Hailes OPS, when she heard a grade one call come up. All decent conscientious cops' ears pricked up at the request for a grade one call. This meant an immediate response to attend was required from all available officers.

"Can any free set attend at Edinburgh College. There is a woman there claiming that someone is stuck down a drain. The informant stated that she heard a female voice and saw small fingers poking out through the drain cover, then nothing after that."

Fran nearly broke Taylor's arm as she grabbed her and took her earpiece out so that Taylor, Marcus and the others could hear the call repeated.

Taylor got on her radio immediately, requesting the public order van to attend with drain cover lifting equipment.

"We need another ambulance to go there too, please. NOW! This is a hurry-up, we need that drain lifted right away."

Sets arrived at the college within minutes of the call, and there was an officer talking to the girl who had made the 999 call. She pointed out the drain where she had seen the fingers.

The first cops at the scene tried to use the jack from their car to get purchase on the drain cover as the public order van was coming from the other side of the city and had not arrived yet. Blue lights and sirens flashed and rang out from all directions as they converged on the scene.

Taylor had made her way quickly to the scene of the sighting, her patience wearing thin at the delay with the essential equipment. She tapped her foot impatiently on the kerb, feeling helpless as she waited. Just as her patience was coming to an end, a fire engine pulled up. It had been on call elsewhere and had not been able to attend straight away.

Two big, muscular men jumped down from the appliance and went to the storage area where they pulled out their lifting equipment. For the first time, Taylor allowed herself to believe there was hope.

As she was leaning towards the drain, she felt an arm on hers, causing her to jump. It was Lana.

"Shit, you gave me a fright woman! Thank god you lot are here. The other team is underground somewhere."

"Good to see you too," Lana said, smiling.

As the drain lifted, Lana moved forward to guide it safely down on to the road. She was the trained medic for that appliance and was ready to respond as the second ambulance had not arrived yet.

The first firefighter donned his breathing apparatus and went straight down the ladder. He had to crouch down and had crawled only a few yards when he saw Sorina. She was half naked. He crawled up beside her. Lana masked up too and crawled in behind him, her eyes agape at the fragile, little woman before her. Lana swiped at the rat that remained on Sorina's face, reluctant to leave its meal. She was disgusted at how cruel nature could be and hoped that what the rats were feasting on was still alive.

Leaning over to put her ear to Sorina's mouth, Lana watched her chest for signs of breath. She couldn't feel anything. Sorina's chest did not move. Lana's heart sank at the thought that they were too late. She was about to pull away as she hadn't felt anything for over half a minute, but it was then that she felt it, a slight puff of air in her ear. At first Lana thought it was just the air travelling through the drains, but when she felt it again she was looking straight at Sorina's chest and this time she was sure. It had risen ever so slightly.

"She's alive! She's alive, more assistance needed down here, she's alive!"

Lana wrapped Sorina up in a fluffy blanket with another space blanket on top for more insulated warmth to try and restore some heat back into Sorina's withered frame. They fitted an oxygen mask to her face to give her pure oxygen and assist her in breathing.

They moved the body onto the scoop stretcher as the other team, who were already down in the sewer, came around the corner into sight, having eventually located Sorina by following her tracks and using their underground maps.

Taylor was nearly in tears with relief as the paramedics and fire service pulled the woman up from the drain, her body strapped in as they had to stand the stretcher upright to pull it up through the narrow space. Taylor looked on in surprise at how thin the woman was, and at the fresh blood that covered her face.

Taylor asked Marcus and Fran to travel with the injured woman to the hospital.

"Thank you, thank you all," Taylor said, praising the firefighters. Their timing had most definitely saved the woman's life. However, the paramedics cautioned that she was still close to death and not out of the woods yet. She still had a lot of recovering to do.

Lana smiled at Taylor, "We'll have to stop meeting like this."

"Do you think?" Taylor said as she turned to leave, but she held Lana's gaze as she made her apologies, smiling at her before making her departure.

Chapter 8
Sorina Costea

Michelle Smith was at her desk in the Public Protection Unit. She had just come off the phone to the immigration department. They had put Sorina's name through their systems and had got a result. It had taken a few days for Sorina to come around in the hospital and, after a lot persuasion, she had eventually given the police her name. She had a lack of trust and a fear of the authorities because she had only had the pleasure of dealing with them once, but that was in Romania, and it hadn't been a pleasant experience, one she had vowed she would never repeat.

Sorina was still not fit enough to be interviewed fully, although she was now conscious and starting to pick up a bit. She had been moved from the intensive care unit to a normal ward but was still on fluids as she had only just started eating.

Calls passed regularly between the Major Investigation Team and the Public Protection Unit as they worked side by side to try and piece together how Sorina had ended up in Edinburgh. They already believed her to have been trafficked to the capital, but didn't know by who or how and when she had arrived in Scotland.

Taylor swept through the office at the MIT at Fettes, a pile of papers in her hands. Fran and Marcus were back at the hospital with Sorina. Detective Inspector Findlay, a rotund man, an old school sexist, was walking back to his office with a bacon roll, scratching at his large belly. The Detective Chief Inspector, Brooke Somerville, was nowhere to be seen. It felt like an age since any of them had been back at the main office, but things were looking better now that they at least had a name to go on.

Taylor thumped the papers down on her desk as she always did and, as she sat down heavily, she had the feeling that she was being watched. She wasn't wrong. Kay was sitting at one of the other detective's desks, closer to Taylor than her normal seat. Taylor must have visibly jumped as she realised Kay was looking at her and Kay noticed.

"I'm not that scary, am I?" she said, smiling genuinely at Taylor, a smile that Taylor had thought she would never see again from Kay after finding out about Fran's little confession.

Taylor gave her usual cheeky smile back, happy inside that Kay was still her normal, kind, caring and very beautiful self. A couple of visible scars, the work of the killer Brennan, still showed on Kay's face. He may have broken her body physically and her mind temporarily, but he had failed to spoil her beauty, and with her inner strength she had managed to find herself again. She was now back, back to what she was like before that living nightmare had taken place at Taylor's house, where Brennan had sadistically brutalised them all. Kay had nearly died from the severity of his assault upon her, which had been his intention. Taylor had come home just in time and she too had sustained some serious injuries as she attempted to protect an already unconscious Kay. The nightmare had affected all those involved and continued to do so, even after Brennan's death.

"How are you, Kay? How have you been?" Taylor asked, with fondness in her eyes. "It's really good to see you."

Kay looked at her with her eyebrows raised. "Really? I've barely clapped eyes on you over the last few weeks and I was starting to think you were avoiding me?"

Taylor gave a comedic response, "Me? Never! Why would I?" she said, knowing fine well that she had been doing just that.

Kay wasn't stupid. "Yeh, if you say so," she said, scrunching up her face in a cartoon-like manner with a 'yeh right' expression written all over it.

Taylor dropped her eyes, guilt now showing on her face, clear for Kay to see. "I'm really sorry, Kay. Fran told me that you had spoken to each other and that she needed to come clean about what happened between us."

"And what about you, Taylor? Were you ever going to tell me? Were you going to sleep with us both, or what? What were you going to do? Do you think I wouldn't have noticed, I mean, really? We're in the same bloody office, Taylor."

"It was only once, and I wasn't going back there, honestly, but that problem was taken out of my hands I'm afraid, in the worst way possible, which I would change in a heartbeat if I could! Fran needed to tell you for herself and her own reasons. It was eating away at her, because she's a really decent person and she genuinely likes you and has to work beside you every day. She felt really shit about it and wanted to be honest with you."

"Funny way of showing it by seducing my lover! She told me it was all her doing, but I'm sure you wouldn't have needed too much persuading, 'cause she is very pretty, right up your street," Kay said, her face a little less friendly than before.

"What can I say? I did it. I'm me. You know me, and it's not an excuse. We were away, everyone was under so much pressure and I missed you, I really did. I wanted company, I wanted you, but she was there, right there, right in my face and she made it very clear she liked me. We had all had a couple of drinks and I thought it was time to leave. She followed me into the lift when I was heading to my room. She kissed me, and it was nice. I wanted to say no, and she kissed me again, and I kissed her back that time and it felt good and I'm so sorry, really sorry. I felt guilty as hell afterwards. She didn't come back to my room. The invitation wasn't there for her and, although it was nice, I knew then it wasn't going to go anywhere. We both knew that.

"Then Brennan, fucking Brennan! He took you away from me and I was ready, really ready to be with you, and I mean be with you Kay! But when you told me we couldn't be together anymore, I was heartbroken. I felt lost, empty. I hoped you would come back to me and things would be alright again, but time went on and we both know that didn't happen. Fran was there and I needed somebody. I was lost, I really did need someone and you were gone. She's a really nice girl, lovely in fact, but she's not you Kay!"

Kay's eyes filled with tears, tears for everything that had happened, losing Taylor, the memories too painful to remember. The infidelity with Fran was a minor issue in comparison with everything they had all been through.

"Do you want to go for a drink, Kay? We need to talk about this, us, everything, talk, talk and then talk some more and certainly not here."

"What about Fran, Taylor? Are you really wanting to break another heart? Are you?"

"I think I have already. She's pretty astute you know and certainly not stupid." Taylor lowered her eyes, a little sad, because she had feelings for Fran, but her heart had never stopped loving Kay.

"DNA, what about DNA, Taylor?" DCI Sommerville's voice boomed out as she strode into the office. "We need the DNA results from all of the corpses from the fire and we'll need Sorina's too please, when you've got a moment that is," she said in a sarcastic tone.

Taylor's head whipped round, a little pissed off at the abrupt interruption and the manner in which it was done, a bit too deliberate for her liking.

Brooke Sommerville's face went a little red, flushing with the misplaced jealousy she felt. She knew she had been abrupt, but couldn't help herself as she watched how close Taylor was with Kay. It was clear from their mannerisms that they were getting on well again. She hadn't meant to sound so bossy, but it just came out that way, almost like being back at school.

"The samples have all been taken and sent. They're at the lab, but it's slow time, and they have the issue of the tissue transference between the bodies. They were pretty stuck together most of them," she said with an equally petulant tone and a look that was openly hostile.

Kay watched and just shook her head. She was tuned in to body language and knew when a woman was jealous. She had been there herself many times and had acted in a similar way on those occasions.

Kay looked hurt, but she was angry too. Her eyes questioned Taylor, who was trying to avoid her hostile stare, fully aware that the timing of this admission could ruin everything.

"Have you slept with her too, Taylor?" Kay rasped at her under her breath. "For fuck's sake! You really can't help yourself, can you? Does Fran know, or is she fucking blind and stupid too?"

Brooke shut her office door with a little more force than intended and the noise made both Kay and Taylor jump.

Kay looked at Taylor, tears visible in her eyes, sadness filling her heart, a realisation that Taylor might not be able to stop being who she was. Taylor's heart may never be hers, or anyone else's for that matter, not exclusively anyway, and she knew she couldn't live with that, not happily anyway.

Kay got up from her desk. Taylor reached out for her hand, but Kay pulled it away.

"I don't know if you're ready, Taylor. I don't know if I'm ready. I don't want to get hurt again. I don't know if I could cope with that, with you. You need to go and think about what you want too Taylor. Is it me? Is it really me? Do you even know yourself? Do you?I don't think you actually do. You're not ready for this, for me, for commitment."

Grabbing her coat from the stand, Kay turned and walked briskly out of the office. She certainly wasn't explaining to DCI Sommerville why she felt sick all of a sudden.

Taylor thought about going after her, but Kay's words had stung her, and she knew it was because they were true.

Chapter 9
Underworld

Nelson Burnett strode from his metallic black Mercedes-AMG GT, a very slick and impressive sports car, bought and paid for through the misery of others, his wealth hidden under the umbrella of legitimate business, his money laundered and his position protected by the queue of wannabes willing to be bought, do his dirty work and take the fall for wealth and notoriety. Burnett rarely visited any of what he called his knocking shops personally, but he had been on edge since the fire and was always looking behind him these days. He wondered who it was that was out to get him, his trust for those around him not as strong as before. He had ordered some of his main guys to do some digging, but they hadn't come up with anything so far. Even on the street, no one seemed to be bragging about the fire. There was silence, no one was taking responsibility, probably because the heat on this one would mean certain death.

Burnett had many enemies. Many a man out there had fingers missing, no front teeth or broken bones, snapped by stamping down on them on the kerb. Others had permanent disfigurements. He was renowned for his brutal retribution towards those that crossed him or failed to pay their debts. There were even a few shallow graves on the outskirts of

Edinburgh where the less fortunate had been dumped like trash and buried, never to be found. Even if they were, the trail would not lead back to him. He always made sure of that.

He walked through the door of one of the saunas in the New Town, a stone bricked, five-storey tenement with a discreet entrance, nicely lit, almost inviting and giving the impression of a legitimate business. The girl at the desk felt instantly uncomfortable. She remembered him from when she was brought over from Bulgaria. She remembered his cruel hands on her face as he gripped it roughly to examine her like a piece of meat, like she was an animal, treating her like a slave. Little did she know then that she would become one, a sex slave. He made her skin crawl with fear and she cowed back instinctively. He was looking for the madam, the formidable woman that ran the sauna and kept the girls in line through fear. Her presence was enough to stop most of them doing a runner, because those that had been caught had been beaten and locked away for weeks, their children taken from them or other cruel punishments.

"Where is she? Where's Shaz? I need to speak to her now!" he barked at her.

The girl at the desk was only nineteen. She had been trafficked to Scotland when she was sixteen, taken from her parents as payment for the debt they owed to the Mafia. They had fallen foul of the extortionate interest rates demanded on their small original debt, the money lenders knowing fine well that it would spiral out of control, which is what they had wanted, what they had planned for on seeing her. They knew that the couple's very beautiful young daughter would repay their debt and much, much more. She was stolen from them, with no choice of her own. She was an object, a commodity. Guns were held to her parents' heads as she was dragged from her home, never to be seen again, stolen into a life of forced prostitution, degradation and brutality.

"She's out just now," she said, her voice trembling, uncomfortable at being there alone with Burnett. "She said she would only be ten minutes."

"For fuck's sake, the useless cow. Get me a fucking drink then, a large brandy, and I'll take it in the lounge area and you can bring it to me personally." He leered at her licking his rough lips.

She scurried through to where the drinks cabinet was, passing many closed doors, echoing with the sounds of grunting men and moans of pleasure as their tensions were eased, and then there were the screams. They came loudly from the last door. The gloomy reddish glow from the light in the corridor signalling exactly what kind of place this was.

She tried to ignore the sounds, but she knew the man in the last room. She had had the misfortune of being his customer. He liked to bite the girls. He liked to whip them, to hurt them, using toys, big toys, revelling in the pain he caused. He liked to tie them up and screw them face down. He liked anal sex ,and he would deliberately not use lube, enjoying the tightness as he fucked them. He liked the pain he felt on his dick as his foreskin was dragged back. He had nearly suffocated her the last time she had been with him when he deliberately held her face down into the pillow. She felt sorry for the girl that was in there with him now, but also thankful it wasn't her, although she was getting worried that the boss man would make his own demands, which he sometimes did, and she feared today might be one of those occasions.

She hurried back through with a large brandy for him, hoping that this would be all he wanted, but as she leant over, she felt his fingers stroke over her crotch. Her body stiffened noticeably as her blood ran cold, and she started to tremble.

"Hey, don't be like that. I just want to relax a little," he said in a low voice, in an attempt to put her at ease. "I won't hurt you."

He didn't actually want to hurt her. He honestly believed that the girls enjoyed having sex with him and were grateful for what he had to offer them, failing to realise it was without their consent.

Pulling her lace pants aside, he plunged his fingers straight into her, finger fucking her to get her ready for him. All he wanted was a quick fuck, a release, and in his depraved mind these girls were his to do with as he pleased. He unbuckled his belt, opened his designer Brunello Cucinelli jeans exposing his erect penis. He pulled her over and sat her down on top of him, facing away from him. She was barely wet and she grimaced as he pushed himself up into her. His cock was big and even though she spent her days being screwed by uncaring punters, it still hurt when she wasn't ready. His thrusts were quick and desperate as if he was in a hurry, and he was. He knew Shaz would be back soon and rape was a pretty low act, even by his standards. He fucked away at her furiously, pulling down recklessly on her nipples, her pert little tits freed by him yanking roughly down on her top. His fingers reached round the front of her and rubbed heavily over her pussy. He liked to feel the wetness her body was forced to produce to help her cope. He tried to force his fingers inside her too, rocking her forcefully back and forwards until his face contorted with a gurn as he tightened his buttocks and came hard inside her. He was panting with the exertion involved. He wasn't as young as he used to be. Abruptly, he shoved her off him. No words were exchanged. She was no longer of use to him now that he was spent, and his mind quickly shut off to any wrong doing on his part.

Adjusting his clothing, he walked through to the front reception area, where he found himself standing face to face with Sharon - Shaz, as she was known, a tall, heavy set woman, visibly strong with a hard and haggard face, a face that even Burnett chose not to get on the wrong side of unless he had to. He wasn't sure of her sexuality either. He'd heard rumours that she had a fella but they both indulged in threesomes, always with other women. She apparently enjoyed these encounters a little too much, according to the gossip, but she didn't want to be labelled a dyke.

She squinted at him, his face still a bit red from his rushed encounter with one of her girls. She was a little possessive and as protective as she was allowed to be with the girls, knowing what they had to endure, but she had a job to do too and that was to bring in the money for Burnett, otherwise she would be in the firing line, literally, or in a box in a shallow grave.

"What have you heard, Shaz? Who the fuck knew about the hide in Sighthill? That place was like fucking Fort Knox and nobody had a fucking clue. Now the fucking filth are all over it. They're still there apparently. What the fuck for, I don't know. The drugs were already in transit, so there was fuck all there other than the girls. Have you asked any of the girls? Have they been wagging their fucking loose tongues, talking to the punters, 'cause someone knew how and where to fuck me right over. All I need to know is why?"

"Cause yer a cruel cunt Nel. There's a fuckin' queue a mile long eager to fuck you over. You're an evil shit. I wouldnae want to get on the wrong side of you, ye dinnae mess around dae ye, and now someone is giving you a taste of yer ain fuckin' medicine, I'm afraid."

Shaz was as blunt as a hammer. She didn't mince her words. She too was hard as nails, but still knew her place. I huvnae heard anyone talking aboot it at all, which is a bit weird tae. Everyone likes tae brag, though eh, but not this sneaky wee cunt, Nel."

The girl at reception came back through. She looked a bit dishevelled and Shaz wasn't impressed. She knew the boss had been in about her and she looked a bit sick. Shaz knew he took advantage of his status and was aware the girls were afraid of him, with good reason.

Nelson winked at her, still thinking he had made her day by screwing her. She just looked down at the desk, not wanting him to think she actually enjoyed being taken against her will.

Nelson wasn't happy either. No news was bad. He needed to find out who it was that had burnt his warehouse to the ground, with all those women trapped inside, and he wondered if the person responsible was even aware that they were inside. If so, it proved whoever was after him wasn't fucking around and was willing to kill.

He turned on his heals. "Keep your eyes and ears open, Shaz. I don't think they've finished yet and this place isn't safe either, nowhere is, so don't trust any cunt right, no one. Do ye hear me, Sharon?" he said emphasising her full name.

"A hear ye, Nel. I'll ask around, but you'll need tae think who ye ken that wid dae this kind of shit. Why the fire? Why you? Think which nasty fuck you've done the dirty on in the last couple of years." She knew fine well that there were many.

He left quickly. His Salvatore Ferragamo, Italian leather shoes clicked efficiently on the pavement as he moved through other pedestrians, none of them any the wiser as to who he was and what he was capable of. Wrapped up in his Marni double-breasted coat, he passed as semi normal, the only give away his boxer-like face, the many facial scars a reminder of his chequered past, wounds from those who dared to fight back, many no longer around to tell the tale.

He slumped into the fine leather upholstery of his immaculate car and just sat there staring ahead of him, his mind racing to all of those he had wronged in the past. As his mind flicked through the memories, his head started to swirl with the list of those he had wronged by taking his brutal retribution out on them or their families. His concern was not for them but for himself and, for once in his life, he was a little scared and unsettled about what might happen next.

His wheels spun on the cobbles as he raced through the lanes that avoided the main routes in town, through Thistle Street, bumping his way down into Stockbridge, up past Inverleith Park and onto Ferry Road, cutting down Crewe Road North and onwards to his penthouse at Waterfront. His mind was still working overtime, his hands gripping tightly to the steering wheel, almost to the point that he nearly came off the road as he spun past the Scottish Gas building too fast for the turn, his mind instantly refocussing.

"Whoa, ya fucker! Get a fucking grip Nel. Focus, and find the bastard," he said to himself as he righted his car just in time.

Chapter 10
Lynne McNare

Fifteen months earlier

"Craig, Craig, answer the phone, please. I've got something to tell you, it's really important, you'll be really happy," Lynne said happily as she called her husband.

Craig and Lynne had been married for just over a year and she was trying her hardest to help straighten him out. She hated some of the stuff he got up to - drug dealing, violence, theft and other petty crime - and she hated the hold that the local hood Burnett seemed to have over him. She was a freelance photographer and had met Craig at Edinburgh College when he had enrolled in an electricians' course, but he had only stuck it out for five weeks, long enough for her to fall for him. He was a cheeky chap with a kind manner. She liked to think she could change people, make them see the good in themselves and she actually felt like she was getting through to him. He was doing less and less for this Nel guy.

Where is he, why is he not answering his phone. He normally does, or at least lets me know why he won't?

The blue lights came on behind Craig McNare's car and he felt the sweat beads forming on his forehead. He was tempted to do a runner, but that would make him look even more guilty.

Fucking scum, how the fuck is it ye never see any of those cunts when ye need one and then when you dinnae want one, they're all over the fucking place.

He tried to act casually as he pulled in innocently. He was so close to the drop off point in Muirhouse. He couldn't believe that he was being pulled over as he was just on Silverknowes Parkway, a stone's throw away.

This was no coincidence though. The police had had him under surveillance for weeks. They knew he was a drug runner for some unknown dealer but had never managed to catch him with anything on him. However, the intelligence this time was of the highest grading. Someone obviously had a grudge and had spilled their load.

As the officers looked in at McNare, they could tell he was nervous, which confirmed to them that this car needed to be dismantled if necessary.

They were casual on their approach and tried to get McNare on side, stating that it was a routine stop and they were just checking his insurance and license. McNare was a wiry type of guy, muscular and very capable, having been a martial arts expert in his teens. He had a calm exterior, bright blue eyes, an expression that gave nothing away. He knew the stop was about more than the shite that the Feds were spouting, and he knew it was now or never if he was going to bolt. He knew every rat run, and every high wall that these guys would never get up and over with all their shit on. Even though they were not in uniform, they still had stab vests on. He stepped out of the car, and the officers advised him to get back in. There was only one on his side of the car. Neither of them had called for back-up yet, assuming he was being compliant.

McNare made it look like he was going to get back into the car but spun around quickly and head butted the officer full on in the nose before booting him in the nuts as hard as he could. He turned back quickly and was nearly knocked over by an oncoming bus, fending it off and bouncing backwards instinctively. Regaining his balance, he sprinted over the dual carriageway and straight into the streets of Muirhouse. The other officer quickly ran around the car to give chase. He too was fit but McNare had a head start, which he was now glad of as he began to worry that he might not get away from this guy. He heard the cop behind him calling over the radio for back up, which slowed him down a little. McNare scrabbled up the first fence he saw and sprang over it with very little effort. The cop was struggling as his baton and cuffs clacked against it. The next fence was even bigger, which was no problem for McNare. He had run from the Feds many times before. He ran through several back greens and headed back over in the direction of Silverknowes, knowing that the cops would check Muirhouse first. He ran as fast as he could and could hear the sirens heading in his direction. He headed round to the row of shops and bus terminus at Silverknowes. There was a bus sitting there. Scrabbling in his pocket for change, he stopped running and began to walk. He heaved in his breath several times and tried to compose himself as he climbed on the bus and said, "One please, mate." He was a little sweaty and a little out of breath, but otherwise he seemed pretty normal and as the bus was just about to leave, the driver didn't think anything of it. He just assumed his passenger had been running because he was going to miss the bus.

The cop back at McNare's motor was still doubled up. His stomach was aching from the strike to his bollocks and there were tears in his eyes from the blow to his nose, which now had blood pissing out of it. He was raging at being caught off guard. He hadn't seen it coming. More police had arrived and a drugs dog too. They would make a thorough search of the car.

Cops swarmed round the streets. The general-purpose dog was on its way to see if it could follow the suspect's scent, but it was looking like he had given them the slip. The two officers that had stopped the car were hoping that he hadn't managed to take the drugs he was couriering with him when he ran for it, or they would be in for a bit of trouble for not calling for back up sooner.

The Springer Spaniel K9 Jess was inside the car, her tail wagging furiously as she stuck her nose in every nook and cranny. She stopped and indicated several times and the cops started unscrewing the panels. They couldn't believe their eyes when they saw what was there - two handguns with ammunition, plus at least five kilos of uncut heroin with a street value of millions. The cops that had pulled McNare over were now a little less bothered that he had given them the slip. Judging by the haul that had been discovered, he was in more trouble from the owner of the seized drugs than the police could ever give him.

McNare knew he couldn't go home. He was now going to have to go to ground. Nelson Burnett was not a forgiving man and would hunt him down and make him pay in a big way. He had already changed buses and was at Waverley Station. He had cash on him and bought a ticket to Manchester, where he had a cousin that he could bunk up with. He would call Lynne and explain away his absence without telling her the truth, the truth that if he didn't carry out the pick-up Burnett had threatened to cut off his balls and shove them down his throat before raping his wife. He owed Burnett and that meant Burnett owned him.

News travels fast in Muirhouse and Burnett was already aware that there was a lot of heat down at the front. A car had been stopped, the chopper was up and the cops were crawling all over the place. When he heard what type of car they had stopped, he flew off the handle, smashing up his living room and smacking Irene hard in the face. He was on the phone immediately and all she had heard was, "Burn that wee fucker's house down and any fucker in it and fucking find that cunting wee coward NOW! I'm going to gouge his fucking eyes out, the fucking useless wee cunt, fucking little prick. He should have fucking bolted, that fucking motor is pretty fucking slick and would have creamed the Feds shitty cars, the chicken livered wee shite bag." His fist slammed down again on Irene's head. He kicked out at her legs, pulled her hair and dragged her to the window to watch the cops buzzing round the area.

***

Lynne answered the door cautiously, hoping it was Craig coming back, but before she could slam it shut again, a huge fist slammed into her face through the gap. She fell backwards striking her head hard on the ground and didn't move. Her assailant wasn't bothered. This just made it easier for him. He poured lighter fuel all over her, up the walls and on the door, before striking a match and throwing it into the hallway without a second thought. He just managed to close the door before a whoosh of flames lit up the small window panel. The flames were already licking up the walls as he moved quickly out and away through the back greens to his car parked two streets away. He was off.

The fire service was quick on the scene at Wardieburn, but the flat was well alight and there was a familiar but hideous smell of burning flesh coming from it. The other residents had already evacuated their flats as someone had pressed all their buzzers and screamed a warning to them.

***

The train was clacking along the tracks and McNare had got his story straight for Lynne, still hopeful that she would believe him and she could join him as soon as she could. He didn't think that things would move that fast. He thought they could both disappear, relocate, because he knew that he was truly fucked and he could never go back to Edinburgh.

He had had his phone on silent. He didn't want any distractions and didn't want to have to lie.

There were four voicemails from Lynne. She seemed really happy, saying that she had something to tell him for the first three messages. On the fourth, he listened and his face tingled with excitement and a huge smile spread across it.

"Craig, where are you? You'll never believe this, but I can't wait any longer to tell you. I hope you get this message soon, because I'm pregnant. Im only a couple of months gone, but you're going to be a dad Craig. A dad! We're having a baby. Phone me the minute you get this message and hurry home. Where have you been anyway? I've been trying to get hold of you all day."

He quickly called her, but her phone was dead, the lack of tone suggesting that there was a problem. His heart started to race, and his head was spinning. "NO, NO, not her, please not her, and the baby, NOOO!"

Chapter 11
Taylor Nicks

When Taylor finally arrived home after another long shift, she threw her keys down on the table, went through to the kitchen, took a Bud from the fridge and slumped down on her sofa. She kicked off her boots and took an unladylike swig out of the bottle. Putting her feet up on the coffee table, she leant her head back, her wavy hair cascading down behind her, the bottle held only by the neck as she tried to find the solution to her predicament. Her head was all over the place, her heart sore at the mess she had unintentionally created.

Taylor had tried to bury her emotions deep inside her, a tactic she used to keep the pain away, never sharing her past with anyone other than her parents. For Taylor, to share her past would open up all of the pain once again, a sadness that very few knew about.

She gulped down the bottle and closed her eyes, drifting off into a light sleep, her mind beginning to wander back to that fateful day, the day she was going to whisk the love of her life away and ask her to marry her.

Taylor had checked the tickets, first class to Paris, Edinburgh to Charles De Gaulle. Two suitcases lay packed in the bedroom, a hotel booked near to the Eiffel Tower for four nights, an evening meal on the most luxurious Bateaux

Mouches, tickets booked for the Lido, Champagne, dinner and a show, plus the Moulin Rouge. Everything was filed neatly into a little pouch along with her Euros, both of their passports and other essentials organised for their trip away. She went into the drawer beside her bed and rummaged right to the back where she pulled out the velvety white box containing a white gold band with diamonds set into it, all the way around. Taylor kissed the box, her heart fluttering at the thought of asking the love of her life to marry her. Taylor and Katherine White had been an item since they had met at police college at Tulliallan five years previously. Their love had grown since these secret liaisons back in their college days. Katherine had no idea that Taylor had sorted out leave for both of them for a long weekend away and that Taylor was about to propose.

Katherine was taking off her uniform and putting the last of her things into her locker, totally unaware that she wouldn't be back at work the next day. She unlocked her phone to call Taylor to let her know that she was on her way home, as she always did. It was just after midnight. The shift had been busy, but for once she wasn't being held on.

Taylor answered, "Hello lovely lady, how was your shift?"

"Not too bad, glad it's over though. There was a sudden death, very sad. He'd lain there for over a month, so I'll need a shower when I get in! You can scrub my back if you want. That's if you want to stay up and wait for me," she said in her warm and inviting voice that made Taylor flutter inside.

"Try and stop me! Of course, I'll wait up for you, I love you, I love every hair on your beautiful head. I can't wait to see you. Drive carefully and I'll have a nice wee nightcap waiting for you. Love you, see you soon."

"Love you too. I shouldn't be too long." Katherine finished the call and carefully put her phone back in her jacket pocket, a tingle running down her spine as the darkness of the lonely street played on her mind.

Katherine walked from Leith police station and along Queen Charlotte Street, round onto the Links. Her car was parked a fair distance away from the station and that was a bugbear of hers, to not have a secure car park for the cops, all of them having to walk out into the night, alone.

Suddenly, she became startlingly aware that all she could hear in the dark and quiet night were her own boots clacking on the pavement, echoing as she walked in the light drizzle. There was no reason for her heightened sense of vulnerability, but her nerves were tingling. She was on edge and felt uncomfortably uneasy, almost to the point of fear, but with no reason to be frightened. To her horror, she heard another set of footsteps not too far behind her on the opposite side of the road, and they were moving in time with her. There was less than 100 metres to go until she reached her car, and she was tempted to break into a run, even though she knew it was just her mind continuing to run wild. The footsteps sped up, and she could hear them crossing the road in her direction, her earlier unexplained fear turning into reality. Her heart was now pounding. Even though she was a cop, she was still very vulnerable and certainly not invincible. She was about to turn round and make the first move before they did and slam her hand into their face, when she suddenly felt a gentle tug on her sleeve, which made her jump back, totally freaked out, her heart now leaping out of her chest as she took a very noticeable gasp of air. An older man was standing there. He was scruffy looking with several teeth missing but not the monster she had created in her own irrational mind.

"Sorry, lady! I didn't mean to frighten ye. Ye dropped yer scarf back there, round near the polis station. A wis quite far behind ye and ah kin barely talk these days. Ma throat is buggered, lass."

Katherine visibly deflated, managing to give a little laugh to herself at how she had become so worked up when the man was just trying to help her.

"Thank you. I wish you'd done something to let me know what you wanted. You gave me the heebie-jeebies."

"A didnae want tae scare ye doll, but a clearly did. Am really sorry, pet," he said before turning and walking back the way he came.

Katherine, now smiling walked to her car, a little bit more relaxed as she climbed in She threw her reunited scarf onto the seat, muttering under her breath at what a fool she had been. She put her seatbelt on as always and checked in her mirrors before moving off. The streets were quiet, practically deserted, as she made her way up Leith Walk onto Pilrig Street and down to the crossroads at the Rosebank Cemetery. The traffic lights were on green as she drove through them onto the junction, below the speed limit.

All of a sudden, her head slammed full force onto the side bar of her car, her skull cracking viciously against it, her neck jerking violently from side to side before flopping limply against her chest. The side of her car was totally crushed and the entangled body of the SUV that had collided with her also lay still, metal from both vehicles entwined as one. A suited man staggered from the vehicle, his head cut from hitting the dashboard. He had his phone out already calling an ambulance as he looked in the car at Katherine's lifeless body, blood pouring profusely from a wound on her head as he opened her door. His heart sank at the reality of what he had done, aware that he had been drinking alcohol earlier.

Ambulance called, along with the fire service, he wanted to help her, but looking at the position of her neck, he didn't dare move her, and he didn't have the medical ability to help. He took one last look at her. Neither car was smoking. He made his decision and left the scene to save his own skin. A conviction for drink driving would ruin him.

Taylor sat on the sofa waiting. Time was ticking on, and Katherine was now too late for her liking. She lifted her phone.

Katherine's phone rang out from her bag, which was now inside the ambulance. She was strapped to a spine board, neck support on, and unable to hear as she was unconscious and in a critical condition. The paramedic working on her reached down and answered it.

The conversation was short. Taylor ran to the bathroom and was instantly sick, tears streaming down her face, clouding her vision as she wiped the saliva from her mouth. She quickly brushed her teeth, washed her face, then grabbed her keys and was about to leave. She spun round and rushed back to get the ring, sadness filling her heart from the truthful words she had demanded from the paramedic. He had tried to skirt round the truth as they spoke on the phone, clearly trying to soften the blow with misplaced hope.

Her footsteps were quick as she rushed into the A & E department at the hospital. She was met by one of her colleagues, who had tears in her eyes. She was also a good friend of Taylor and Katherine.

"How is she, Lindsay? What are they saying?" Taylor asked, trying to hold back her tears.

Lindsay took hold of Taylor and held her tight as she whispered in her ear.

The words stung and her heart felt heavy, like a stone. She could barely catch her breath and she dropped from Lindsay's arms onto her knees, giving out a guttural wail as the news cut like a knife.

A nurse came over to help Lindsay get Taylor back to her feet and lead her to where Katherine was being treated.

Taylor walked with them to where Katherine's lifeless body lay, machines busily working to keep her alive. She reached for Katherine's hand and held it tenderly. The nurse brought a chair so she could sit by her side, as they continued their efforts to save her.

Taylor spoke to her beloved partner, loving words, sincere and filled with hope of their future together, the harsh reality of her injuries pushed to the back of her mind. There was desperation in her heart as she willed her soul mate to live.

Minutes passed as she continued talking to Katherine, the consultant now telling her of their plans to put her into an induced coma to try and stop the swelling in her brain, which would give her a chance of survival.

Taylor begged them to wait a moment as she had a question to ask Katherine before she was sedated. She was granted her wish.

Katherine had been totally unresponsive since her arrival at the hospital, and the doctors didn't think there was much hope of her being able to respond prior to their medical intervention.

Taylor took Katherine's left hand and spoke softly and clearly into her ear, telling her she had something to ask her as she kissed her cheek gently. There was no response.

This didn't deter Taylor as she got down on one knee, tears rolling freely down her cheeks. She sniffed loudly as she wiped them away and composed herself.

"Katherine White, will you marry me and make me the happiest woman in the world?"

There was silence, not a flicker of movement from Katherine.

Taylor was not deterred. Tears streamed down her face. "Sorry, I don't think you heard me. Will you marry me, Katherine?" she said with a tone and volume that took those around her by surprise, but they were even more surprised by the very obvious flicker of Katherine's eyelashes.

Taylor moved right up to Katherine's ear and asked, "Can you hear me? Squeeze my hand if you can hear me."

Taylor sat in silence and watched as Katherine's hand curled round hers, a very definite motion of response to Taylor's request.

"Oh, Katherine, I love you. Please fight, please don't leave me. I need you," Taylor blurted out in realisation that she could be heard.

The consultant gently pressed on her shoulder to remind her that they must act quickly to save her.

Taylor's face was filled with pain. Katherine's response had been heart-warming, but the desperation of her situation was still obvious, her fight for life very real, and time was not on her side.

Taylor turned back to Katherine and asked again the question she so desperately wanted answered.

"Katherine, Katherine White, will you do me the honour of becoming my wife? Will you marry me?"

Taylor could barely breath as she waited and waited. Eventually, a whisper escaped from Katherine's lips. It was weak and very faint, but it was clear for those beside her to hear.

"Yes, yes, I would love that. I love you Taylor Nicks, I love you with all my heart."

"I love you, I love you too. Please stay with me, and thank you. You've made me the happiest woman in the world," Taylor said, the emotion in her voice clear as she looked at Katherine properly for the first time, her injuries now screaming out. Katherine's face contorted a little, a tear now visible in the corner of her eye. Her hand gently released Taylor's.

"No, no, noooo! Don't leave me, please don't leave me!" The reality of how injured Katherine was was hitting her hard.

Taylor was shaking as she fumbled in her pocket for the ring. She gently pushed it onto Katherine's finger. It fitted perfectly.

All those around her were clearly moved by the very touching moment they had been privileged to have been a part of, but they needed to act now.

One of the nurses took hold of Taylor's arm and led her out of the cubical as they rushed Katherine away to theatre.

They sat Taylor down in the visitors' room and asked if there was someone they could call for her.

"No, thank you. The person I would have phoned is lying through there," Taylor replied as she started to cry.

Time passed slowly, every second excruciating and it seemed to take forever before she saw anybody, but this visit was the one she had been dreading.

The consultant walked in, and Taylor knew the minute she began to talk that the news was not good.

Taylor remained seated as the consultant explained how catastrophic Katherine's head injury had been. The bleed on the brain had been too damaging, the injuries just weren't survivable. They had tried everything they could, but it was now only a matter of time. She asked Taylor to come with her through to the theatre. Taylor's face was awash with tears, her nose running. The pain in her heart was indescribable. She felt it was tearing inside.

Taylor stood silently beside the bed, taking hold of Katherine's hand with both of hers. She fell to her knees as she slumped down beside her, her cheek against Katherine's hand. She kissed her softly with whispered words of love. Time passed by as Taylor hoped and prayed for a miracle. The consultant appeared and softly gripped her shoulder, squeezing gently. "She's gone now, she's away," she said. "I'm so sorry." Taylor looked up at her, tears rolling down her face, her eyes submerged in tears, gazing up in disbelief at the consultant's words. Taylor couldn't believe Katherine had died. Her shoulders heaved up and down uncontrollably, her sobs becoming louder. The consultant took her arm, gently helping her to her feet and then holding her tightly, absorbing Taylor's distress, her strength welcomed by Taylor's need for comfort. Her world had been torn apart, never to be the same again.

***

Taylor woke up with a start. Her beer had spilt on her chest, which made her jump forwards. There were tears in her eyes, the reality of the dream still tormenting her as she relived the worst day of her life once again, sending a wounding pain searing through every fibre of her being. She was really upset, the pain still physically sore within, but she was also frustrated. She thought she had dealt with this, and that her emotions were locked away in a safe place. Clearly this wasn't the case.

Chapter 12
Another Day in the Polis

Response cops were sitting in their briefing room, going over the who's who of recent crimes. Page after page of familiar faces filled the screen, each with a similar story. Who hated who, who had weapons, assaults on police, the never-ending feuds for ultimate power in the city and of course the never-ending terror threat.

The radios shone brightly as the control room requested an available early shift set to attend a fire at a house in Leith. Persons were reported within, further details to follow.

The Response Sergeant allocated two sets to attend immediately. They were to report back with an update as soon as possible. Further sets would only be sent if it was not a hoax call.

On arrival there was a good going blaze at the second floor flat in Cables Wynd House, a long high-rise block of council flats, that loomed over Leith, a real mix of people living within. The first officers on the scene requested a further ten officers as a minimum response.

The fire crews were already there, firefighters in breathing apparatus working their way into the flat which, luckily for the other residents of the block, was contained within the concrete surrounds of the flat's self-contained unit, but the usual caution was necessary in case of an explosion.

Officers evacuated the flats nearest to the fire, set up cordons and began their wait for the fire service to extinguish the blaze and make the locus safe. Ambulance crews also waited for any news of casualties.

It wasn't long before a firefighter appeared carrying a man, who was naked from the waist down. Another firefighter emerged with a second man. He wore the remains of a suit. The material was charred, the white weeping wounds of his burned legs there for all to see. Their faces were blackened from the soot of the fire and they had severe burns to the remaining unclothed parts of their bodies that had been exposed to the intensity of the fire.

Paramedics began working on them immediately,. Another unit was called to attend as well as medic one, so catastrophic were their injuries.

The fire crews on scene continued with their ominous task of search and rescue. The next time a firefighter emerged, there was a small Jack Russell terrier in her arms, its white coat not visible due to the amount of soot that covered its lifeless body.

The fire was nearly under control as the officer removed her breathing apparatus and put her mask over the face of the dog, rubbing it roughly around the chest area. Minutes passed as she continued to work on it. Then, to the relief of the cops and other firefighters watching, the dog began to breathe, whimpering and coughing as it tried to clear its airway.

The two men who had been found inside, were not as fortunate. The one with no trousers had been injecting heroin into the only viable vein he had left, which was the one in his penis. A thin needle was still buried deep into it, creating a certain amount of interest for those in attendance. Under their breath, they couldn't resist some chat at his misfortune at being caught with his trousers down.

The cops knew him as a regular dealer and user. They were always amazed that he had managed to stay alive as long as he had as he was so skinny and ravaged with the effects of drug abuse.

The other male that had succumbed to what they thought was the fire and smoke inhalation looked out of place for where he was and who he was visiting. His clothing was charred, but they could see he was wearing a suit.

The Sergeant from Leith was now on scene. He contacted the CID for their attendance as soon as possible. The ante in this crime scene had gone up considerably with two deaths confirmed. Everything was pointing towards foul play, with the unlikely mix of casualties, rather than accidental death.

DC Steve Shack, the newest member of the team, and his reluctant partner DC Andy Foster arrived on scene. DC Shack had become a very insular individual, and Andy already had concerns about him. He believed that he was a bit shifty and always seemed preoccupied, like his mind was elsewhere and not really focussed on the job.

Both got to work on the crime scene once the fire service had given it a satisfactory venting and ensured that the embers couldn't reignite.

Steve and Andy wore full forensic suits, gloves and masks. The smell of burnt flesh was unpleasant, and Steve was already retching as they turned one of the bodies over to examine him further.

As the man's face became visible, Andy noticed that Steve had become almost rigid, as if he'd seen a ghost. His retching became vomit and it sprayed out over his mask and onto the corpse, narrowly missing Andy's shoulder.

"For fuck's sake, Steve! What the fuck's got into you? You've totally contaminated the fucking body, ya div."

The uniform cops looked on and then at one another, mirth in their faces at his reaction. They made facial gestures to each other and then looked away, trying not to be seen laughing, both ripping the piss out of Steve's reaction.

Steve moved away from the body and vomited again, this time missing both corpses. He seemed to be shaking a bit. Not only had he recognised the man, but he also saw that there was a very small bullet hole in the front of his forehead.

Andy also examined the skull, noting the bullet hole in amongst the soot and charred flesh.

He radioed his DS with the facts. This was now a firearms enquiry, a rare occurrence on the streets of Edinburgh. He also contacted the Major Investigation Team to get them to come down and join the party. There was certainly more going on here than first met the eye. This wasn't a couple of junkies killed in a house fire any more.

"Steve, are you okay? Do you know him or something? You're acting pretty weird, mate," Andy said, concerned at how much this was affecting his colleague.

"I'm not your mate, and I'm fine thank you, Andy, mate! Just drop it. I hate fucking burnt flesh, alright? It fucking stinks. That's it, mate!" he rasped through gritted teeth, shitting himself at what he had just seen.

"Alright, Steve, keep yer fucking hair on. I was just asking what was wrong with you," Andy said angrily, now a little uneasy at his partner's overreaction and outburst.

There was an uneasy silence between them as they waited for the MIT to arrive, both avoiding any further conversation.

A short time later Taylor, Marcus and Fran joined the CID. All of them showed signs of repulsion at the disgusting smell from within. The filth that had accumulated in the flat, having never been cleaned, and the smell of burnt flesh mixed together was pretty putrid even for the police.

They had suited up forensically prior to coming up except for their shoe covers. Crowds of locals had gathered for the show and were deliberately winding up the cops on the cordons, trying to get a rise out of them, the usual tracksuit wearing mob, baying for a reaction.

The firefighters had gathered up their equipment and were moving out between the detectives. One deliberately brushed against Taylor, gently, but very deliberately. The firefighter was still in full kit, a fire hood hiding their face.

"Excuse me," Taylor said sarcastically, expecting an apology for the unnecessary nudge, but the firefighter just turned around and pulled the cover from her face and smiled.

"Oops, sorreee," Lana said with laughter in her eyes. "Are you following me, ma'am?" Lana's eyes were totally focussed on Taylor's.

Taylor smiled back, a slight flush on her face. "I must be. You seem to be everywhere I go these days. I hope you don't mind!"

Marcus and Fran looked on in disbelief. It wasn't Taylor's fault that she was here but her reaction and obvious flirtation was open for all to see.

The encounter was brief, but the cops on the cordon had also captured the moment, watching on because they were cops, and cops loved to gossip.

Taylor turned back around quickly and pulled on her business face once again. The others said nothing. Fran felt a little hurt, but refused to show it. Marcus just shook his head. He loved Taylor but was saddened by the fallout that came with her behaviour.

Taylor inspected the scene. The two bodies were on display after the medics had finished with them, now safely under tents. Instantly, she turned to Marcus and Fran, "This doesn't add up here. Who's the suit?"

Marcus nodded, fully agreeing with his boss. "This boy's totally out of place. What is he? A repo man or something?"

Andy came through from the back room. "Hi, I'm Andy Foster, CID. Are you ready for an update?" He hesitated, waiting for Taylor to introduce herself.

"DS Nicks, Taylor Nicks, DC's Black and Andrews. What have we got so far?"

"The suit's got a small entry wound on his forehead," Andy began to explain.

"Has he? I never noticed." Taylor looked a little taken aback.

"Yeh Serg, it's charred over a bit, and we had to really stare at it to see it. Come over and take a closer look."

Taylor knelt down beside the corpse and on close inspection saw a very small bullet hole within the black charred flesh. There was no obvious blood surrounding the hole due to the smoke discolouration.

"Shit, that changes things a bit. Even here, there aren't that many people prepared to use a shooter," Taylor said to Andy, who nodded in agreement.

"I bet the autopsy on the junkie will not be as it seems either. Why would you inject in your dick if there is someone else there? Even a junkie would probably wait till they were alone. It's as if it's been done to shock, to make it look like a very obvious overdose to stop us looking elsewhere, but I think someone else got to the party before the gate-crasher had left. Make sure the contents of all the cups are checked, all of them, even the really manky ones."

Just as Taylor reached for her radio to get scenes of crime officers down, DC Shack came through, still white as a sheet and looking like shit.

DS Nicks looked at him, and her expression changed to one of curiosity. She'd never met him before, but his appearance was enough to make her hesitate with what she was saying.

DC Shack looked up at her, noticing her puzzled expression and obvious hesitation. He was an astute guy and well aware of how everything worked in the police force.

"You alright? I'm DS Nicks, and you are?" Taylor offered her hand to introduce herself.

Steve nodded at her and gave his excuses for not shaking her hand. Taylor looked down and saw the vomit trails still on his chin and on the back of his hands. He gave a weak smile of apology, a little embarrassed.

Scenes of crime arrived at the locus and Fran was asked to corroborate the evidence gathering, plotting, marking, packaging, labelling, everything meticulously documented, and then the gruesome task of forensically recovering one body with another unfortunate officer assigned to the other to avoid any cross contamination.

Taylor contacted DCI Sommerville to give her the full update and offer her the opportunity to visit the scene. Sommerville declined, not through disinterest. She trusted the team and was buried in her own urgent paperwork. Instead, she asked for regular updates to allow her to coordinate proceedings remotely.

Chapter 13
Desperate Times

Two months previously.

PC Shack was in the rear room of a dealer's house in the Muirhouse area of Edinburgh. The other officers attending were elsewhere in the house. The guy in cuffs looked up at Steve from his chair and whispered under his breath. His eyes were dark and serious as the words came out.

"Twenty-five G, if you make this go away."

"What the fuck did you say?" Steve growled initially, annoyed at the audacity of the suggestion. "We'll add this to the charges - trying to bribe a cop!"

"Thirty-five, and more to come if you can share a bit of info," the guy repeated his offer with interest. He was deadly serious and not at all perturbed by Steve's first reaction.

Steve was about to call the others through but, against everything he stood for, he hesitated, thinking of his life at that moment. They were struggling as a family and cash flow was virtually nil.

"Thirty-five big ones! The main man is very generous. I don't want to do fifteen straight and he won't want me to either." The dealer had seen Steve's hesitation, watched the cogs whirring in his head, and he knew his offer was being considered.

Sweat beads blew up on Steve's forehead as he began to seriously consider the offer. He thought of his wife and their three young children and how they could benefit from such a sum of money, especially as their youngest was unwell and needed to travel for specialist treatment.

The guy in cuffs stood up. He was wiry, his taut frame impressive despite being involved with drugs. He clearly wasn't using any of the gear and only selling the misery on to others for profit.

Steve could feel the pulse in his temple, heart now racing as if he was about to be caught out on the spot. He felt that his thoughts were transparent, written on his forehead for all to see, as his colleague came through the door.

"We need to get these guys up to the cells. We've found thirty kilos through there. There's going to be repercussions. We'll need to get the public order unit down into the area just in case!" "Are you good to go? Steve! Are we good to go?" The other DC had to repeat himself before Steve snapped out of his trance-like state to acknowledge and respond to his request.

Steve gripped the suspect under one arm and without words signed a deal with the devil.

Chapter 14
People Need Friends

Taylor popped her head round the office door at the PPU. Michelle swivelled round on her seat to see who was there.

"Hi, how are you? I've not seen you for a while. How are things going with the fire enquiry?" Michelle asked, already knowing the answer.

"Slowly. Everyone is tight-lipped and clearly too scared to speak out, because they know who's behind it all. We have our thoughts on it too, but proving it is another matter." Taylor was flagging a bit with the stress and pressure of her recently increased workload.

"Any more about the shooting, what's the story there? Is there a connection? Seems a bit severe from the norm in Leith, and fire involved again. There's clearly a bloody pyro out there with a vendetta!" she said with a little humour, unaware of how close she was to the truth.

"Not yet, but someone is certainly out to make their mark on Edinburgh's drug scene, and they have certainly ruffled a few feathers lately. The boy in the suit was clearly assassinated, There is fear out there just now; the dealers are clearly rattled. Let's hope someone starts squealing soon," Taylor said hopefully.

Michelle smiled at Taylor. "Pete's a lot better now, just for your info," she said coyly, a flush coming over her face.

Taylor grinned and pulled up a chair next to her, knees pushing into Michelle's thigh. "Tell all," she said. "What do you mean by that, lady." She playfully squeezed Michelle's side, tickling her ribs, knowing fine well what she meant.

"Spill the beans, madam. I want details, all of them. Mind you, that smile says it all. That is brilliant, brilliant for both of you. I saw him the day of the collision and even I thought he wouldn't make it, far less make a full recovery."

Michelle's eyes watered as she was reminded of the day of the crash. Pete was very badly injured, clinging to life, with blood pouring from his broken body. She had held his hand so tightly, two strangers that were now lovers, pulled together by tragic circumstance .

Snapping back to reality, she smiled again. "That's in the past now and he is more than better now." Her mind wandered back to the intimate evening they had shared that week.

Taylor leaned in and gave her a warm hug, filled with genuine and honest affection. She was glad that there was a happy ending, when so many times in their line of work there wasn't.

Both women shared a bond and mutual respect for each other like many officers in the service, sharing experiences that normal people would never have to face, an invisible force keeping reality away from the public.

"Anyway, stop your love chat, I'm jealous," Taylor said with an exhausted and emotional look on her face.

Michelle had known Taylor for years, her lifestyle, her flighty nature, her good humour and bubbly personality, and she had never seen her look so exhausted and down.

"Your turn. What's going on with you? I thought you were with Fran these days, and happy?"

"I was." Taylor hesitated.

"Well?" Michelle turned her head slightly, waiting for the 'but'.

"Kay's back."

"Oh."

"I know, but it gets worse."

"Why is that?" Michelle looked straight at Taylor, eyes encouraging her to say more.

"The DCI."

"What about her? No way! You're kidding. Not Sommerville? Wow lady, you really are a dark horse. No wonder you're walking around like you've been hit by lightning."

"It gets worse," Taylor said, a little embarrassed.

"How, is that possible?" Michelle replied cheekily.

"They all know, and they are not happy with me and neither am I. I want Kay, but she is really disappointed in me, and Fran is really hurt. Brooke is totally moody and has a dig at me at every opportunity. I'm caught in the middle, and it's very uncomfortable, although I deserve it!"

"That's not good. Can't you try and sort things out?"

"There is also this firefighter that keeps cropping up too. Seems that everywhere I go, she's always there," Taylor added, shrugging her shoulders and trying to make light of the mess she was in.

"Bloody hell, Taylor! Here's me thinking that my life was a bit of a story."

"I'm not happy about what's happening. I just seem to screw everything up. I really don't mean to be such a shit. I hate hurting people."

"Taylor, you need to decide what you want. I mean really decide who you want to be with, if anyone. The answer will come, circumstance will show you the way."

"Really? I hope so, because the door I want to go through might be closed and closed for good."

"You either commit or carry on. Only you can decide. Rather you than me though."

"Shit! It's not that easy. Kay has totally lost it and doesn't want to know."

"Can you blame her?" Michelle said with raised eyebrows.

"No, I don't. Well actually, I do a bit if I'm honest. I did commit, and she let me go. We were both so broken, so I moved on because she told me to. I had to for my well-being too, and that was what she told me she wanted, in fact, demanded."

"Wow! That hurts." Taylor had tears in her eyes. Michelle gave her a tight hug and Taylor's shoulders began to move up and down as she let herself cry, releasing what she had been holding in for so long."

Michelle was taken aback because Taylor always came across as a woman in control, but this time she was clearly broken.

After a while, Michelle let her go and handed her a tissue. "It'll be alright, Taylor. You're a good person, and you know it, and what will be will be. Don't force anything. Give it time, give everything time, and watch you don't hurt anyone else, including yourself."

There was a pause. Taylor sorted her blouse and wiped her eyes, then turned to Michelle, trying to look more business-like, and they both burst out laughing.

Taylor spoke first. "We'll need more than a shift to solve my life's problems."

"And some," Michelle said as she elbowed Taylor gently in the ribs.

"Work! Let's do it. Now let's get back to what we have. What's the update on Sorina, how's she doing?"

"She's a lot better, but she's not talking. I think she knows more than she's letting on, and she's terrified."

"Of what though? I bet she holds the key to this whole syndicate. I bet she's seen or had contact with the head of all of this and is frightened of what he can do."

"What about the kid, her kid, the one she was talking about when we first found her?" Taylor quizzed.

"We've put his names through all of the systems, but nothing has come up yet."

"Just the name? What about DNA? have you taken samples yet?" Taylor asked, hoping that this had been done.

"She won't let us take it. She's really apprehensive and certainly doesn't trust the police, and no wonder with what's happened before."

"You'll need to spend time with her, Michelle. Get her to trust you. We need to find this kid, or at least the connection, and we could maybe get her to talk if she knew he was safe. Get to work, use your charm," Taylor said with renewed hope.

"I will, but why don't you try and speak to her. You're good at that sort of thing, maybe she'll open up to a different friendly face, someone that can offer her more reassurance."

Taylor thought about it for a moment and agreed. "I will. Let's get it arranged. Where is she just now?"

"She's in protection, and even you aren't on the list to know." Michelle smiled at Taylor.

"Well you'll need to sort that then or' your little plan stops here," Taylor said cheekily.

"Okay, I will, but the security with her is pretty high. The bosses have pulled out all of the stops due to her connections and the risk she poses to one of the top drug rings."

"Good, so they bloody should. Make sure she's alright, but work on it,'Chelle, don't let me down." Taylor squeezed Michelle's leg and smiled. "Thanks for listening to my sob stories, and I'm glad you and Pete are doing well. I mean it, I'm truly happy for you both."

Michelle grinned and said, "Look after yourself and come back soon once the interview is sorted."

"I will," Taylor said, smiling as she left the office.

Chapter 15
Caught in the Web

Fran and Marcus were in the office, their desks close to each other, both working hard, with the occasional interruption for a little tomfoolery and dark humour. The office was a hive of activity, numerous desks in an open plan setting, no privacy, even the Detective Inspector and Detective Chief Inspector's office was glass fronted and anyone could look in. This worked well though, as everyone had to know what was happening in relation to the cases they were dealing with without having to go and search for information.

Taylor's desk stood alone but was positioned to have a view of the whole office and the evidence boards, and the officers in her charge. Phones rang all through the day, so when Steve Shack's mobile rang nobody paid any attention, but Steve did. His face flushed red and sweat beaded on his forehead when he recognised the number. He put the phone to his ear and squeezed it tight to his head as he listened.

"Stevie, my boy, how the hell are you? We need more info and we need it yesterday. Someone's fucking with us and we need it stopped."

Steve felt sick. He thought his guilt was shining out from him like a fluorescent light, but Fran and Marcus were still chatting away to each other, unbothered that he was sweating in the corner.

"Who the fuck are you? It was a one-off. I fucking told you that!" He thought he had whispered discreetly.

But it was his anguished whisper that made Taylor look up from her desk and see he was flustered.

Steve noticed her and didn't speak again, hanging up. He put his phone away quickly, missing his pocket first time, clearly stressed. He felt ill and got up from his desk and went to the toilets to throw up. Taylor watched him as he went. She had noticed the change in his demeanour. She had never been sure of Steve. He had recently joined the team from CID and she hadn't quite got the measure of him yet, but there was nothing she could put her finger on.

As he reached the rest rooms, the phone sang out once again, vibrating against his thigh. He knew it was them again.

He wiped the string of saliva from his mouth after throwing up. The phone kept ringing, over and over until he answered it again, this time even more reluctantly.

"Don't hang up Steven. I mean it. We need to talk, or you do anyway!" the voice rasped threateningly on the other end of the line.

"I've got no more to say to you. I needed the fucking money, right. It was a mistake, a fucking big mistake, so fuck off and leave me the fuck alone! You're getting fuck all else out of me!"

"Well that's where you're wrong mate. It doesn't actually work that way. You work for us now and you do what the fuck we tell you to do, aw-right!"

"The fuck I do! You're getting no more from me, ya deaf cunt, do you get it! Now away ye go and take a flying fuck to yourself!"

"Okay, fine Steve! Have it your way, We'll just have to give your wife Kim a little visit then, your lovely children too. Sorry we couldn't sort something out." Silence followed.

"The fuck you will. You leave my fucking wife and kids out of this. Touch them and I'll fucking kill you, and we'll lift all of you fuckers!"

"We? What the police will have us? You're kidding, right? Who's gonna fucking tell them - you? Go on then, tell them!

See how far you get. I'm sure your boss, yeh the big leggy bitch, I'm sure she'd be very interested in what I had to say. She looks like a real ball breaker!"

Steve felt his shoulders slump. He knew they had him by the balls, and asked with apprehension, "What the fuck do you want? I did what you fucking wanted, and that was fucking risky enough!"

"Sorina Costea, that's all!"

Steve froze on the spot, his heart pounding. He knew what they were asking and why, and the consequences for her if he gave her up.

"No way, no fucking way! She's too well protected. You'll never get near her."

"You're right, we won't - not without your help anyway, Steven."

"I won't do it, I fucking won't!"

"Now listen here, ya daft wee prick, av hud enough of your shit. It's time for you to listen to me now, right! Don't be a spineless wee bastard. You'll do what the fuck I say or I'll fucking do your wife with the kids watching, and your wife will die. It's as simple as that! You know we will do it, and you can't be with her 24/7 now, can you? And accidents do happen!"

Steve slumped down on the toilet seat and started to cry,. He knew he couldn't tell anyone, although he desperately wanted to, and he knew these guys were ruthless and more than capable of carrying out their threats.

"Stevie, STEVIE! Are you still there, mate. I can still hear you whimpering, you snivelling little shit. Get back on the phone and speak to me you dumb little fuck, or I'll come up there and rip your fucking shrivelled up wee balls off! Dae ye hear me?"

Steve put the phone back to his ear and said, "One hundred grand - that's the price."

After a short pause, Steve heard a sinister laugh escaping from the phone, making his blood run cold. Steve was confused.

"What's so fucking funny? That's how much I want, if I'm going to do it, right."

"No, no, no, nooooo Steven, you're so wrong. You're gonna do it for fuck all! The first payment was the temptation to turn you bad and that's why it was a good one. We now have you by the short and curlies son, and you'll do this for fuck all, fuck all ya daft little cunt. Now listen, and listen very carefully, get this fucking sorted or your wife is FUCKING DEAD, and I fucking mean it!"

The line went dead and the colour drained from Steve's face. He knew now that he was their puppet and that there was nothing he could do about it without going to jail himself, and they'd kill his wife anyway so he had no option.

The door to the rest room opened and Steve froze. He felt like shit and knew that he looked it too

Marcus came in and noticed the second trap was shut and carried on with his business.

He heard a sniff from inside the cubicle and turned and called, "You alright in there?"

There was silence at first, then Steve responded, "I'm fine Marcus. I just feel like shit, I'll need to go home. Will you let the Serg know?"

"Yeh, okay What is it, you eaten something rotten?"

"I think so mate, it must be something like that. Will you let her know and apologise too? Thanks, mate."

Marcus washed his hands and left.

Taylor raised her eyebrows when Marcus told her and said, "He was fine earlier, although he looked a bit off when he took a call a short while ago. Is he okay?

"Not sure, he sounded like shit. He actually sounded like he was crying, but I could be wrong?"

"What do you think of him? He talks more to you than me."

"He's okay. He's pretty quiet and doesn't really join in that much, but that might just be because he's new to the team and a little shy."

"You're too fucking nice, Marcus. I'm not so sure. Keep an eye on him. I think he's a bit odd and, with all the shit we're dealing with just now, we can't afford to have anything go wrong."

"Do you think?" Marcus said questioning her.

"I do think, Marcus! Trust me on this one. Keep an eye on him, nothing heavy, even if it's just to check he's okay, nothing sinister, duty of care and all that…"

She squeezed his arm. "Trust me." Taylor's tone was serious.

"Anyway, enough of that. Do you want to head out for lunch? We've not had a chat for ages?"

"Yeh, sounds good. How about The Raeburn?" Marcus replied happily at the prospect of lunch away from the office for a change.

Fran was at her desk working away, but had heard the offer of lunch. Marcus poked her in the shoulder in his usual playful way and asked her to join them.

"Two's company, three's a crowd," she said with sadness in her heart, not wanting to go because of the way things were between her and Taylor.

She sat for a while and then watched when they both left the office, her heart heavy with acceptance that she had lost Taylor.

Chapter 16
Chance Meeting

Taylor and Marcus walked into The Raeburn Bar and Bistro. It had been recently refurbished, it's modern fittings and layout welcoming to all who entered, classy tables and seats, leather upholstered booths, immaculate staff and a bright well-lit central bar area, shining with the pristinely polished variety of spirits on display.

Taylor and Marcus chose to sit down at a booth, a more dimly lit cosy area, allowing them privacy.

Taylor fiddled with the fashionable salt and pepper cellars. She smiled and gestured towards her pockets as if she was going to pinch them.

"Don't you dare," Marcus said laughing, knowing that she was only joking.

"How's Maria, Marcus, and wee David? Has he gotten over his ordeal yet?" She paused. "Have you?"

"Just! We're getting there, but I don't think Maria will ever be able to relax again, not fully anyway."

"No bloody wonder. Do you blame her? What happened isn't just run of the mill you know. I think you need to get away, all of you. A little time away will help, don't you think?"

"What, with this enquiry going on?" Marcus looked at her a little disbelievingly.

"Yes, even with this enquiry going on. I think you need it. You're going to burn out Marcus." Taylor knew that Marcus was a committed worker, but she also knew that he needed time away to heal, time to be with his family.

"At least take a long weekend, what do you think?" Taylor said with affection in her eyes.

Marcus thought for a while, then looked up with a smile on his face, his handsome features a little more worn than they used to be. The stress of the kidnap of his son had taken its toll over the last couple of months.

"Okay, I'll see what's available on-line, a last-minute thing. We do need it, Maria needs it. Thanks, Taylor," he said with a distracted look in his eyes, already planning where they could go. He loved his family more than life itself and what had happened to them had nearly broken him. He had been pushed to the absolute limit and at times had felt he was losing it.

Taylor loved him, and had watched him crumble. She thought that he was going to have a breakdown and, had there not been a positive outcome, she believed he wouldn't be here today. She smiled at him and squeezed his hand.

Just as she was doing that, Lana came up behind her and squeezed her ribs quite forcefully causing Taylor to squeal out loud and jump up. She was about to get angry with whoever had invaded her space but, when she looked up and saw that it was Lana standing next to her with a huge beaming smile, her mood changed.

She couldn't help but smile back. "Hey, how are you, you look different without your equipment on, almost human."

"Gee, thanks! Did you think that I actually filled the suit, you cheeky mare," she said with laughter in her voice.

Taylor laughed back, and tried to backtrack a little, but it was too late.

Taylor looked up at her. Lana was tall and athletic with strong muscular shoulders and a tight torso. Her jeans hugged her legs perfectly and a white cotton round-necked buttoned top clung to her. This didn't go unnoticed by Taylor. Neither did the woman that came rushing in, clearly late and a little flustered. She came right up to Lana and apologised.

Lana squeezed Taylor's hand, deliberately lingering before she swept her fingers up Taylor's arm and turned, going further into the bar to find a seat, one that allowed her to keep an eye on Taylor.

Taylor only snapped out of it when the waitress came to take her order.

"Hi, what can I get for you, or do you need a little longer?" she said.

Taylor read her name badge. "Joy is it? We are ready indeed. You go first, Marcus, and leave some food for the rest of us."

Marcus gave a dramatic gesture and with a big beaming smile ordered the biggest burger with extra toppings, three sides and a pint of fruit juice.

"See! You are a pig. You should be the size of a house." Taylor smiled at him and said, "I'll have the same."

The waitress looked at Taylor and asked, "Are you sure?"

Marcus laughed at her, knowing fine well she would eat all of it. They both trained hard and enjoyed the benefits that brought.

Joy smiled as she left to get the monstrous order. Taylor watched Lana and her friend laughing together in the corner, and her mind started to wonder.

Chapter 17
Home Alone

Steve's wife Kim was upstairs in their four bedroom house in Silverknowes. The two older boys were already asleep as she began the sleep routine with the youngest one. Steve and Kim's little girl suffered from biliary atresia, a rare disease of the liver and bile ducts. Her bile ducts had been damaged by her body's immune system in response to a viral infection acquired when she was born. Unfortunately, the procedure to re-establish the bile flow from her liver into the intestine had failed and now she required specialised treatment, both at the Edinburgh Royal Infirmary and at a private hospital in London, until a liver transplant could take place if a donor could be found.

Kim's soft, melodic voice hummed away as she sung little's Maisy's favourite nursery rhymes to her. Maisy's face, although discoloured and tinged with jaundice, was angelic and happy. It took all of Kim's strength to smile without showing her inner sadness and fear that her precious little girl might not make it to her next birthday.

Maisy gripped her mummy's hand, her eyes wide and filled with fear. "Mummy, what was that noise?"

Kim's eyes remained fixed on her daughter, the hairs on the back of her neck rising, but her smile was unwavering as she said, "It's nothing honey, it's windy outside," openly lying to allay her little girl's fear, while also trying to convince herself that that was the case.

She listened intently, hoping not to hear another sound. Minutes passed, but she heard nothing, which allowed her to relax once again, reassured that it might actually have been the wind.

Little Maisy finally fell asleep, her mum knowing that she would be up numerous times to tend to her and comfort her during the night. She didn't mind. She would do anything for her children.

As she reached to adjust the nightlight, she heard the noise again, and this time her white lies that it had been the wind, meant to comfort her daughter and herself, were clearly not true. Whoever, whatever was making that noise must have been there for some time. Waiting, but waiting for what?

She went through to her bedroom and reached for her phone. Her hands were shaking. The noise came again and this time from the glass porch area at the back of the house. She reached under the bed and pulled out her hockey stick, then dialled 999.

She checked her boys and shut both doors to where her children innocently slept, her feral instincts bristling, the protection of her children her uppermost priority.

She stood at the top of the stair in silence, the hall lights off to secrete herself in the darkness, but this brought out her fear of the dark and what lurked within it.

She could see the glass porch from where she stood as still as a statue, fear gripping her stomach brutally tight, terror creeping up her spine like skeletal claws tip toeing up her back. She shook it off and tried to focus, *Where the fuck are the police?* she thought to herself, knowing from what her husband Steve had told her that there might not be someone available to come. She dialled his number, and when he answered whispered, "Steve, help me, there's someone outside the house!"

"Fucking hell! I'm coming home right now. Have you called the police?"

But there was no answer from Kim. Steve's blood ran cold, colder than ice as he reached for his jacket, while telling the others where he was going. His house was only two miles from Fettes. The threats made to him on the phone the other day were fresh in his mind and fear stabbed his face like needles being pushed into his skin. Marcus and Fran went with him without hesitation.

The phone shone brightly in front of her as she saw the masked face pushed up close to the window, eyes peering in through the glass. A second person appeared. Kim shoved the phone against her chest to hide its light. She could still hear Steve but dared not answer. Torchlight from outside swung round and into the house, probing into the darkness, creating eerie shadows downstairs. Kim held her breath as terror filled her heart. The invasive light made its way slowly up the stairs, climbing steadily up towards her. Unable to move, frozen to the spot, the beam shone straight into Kim's face, the phone dropping down from her chest from the shock.

Both froze, Kim with terror and the man outside with a little jolt of unexpected attention. He had believed the house to be empty due to the minimal lighting and lack of movement from within.

He lifted his hand to his throat and drew it menacingly across from ear to ear. Kim simply stood there, terror struck initially, but then her maternal instincts took over. She suddenly flew into a maniacal rage at the threat to her and her children sleeping upstairs. She wasn't going to just stand there and do nothing about it.

Without thought or fear of the consequences, she rushed down the stairs straight towards the men, who were both taken aback at her reaction.

They had no intention of sticking around anyway. They had done what they had come to do and the Feds would be on their way anyway. Kim grabbed at the many locks on the back door and tried her hardest to get at them. The time it took turned out to be a godsend for her as the intruders were tooled up with large hunting knives and they were more than prepared to harm her if she got in the way of their escape.

Their trials bikes roared into life as they revved up the powerful engines and shot down Silverknowes Road, veering off road onto the council run golf course before Kim's assistance arrived at the house.

Response cars pulled up moments later, sirens blaring and lights flashing, four sets in total. It had seemed like an age, but in reality, it had only been minutes since her call to Steve. One set had come from Leith, one came down from Broomhouse, and another all the way from Queensferry. None of the local Drylaw sets had been available to respond, already dealing with other incidents. Steve, Marcus and Fran pulled up along with the other officers and were met by a frantic Kim, her eyes streaming with tears, her hands shaking with fear, rage and desperation as she ran to Steve. He held her tight, anguish and despair now filling him with dread.

"Are you okay? Where are the kids? Are they okay?" Steve said, running into the house to check his children.

"They're fine, they're all fine. I wouldn't let anything happen to them, even if I had to die doing it."

Steve looked at her, sadness and guilt twisting and tearing his stomach into knots, knowing that in his bid to make their life a little easier, he had done the exact opposite and may even have threatened their lives. He dropped his eyes to prevent her noticing what was going on in his head. He knew his wife would have done anything to save their kids, and if that meant death, so be it.

Marcus looked around the side of the house and saw the petrol cans sitting there, the side gate ajar, its padlock on the ground, having been cut. A pair of discarded bolt cutters lay beside it.

"What the fuck? Steve, get round here! These guys meant business. Who's fucking cage have you rattled, mate? They weren't fucking around, you know! If they had lit this, with this amount of accelerant your house would have gone up in seconds with your family in it!"

Fran was already on her phone to the Scenes Examination Branch and CID. She began to cordon off the area and asked for air support and any roads policing sets that could assist in trying to trace the bikes, knowing full well they would already be dumped and the assailants miles away, virtually untraceable, time delays always favouring the criminal.

Fran also phoned Taylor, who was initially abrupt when she came on the line, most probably harassed in the office, but she softened when she heard it was Fran.

"Hi, what's up?" she asked, unaware of where they were and what they were dealing with.

Fran whispered, deliberately avoiding broadcasting her call to their boss, but she felt Taylor should know what was going on, sooner rather than later.

Taylor's eyebrows lifted as she listened intently.

"Thanks Fran, the heads up is appreciated. What do you think? Why his house?"

Both of them were deep in thought by the end of the call. They were perturbed by the level of threat made on Steve's family and puzzled by the reason behind it. They chatted away like they used to, both appreciating their similar ways of thinking, until the end of the conversation when Fran felt the cruel ache of her loss as it became clear that the call was just work.

Chapter 18
Same Assailant

The team that were working on the deaths in the Leith flat had scoured hours and hours of CCTV footage and there had been many leads found and followed up, all negative. They had recently come across footage of an unidentified male in the area. These images had been circulated throughout the police systems with the hope he could be identified by officers on the street.

Eventually a name was put forward from a cop in the Drylaw area - Craig McNare.

The name had been a regular feature on office boards in years gone by, but had disappeared off the face of the earth after a drug stop in the Muirhouse area, several years before. McNare had successfully evaded the police since then. He seemed to have gone underground, completely off the radar, believed to be living down south, out of sight and out of mind. The police believed he was hiding from them and evading arrest. In reality, he was saving his life. There was a massive bounty on his head. He knew the police would never kill him, but Burnett would.

Taylor was very excited about the sighting of McNare in the area around the time of the incident believing that there was somehow a connection, although there was nothing to suggest that.

Officers carried out more research into McNare. The death of his partner in a fire came out, which was very significant especially the way in which she had died, giving the coincidental sighting of McNare near to the recent fire a more sinister turn. The post mortem results had shown she had been pregnant at the time of her death. Taylor started pushing for further enquiries to be made further afield in relation to the incident and also the major blaze at the warehouse in Sighthill, her mind ticking over, the common thread being fire.

Taylor knocked and entered the DCI's office blurting out, "We need to find him." DI Findlay barely raised his head up from his computer, totally disinterested in what Taylor had to say, their mutual dislike for one another very obvious to see.

Brooke Sommerville on the other hand was very interested in what she had to say and couldn't help but notice how nice Taylor looked. Her heart still skipped a beat when she was around, although this annoyed her as she didn't want to feel like that.

There was a slight hesitation by both of them, their illicit encounter several months before still clouding their working relationship and still creating an invisible tension between them, a mixture of desire, mutual respect and a few what ifs.

"Why him? Is he not just a junkie crawling the streets to get a fix or looking for his next deal?" Sommerville questioned.

"I don't think so, I think it's really significant, ma'am. He's not been around for years. That's a coincidence in itself, but here he is close to an assassination and another unexplained death. Do you not think that's significant? I mean he was a big player in his day, handling really big quantities of drugs. I don't think he was the main player though."

"Drug dealing is very different to murder though, Taylor. That's quite a big step up, don't you think?" Brooke's eyebrows were raised, as if pushing Taylor to try harder to convince her.

"His partner and unborn child were killed in a fire shortly after police pulled him over and found a large quantity of heroin in his car, its street value worth hundreds of thousands of pounds, and some! Funnily enough, some local youths took the fall for that. Claimed they were just arsing around and they didn't think about the consequences, and if you believe that, well… That makes his reappearance a bit more significant, don't you think?"

Brooke's face changed a little as the cogs began to turn and a smile appeared, a smile that changed her whole appearance, a rare thing these days with the continual pressure they were all under.

Taylor got a sense of satisfaction and smiled too, sharing her hope and thoughts about wanting to widen the search regarding the the fire at Leith to see if they could find a connection with the Sighthill fire. Arson was not the normal method for murder in Edinburgh, or a common crime in the capital for that matter. Two fires in such a short space of time, had to be significant. There had also been more homicides in the past month than there usually were in a year

"Get hunting for McNare, Taylor. Find him! I don't know what he's up too and why, but this level of violence is for a reason and it has to stop."

Chapter 19
Warning

Shaz was a rotund woman. She wore large men's shirts, had a face like an old bull dog, and was a woman who knew how to take care of herself. Her expansive backside rubbed past the door frame as she turned to lock up the sauna, alarm set, tired from her long day. Dealing with the girls and the punters all day and half the night was wearing on her. Some of them she truly hated, their depraved dirty, cruel needs being played out day after day on these poor girls. She didn't agree, but Nelson knew that the money paid was always higher for things a little bit more kinky and sadistic. She herself was paid well too, and she knew when to keep her trap shut. The girls had already been collected and taken back to where they were housed. She knew that they had all been trafficked into the country with no hope of ever breaking free. This too didn't sit well with her, but her fear of Nelson far outweighed her concern for the girls. Shaz knew she would be nose down at the bottom of the water of Leith wearing concrete boots before she knew it if she didn't keep her mouth shut. Her loyalty lay with him through fear not respect.

The New Town streets, with their cobbled roads, were quiet, as they usually were at 1.30am. There were a few lights still on at the four-storey stone-built dwellings, curtains drawn, the city's wealthy folk enjoying the comfort of their multimillion-pound homes. There was nothing modest about this area, the cars lining the streets also a testament to wealth with very few below the fifty-grand price mark.

Shaz's car was a little further away. She did not have a parking permit for the area close to the sauna and had to walk a short distance down the road to get to it. This didn't bother her. She was tough and her ungainly swagger was usually enough to deter any negative attention developing into danger, but not tonight.

She swivelled round threateningly on her comfy shoes, her head turning quickly to see what had made the noise behind her, ready to take on whoever it was invading her space, but to her surprise she couldn't see anyone there, not a soul in the street.

She shook her head muttering, absolutely sure that there had been someone behind her. *You're fucking losing it woman. Just get your arse home, and put yer feet up.*

Her walk down the desolate street continued, this time a little quicker, but McNare's pace was faster and this time his footsteps were silent on the pavement, his martial arts training helping with his stealth. This time he made sure there was not a sound to be heard. The thick plastic bag went right over Shaz's head, a savage tightness round her neck instantly restricting her breath. Her fingers gripped at his powerful hands in a futile attempt to free herself, her legs kicking out viciously backwards to try and boot him heavily on his shins, but he swept her legs away from her with ease, skilfully dropping her to her knees.

He made sure he kept her face facing forwards as he spoke menacingly into her ear, his voice cruel and threatening, his words harsh with violent torment, enough to put the fear of death in her. His warning was for Burnett and it had been received loud and clear.

Shaz was now gasping for air, her mouth gulping in an involuntary motion desperate for breath, the carbon monoxide in the bag eating away at the remainder of the oxygen, her head dizzy, consciousness slipping away.

The jolt was brutal as her head was yanked backwards. A burning pain seared through her as the knife sliced her face. Blood poured out of the wound. Life-saving oxygen flowed back in through the slash in the bag as she lay wounded on the street, footsteps light as they moved quickly away from her, his departure as discreet as his arrival. McNare's path took him back past the sauna. The accelerant he had left by the door was sprayed through the letter box and ignited. It only took seconds to take hold and light up the night with an orange glow. He watched long enough to savour the moment, then ran as fast as he could, making sure he stayed off the main streets.

It wasn't long before a taxi drove by. The driver saw Sharon slumped on the street, the bag still over her head. She was clearly in shock, blood now covering her light jacket and continuing to pour from the deep disfiguring gash in her face, a large fold of skin hanging down, exposing the inside of her mouth.

The driver was already calling 999 as he jumped from his cab and went to help her. Her head was fuzzy, the blood loss and terror from the attack overwhelming her, but she was still with it enough for her heart to fill with fear when she heard the driver speaking to the services, knowing that the police would be there soon.

"I'm alright, I'm fine, thanks. I'll manage. My car's just down here. I just need to get home!" she said desperately trying to get up on her feet.

The driver felt obliged to help her up as she was clearly going to try to get to her feet. He instantly realised it was a big mistake as he tried to hold her weight. She fell heavily back to the concrete, hitting her head on the pavement, causing further injury. This time she did not move. Although breathing, she was no longer conscious and unable to escape the unwanted scrutiny the police would put her under.

Blues lights and sirens filled the scene. Shaz was lifted into the ambulance as smoke billowed out from the sauna doorway.

Chapter 20
Home

Taylor arrived home, very late as usual, and headed straight for the shower, blissfully unaware of what the night shift were now dealing with.

The hot water cascaded over her face. She tilted her head back, letting it pour vigorously onto her, enjoying the strength of the water as it flowed over her needy body. The water continued down the contours of her body, sliding over her lithe and athletic frame, long limbs perfectly formed and weary from another long day at work. Her mind raced with everything that was going on at work and in her troubled non-existent love life.

Once out of the shower, she headed downstairs wrapped in her lightweight, knee length dressing gown. Her phone pinged with a message. Surprised and wondering who could be texting so late, she opened it warily, fearing it was bad news.

The number that had come up was unknown, and this made her even more curious. The text was short but made her eyebrows rise. *How had they managed to get my number?* Taylor thought as she read the message. "Are you up? Do you fancy a night cap? I've had a really long day and I think you might be interested in hearing about it - not that work is all I'd like to talk about!"

Taylor's eyebrows lifted even higher when she read the name at the bottom of the text. It was Lana. Taylor gave a little smile, her mind wondering once again.

Taylor's reply took little thought, as she had already allowed herself to think about Lana in that way. "I'm still up, and there's a beer in the fridge for you," she typed.

"Where do you stay? They weren't as easy to persuade to give out your address, or will I just continue to drive about aimlessly a little longer?" Lana smiled with hopeful anticipation as she wrote back.

Once Taylor had given Lana her address, she shut her eyes and thought, *What am I doing, my life's a bloody mess already, as if I need this, but I do need this?*

She knew, if she was honest with herself, that she had wanted this for quite a while now, but hadn't thought it would ever happen, because she herself was not going to pursue it.

Her instinct was to hold back and be conservative, but her daring less sensible side made her want to see what would happen. Against all of her better judgement, her mind convinced her that she was single and that it could do no harm. It was just a harmless drink, *at 3am in the morning!*

Taylor didn't bother getting dressed. She gulped down a bottle of Bud and then reached for another. She hadn't eaten much during the day, so the beer went straight to her head as she glugged greedily at the second one.

The doorbell rang and Taylor moved to the door, her thighs exposed with every step she took, her silky smooth, olive skin a contrast with the pure white of her cotton gown. Her hair was still damp, her light curls lying as spirals on her shoulders. She didn't have any makeup on, but she still looked good, her big brown eyes with their naturally long lashes a draw into her gaze, her full lips a little wet from her beer and her deliberate brush of them with her tongue. The material of the gown, pulled in by the tie, showed off the shape of her toned body, leaving not a lot to the imagination. Taylor's apprehension had already turned to excited anticipation. She had had a traumatic few weeks, her heart was sore and she had not been intimate with anyone for a long time. Her mind was made up. She wanted more than a drink and was sure that that was Lana's intention too.

She opened the door and Lana stood there, six foot tall, long fair hair pulled into a pony tail, slim, athletic with muscular shoulders, feminine features with a masculine hint because of her physical structure. She wore fitted skinny jeans, trainers and a loose cotton round neck white top button opened at the front, slightly revealing, all unisex nondescript clothes. She wasn't Taylor's usual type, being quite similar to herself in nature and character, and not the sort to be controlled.

Lana looked at Taylor, flowers in hand from the all-night garage, her smile broad and genuine as she stood on the doorstep. Taylor smiled back, and for once felt a little vulnerable as she recognised the familiar look in Lana's eyes, a look she imagined herself to have when she felt that way.

Lana looked at Taylor's bare legs, her gaze travelling up to where her breasts were pleasantly and slightly exposed, before moving on to Taylor's long neck, defined jawline and then to her eyes. Their eyes locked and not another word was said. The flowers were dropped to the floor as Lana's strong but soft hand stroked gently up Taylor's outer thigh all the way up to her perfectly rounded bottom. She pulled herself up the step to the same level as Taylor, and they both moved inside the hall. Taylor was barely able to shut the door before Lana kissed her, pulling her closer with her hand cupped round Lana's cheek. Taylor's body pressed against her, Lana's thigh now between Taylor's legs. She could feel the material of Lana's jeans rub against her, and it felt good. Taylor felt her head spin, a little taken aback at Lana's confidence in coming to her house and taking her like this, but Taylor found herself wanting to be taken.

Their kiss was intense, passionate, very needy and a little desperate, but completely thrilling. Lana's hand now replaced her thigh, her pleasure audible when she felt how wet Taylor was. Taylor's response was even more expressive. She moaned loudly at the intensity of sensation. Taylor gripped Lana's shoulders as Lana rubbed over her with the perfect pressure, several times, before pushing deep up inside her. Taylor's legs gave way a little at Lana's intimate touch, the pleasure very powerful. Taylor was a little taken aback at how good this felt and how out of control she was now acting, and Lana seemed to know it. She kissed Taylor deeply, her tongue delving into Taylor's fully responsive and inviting mouth. The kiss was as good as Lana had imagined it would be during all of their previous meetings. Lana had found Taylor incredibly attractive from their first encounter and had hoped she would have the opportunity to savour Taylor's beauty. Her heart raced as her dream was coming true, Taylor had managed to pull Lana through to the living room, and she was now lying on her back, her gown open, the tie lying across her taut stomach. Lana made love to her, her fingers pleasuring Taylor deep inside. She licked her, and the intensity grew. Taylor rocked her head back and moaned out loud, the pleasure mounting. She was finding it hard to hold her orgasm back any longer. Lana's fingers gripped tightly on one of Taylor's nipples as her tongue continued to swirl on her clitoris, her other fingers pushing deeper into Taylor with more force. Taylor let out a squeal of pleasure as her climax spiralled deep inside her, her body moving down towards Lana, forcing her deeper into her. Taylor's body kept on responding as she came hard again. This time Lana came up from being down on Taylor and kissed her, their mouths wet and needy, tongues and lips full of desire and out of control, Taylor enjoying the taste of her own pleasure. Taylor feverishly responded, lifting up Lana's top and pulling her bra down relishing the perfect vision, taking Lana's nipples into her mouth, her hands pulling desperately at her jeans. She wanted to have Lana too and to give back the same pleasures she had just enjoyed.

She managed to pull Lana's jeans down far enough for her mouth to savour her, to taste her intimacy. The tingling sensation and the fact she was still trapped in her clothing turned Lana on all the more. Taylor followed her mouth with her fingers.

The restriction of movement was even more thrilling. Obviously turned on, Lana helped Taylor undress her. Their naked bodies slipped up against one another, a perfect blend of skin tones and physical perfection in two women. Taylor's hands cupped Lana's strong buttocks as she pulled her into her, pushing against each other's intimacy. Taylor licked the length of Lana's body before turning her onto her front. Her teeth gently gripped Lana's strong buttocks and the back of her thighs, her skin soft and silky as she stroked her pussy underneath. Her fingers glistened as she pleasured her, then she pushed up into her as she licked gently over her ass. Lana jumped instinctively forward, and let out an unlikely giggle as the sensation was exciting and unexpected, but then she relaxed back at the pleasurable motion of Taylor's tongue upon her, Taylor's firm hands and skilled fingers ensuring a mind blowing orgasm followed, Lana's expectations of their first encounter fulfilled. It had been both exciting and addictive.

Their lovemaking finally ended, and they sat up straight on the couch smiling. Taylor offered Lana a drink, then threw her clothes at her and said, "You'll get cold. I don't want you to catch a chill," laughing kindly as she did so.

"I don't think that will happen any time soon." Lana smiled back at her, comfortable sitting there in a state of undress, confident in her appearance without many clothes. Taylor was a little disappointed that Lana was half-dressed when she came back through. She had tied her gown and was also now semi-decent. She considered straddling Lana as she sat there, desire still coursing through her, her guest totally unaware of her thoughts, but in the end she just sat down beside Lana on the couch, allowing her robe to open slightly.

Taylor remembered Lana had news for her and decided not to reignite their lust, not yet. "Right, what was it you said - a long hard day and you had something interesting to tell me about what you were dealing with tonight?" Taylor said jokingly, with a contented look on her face.

Lana laughed at her and patted the space beside her, inviting her to sit really close to her, which Taylor did willingly.

"We were at a fire tonight, another deliberate one, and the madam from the premises was seriously assaulted less than 100 metres from the door. Now that's a little suspicious don't you think, a bit more to that than meets the eye? I was hoping you would have been there. I was hoping to say hi."

Taylor looked at her, mirth in her expression as she said, "Hi! Even I get a day off sometimes. There are other cops you know."

Her focus returned to what Lana was saying. Lana reeled off some of the details of the night - timings, injuries, some thoughts given by the cops she had known at the scene, which Taylor seemed particularly interested in.

They chatted long into the night and retired to bed together, Taylor's unfulfilled needs finally addressed as they shared several more hours of unbridled, intimate sex until dawn.

Marcus was tucked up in bed with Maria, their precious son David safely asleep in his room, both fresh from the excitement of Marcus telling them that they were going off to Paris at the weekend for a short break, just the three of them. There had been a real buzz of joy in their house. Time was always of the essence and, with work taking up most of it, not enough of it was spent together these days,.

His mind floated back to their lovemaking earlier that evening. A couple of glasses of red wine had set the mood, faces flushed with the alcohol as Maria kissed him while they caressed one another, clearly relaxed with the effects of the wine. Their lives had not quite got back to the way they were before David's abduction earlier in the year. But, tonight had felt different with the excitement at knowing they were going away, uninterrupted time away together, just their little family, so precious, and even more so after thinking they had lost wee David, possibly forever.

He thought of her pulling at his shirt to get him to follow her up to the bedroom. He had had no hesitation in doing so. It had been a long time since they had really taken the time to enjoy one another.

Marcus held her face as he pulled her close to kiss her, their mouths tuned to one another. His kiss was full on and wanton, his arousal already at a peak. She knew this and pulled him towards her and took his hand between her legs, his strong gentle touch sending ripples of pleasure through her. She was really turned on. She had missed him and the pleasure he brought her, but her heart and head had not been able to allow it for such a long time. He skilfully brought her to a climax with his strong hands, before he couldn't hold off any more. He lay her gently on her back, pulled off her underwear and kissed her intimately, intensifying her need for him. He pulled himself up onto her and gently but firmly entered her, his first thrust slow and deep, then another, pushing as deep as he could go. Maria raised her body up, wanting all of him, taking him into her. His thrusts quickened as his desire unravelled. Maria groaned as he made love to her, their bodies joining in perfect intimacy, a forgotten harmony as their bodies became one again, both of them freed at last from the invisible binds of tension, fear and the stress they had suffered for months. They had both been caught up in the year's events, blocking each other out, especially the need to be intimate, something they were used to, but it hadn't felt right, until now. They lay in each other's arms, exchanging soft tender kisses, a closeness they had longed for once again shared.

They knew that this was a turning point for all of them, and that they could start living their lives again. Their lives had been touched by the Devil, but this had only made them stronger.

Chapter 21
Unwelcome Visitors

Burnett was out on his balcony when he saw two cop cars pull up down below, outside his block of luxury flats.

"Irene, that's the bacon here. What the fuck to they want?" he growled through to the bedroom, almost blaming her for them coming to his door.

There was a loud knock at the door, and Irene was sent to open it. She had to rush to dress and was a little dishevelled as she went to answer it.

Two well-dressed detectives stood before her, and she casually asked what they wanted, fearful of what was to come.

Taylor and Marcus showed their ID cards and Taylor asked politely if they could come in.

"NO! THEY FUCKING CANNAE COME IN, HAVE THEY GOT A FUCKING WARRANT? IF NOT, TELL THEM TO GET TAE FUCK," Burnett yelled through from the balcony, with his usual polite response to the police.

Taylor noticed the faded bruising on Irene's face. They looked at each other, Taylor giving her a knowing expression, which told Irene she knew it had been Nelson that had injured her face. Another shared look passed between them, one of exasperation from Taylor, she herself a strong and independent woman, who in her time in the police had never understood why women stayed with their partners that hurt them over and over, controlling them in every way.

Taylor raised her head up and spoke loudly back to Nelson, "We won't be needing a warrant, we just need to talk to you Mr Burnett."

"WHAT THE FUCK FOR, WHY WOULD I WANT TO TALK TO YOUSE CUNTS, NOW GET TAE FUCK AWAY FROM MA HOOSE!"

"Actually, I think you might want to hear what we have to say Mr Burnett, as it involves your premises in the New Town."

"What about them? It's all fucking legit. I have all the permits, licences, it even has the right fire safety certificate, so fucking do one."

"Fire certificate you said? Because that's a bit of a pity really," Taylor said a little too sarcastically. She was getting fed up standing out on the landing being abused by this man, who thought he was above the law.

She could hear heavy footsteps marching through from the living room, and that made her smile. She straightened up, readying herself for their meeting, not scared, but a little wary, as he was known to be violent with the police, male or female.

His face was flushed and angry when he came face to face with Taylor, deliberately walking into her personal space, his face virtually touching hers.

"What the fuck do you mean by that, you smug looking boot?"

"Mr Burnett, please try and refrain from being abusive to us, or you'll end up getting lifted for a breach," she said with a serious face, moving even closer to his face, noses touching momentarily, her intolerance of intimidation and ignorance making her bristle with anger and resentment, fully aware of how connected this man was and that he could turn on her at any moment, but still not willing to back down.

"Aye, so ye will ya fucking jumped-up smug-arsed bitch. My lawyer would have me out in no time." He sprayed saliva into her face as he spoke, which she thought was deliberate.

Not budging an inch, Taylor just wiped her face and continued to talk politely to him, causing Marcus to move up by her side, his face tightening. He hated people like Burnett who threatened women.

This was like a red rag to a bull. Burnett was barely tolerating Taylor, but a man was a step too far. "Who the fuck do you think you are, ya wee tosser, movin' up to save yer burd here, eh? I'll fuck you right up, ya cunt. What do you think you're gonna dae anyway, ya wee fanny?" Burnett's posture was now fully threatening and intimidating, itching for a reason to fight.

Irene was standing behind Nelson. She knew he was going to go mad. He had been on the coke all night and it was either her or them that was going to get it.

Marcus just held his stare, unafraid. He had met many people like Burnett and he could feel the situation was going to boil over, but he could hold his own and was ready for it.

Before Taylor got the chance to explain why they were there, Burnett lunged at Marcus, shoving Taylor back hard against the wall in the process. She didn't like this one bit and pushed herself back up as Marcus avoided the first punch, but Burnett caught him with the second, sending him reeling backwards onto his backside. Burnett lunged forward leaning over towards Marcus. Taylor struck the side of his thigh full force with her baton, giving her time to press the emergency button on her airwave terminal and shout for back up. Burnett buckled on one side, pain searing through his dead leg, now raging at her. He tried to turn around to get at her, struggling to regain his balance.

"I'LL FUCKING HAVE YOU, YA SLUT. I'LL TEACH YOU SOME FUCKING RESPECT!"

The words were barely out of his mouth when Taylor struck him on the upper arm as hard as she could. Marcus grabbed him round the legs and managed to topple him to the floor.

"IRENE, PHONE MY FUCKING LAWYER. HELP ME OUT HERE, YA DAFT WEE COW. FUCKING HIT THE BITCH!"

Irene moved towards Taylor, thinking about doing as Burnett had ordered, but just one look from Taylor with her baton raised over her shoulder and she chose to move back again, knowing that Taylor wouldn't hesitate to use it.

Two cops came running up the stairs and helped to restrain Burnett. They finally got him under control using leg restraints, handcuffs and a spit hood. He continued to struggle violently, refusing to go quietly, and they had to carry him down four flights of stairs to a police van that was now arriving. He was clearly too unruly to transport in a car.

Taylor cautioned him and told him he was under arrest for police assault, telling him that this needn't have happened.

She walked with the cops that were struggling a bit with his weight, and went on to tell him why they had been at his door in the first place. She told him about the sauna, the fire and the serious assault on Sharon near to the premises, knowing full well that this would make him even angrier, but she was beyond caring. Burnett was a vile individual and she had been more than patient with him. He had bruised her shoulder and assaulted her partner Marcus. She was done pussy footing around with this complete arsehole.

Once Burnett was safely in the van, Taylor turned to look at Marcus and saw that he had a fat lip, so she pushed hers out further to copy him and tease him about his new look.

"Fuck off, Sergeant Nicks, with all due respect," he said. They were now able to laugh about the incident as they were both safe and had Burnett's full attention.

"That went well then," Taylor said sarcastically, the adrenaline still flowing in her veins. She had yet to calm down after the rush, and her hands were still shaking.

"Tits up you mean. Fucking hell Taylor, he could have knocked your bloody teeth out."

She smiled at him and said, "Lucky he chose yours then." She poked his lip gently.

"Ha bloody ha, but it was pretty full on eh. Good job we came out on top," he said seriously, knowing that Burnett could have knocked him out.

"Never a doubt in my mind who would win," Taylor said, truly confident in their ability.

"Well, let's go and speak to the fine gentleman we now have in custody." Taylor smiled, falsely beaming at the prospect of having to speak to Burnett again, knowing he would be livid.

Chapter 22

Questions Need Answered

Taylor and Marcus arrived at the cells complex at St Leonard's Police Station and waited at the door to be buzzed in. Instantly, the smell of cheesy feet and sour body odour hit their noses. People were shouting and swearing at one another from cell to cell, or just generally wailing to vent their anger and anguish. The magnolia walls were covered in scuff marks, spit, blood, faecal matter and other body fluids. They moved through to the booking area and watched as another couple of Edinburgh's poor souls were booked in for the night, each with their story to tell and marks and scars from their eventful lives to prove it.

They spoke with the cells Sergeant, Katriona McVay, to let her know what they had brought in. The cells officers looked up at the suited officers and noted the bruising on Marcus's mouth. Taylor met their interest with a polite "Hello, how's things today?" and relayed their tale and why they were there, always taking the time to talk to people, taking away the chance of whispers and impressions of them as unknowns. Lors walked through. She was a friend of Taylor and they greeted each other with a warm smile. Lors was a long serving officer in the cells, and took no shit from anyone

They asked for Burnett to be taken out of his cell, Taylor told them the task would be interesting to say the least. He was likely to fight or resist at best and she wanted to ensure the safety of the cells officers.

"Is his lawyer here yet? I take it he wants one?" Marcus asked, knowing the answer.

The rather stressed Sergeant looked up. She was a strong woman, attractive, very capable and someone you would not want to mess with. She said, "They're already here, suited up and clearly pissed off. He has a face like he's been chewing a wasp and walked in like he owned the bloody place."

Taylor smiled at Katriona, meeting her stress filled gaze with a knowing look, one that said she had seen it all before. "Coffee?" Taylor asked.

"I'd love one," Katriona replied as her eyes led Taylor to the piles of paperwork on her desk. Taylor squeezed her shoulder and went through to the kitchen to fulfil her promise.

Shouting and bawling came ringing out from the corridor outside and Taylor peeked her head round the door to watch as one of the prisoners swaggered naked down the corridor, yelling at the top of his voice in protest at being held in custody. He was being taken back to an observation cell, voicing his intention of self-harm. The officers that held his arms were exasperated with their struggle to prevent this, spit in their hair from his last attack towards them. When the male noticed Taylor looking at him, he smiled at her and thrust his hips forward at her, causing his penis to wave up and down towards her.

"Want some, darling?" he said with a menacing look in his face, continuing to thrust his hips at her.

Taylor just smiled, unperturbed, with an expression of sarcastic mirth on her face. She had seen it all before in her lengthy service, to rise to this insignificant little twerp, but chose to respond anyway. "Eh, no thanks, I've already eaten today," she said sarcastically," putting his gas at a peep.

The custody officers directed him away as Lors was heading down to check on the other prisoners, and his focus shifted onto her, delighted that he could continue with his sexual harassment. He thrust his hips again as quickly as he could, his manhood barely 10 feet away from her, but the verbal well versed onslaught he received from Lors, left him in no doubt about the inadequacy of the size of his appendage, and he allowed himself to be more easily directed away from her, to try and save face.

When the officers turned him round, Taylor was still there, so he continued trying to get her attention but failed miserably. The officers had to use a little more force to get him away and into his new cell, this one fitted with cameras to prevent him injuring himself. They offered him the chance to put on his anti-ligature suit, but he chose to remain naked and began masturbating in full view of the camera, shouting obscenities at the cops and more vile offers of sexual delights to Taylor.

"How do you cope being in here all day? You must get cabin fever." Taylor smiled at the worn-out looking officer sitting there.

The cop smiled, a genuine smile, and replied, "At least I get to go home at the end of the day. They don't."

Burnett was brought through from his cell. He was walking independently but with a limp, the result of Taylor's baton strike. Officers flanked him on both sides, Burnett choosing not to get into any further physical altercations on this occasion.

Taylor watched as he was brought closer. He snarled at her, mumbling about suing her, but continued into the interview room where his lawyer was already sitting.

As Taylor walked into the room, the lawyer said abruptly that they wanted a private consultation and rudely dismissed the officers from the room. He leant back and smiled. They left the room deliberately slowly, but this was Burnett's right, so they had to go.

Taylor wasn't bothered. She hadn't expected a friendly face but whispered, "Rude prick," under her breath to Marcus, and they chuckled like little kids. "Good, more time to finish our coffee and chat." They asked the officers standing by at the door to give them the heads up when he was going to be ready. Both smiled and obliged.

The cells Sergeant had a queue at her desk, officers relaying their custodies to her for her decision to be made on their status. Taylor peeked over and pointed to her cup. Katriona crossed her eyes and pretended to pull her hair out but nodded for another.

Eventually, a young fresh-faced male officer came through, blushing slightly as he interrupted their chat. He told them that Burnett was ready. Once allowed inside the room, Taylor was blunt. She knew politeness hadn't got her anywhere before with him, and he was clearly bristling for round two.

"Mr Burnett, this is not an interview. It is just a chat about what happened at the sauna last night as I already explained to you at the house when you decided to attack us."

"Attack youse? You fucking went for me first, ya daft fucking bitch, and I have a witness tae prove it. I'm going to sue you for criminal damage, and you know I'll get it!" Burnett said smugly.

Taylor's blood was already boiling and this accusation, although expected, punched right into her ribs. She knew that a slime ball like him probably would be awarded compensation.

Ignoring her thoughts, she said, "I think you are forgetting why you are now under arrest Mr Burnett, and if you choose to make a counter-allegation, I wish you luck with that. However, can we get back to the point?" Taylor's voice was raised and full of conviction with a hint of controlled verbal aggression.

"Mr Burnett, it is pretty clear to me that someone appears to be wanting to harm you and your business interests, what with the fire, the assault and the tragic death of an associate of yours?"

"What fucking associate of mine, ya daft cow? Stop talking shite! What the fuck are ye talking aboot?" he said, knowing full well she was talking about the deaths in Leith.

He turned to his lawyer and whispered to him, ensuring she couldn't trip him up and incriminate him.

Taylor stayed silent for a little moment, watching him and his reactions, a little sweat, eye-contact avoidance, assurance from the lawyer, all the traits of guilty knowledge, regardless of what shit would come out of his big foul mouth.

"Mr Burnett, the gentleman was called Gordon Wilson. He was a defence lawyer, and your name and number were in his phone. Are you prepared to explain that?"

"No! I'm not under arrest, and I'm not here to answer your fucking questions. Am I right or am I wrong? I am here for a so-called chat, so get fucking chatting, or I'm fucking going back to my cell!"

"As I said, Mr Burnett, someone appears to be targeting you. Do you have any idea who that may be? Why would someone want to do this to you, the sauna, your work colleague? She is pretty shaken up, disfigured. Someone is going out of their way for you to notice them and keep you looking over your shoulder?"

"No idea, bewildered really, and nobody makes me look over my fuckin' shoulder, hen, 'cause if they are there, I'll fucking kick the living shit right out of them. Whoever it is will get his bollocks ripped off and jammed down his throat," he said with his voice full of arrogance and vengeance.

"What makes you think it's a man, Nelson?" Taylor deliberately baited him into another angry outburst.

He just glared at her, his silence enough to let her know that he thought women were not on the same level as him and not up to any sort of relevant challenge to his superiority and they wouldn't dare to anyway.

"We can help you, if you help us," Taylor said honestly, despite being full of resentment towards this twisted controlling man, a man that was capable of truly horrific crimes of violence.

"Why would I need your help? You lot are fucking useless, and I've done nothing wrong anyway, nothing at all!" he growled, the little patience he'd had now completely gone.

"So, you've got nothing to say then? Well, if you need our help, you know where we are, Mr Burnett."

Taylor nodded to the officers outside to take over, and she and Marcus got up and left the room, Taylor's face a little red with exasperation at just how much of an arsehole she thought he was.

Burnett was also red faced and a little flustered. He was taken back to his cell. He was very aware someone was after him, as well as the cops, and he would need to be very careful for a while until whoever it was was caught. He would put the feelers out to find out who was trying to fuck him over, and he would use that snivelling little bent cop Shack to find out what the Feds knew and allow him to get one step ahead of them.

Chapter 23
A Hand is Forced

Kim sat in her living room having just fed and medicated Maisy, tears in her eyes, fear in her heart. She didn't believe the other night was a random threat; it had been a very real and direct threat. Maybe they had actually been trying to kill her and her whole family, but the sirens had stopped it from happening. The question kept stabbing her head to the point she could actually feel a pain piercing her brain. Her nerves were shot to pieces, her hands shaking at how wrong it could have gone for her family, for her if she'd managed to get out of the house to try and get at them. Had they set the fire, could she have saved her innocent little children? She wanted to move away, get away from the city, take some action, but most of all she wanted to speak to Steven. He had seemed off lately, hard to talk to, on edge, and now this. He knew more than he was letting on.

Steve came down the stairs, straightening his tie, clean shaven and ready for work. He kissed Maisy and then went to kiss Kim, but she pulled away, out of reach. He was taken aback.

"What's wrong, Kim? I know you're still upset about the other day, but this case we are on has obviously got the underworld feeling uncomfortable. It wasn't personal. They somehow found out one of our addresses and are trying to intimidate us, the police that is!"

"Not bloody personal? Intimidate us, INTIMIDATE US! For Christ's sake, Steven, they did more than that. They were going to bloody KILL US! I know it. They went a bit too far for just one of the cops on the team. Why us, Steven, why? Have you got something to tell me? What have you done?"

"Nothing, I haven't done anything! I haven't, honestly! What are you saying? That's so unfair Kim. I know you're angry at what happened the other day, so am I, I'm bloody livid in fact. They are scum, pure scum. They have cops out there now 24/7 for our protection, and they will do until they find out who was behind this, and I will work every waking moment to get them behind bars," Steven exclaimed as truthfully as he could muster, but inside his guts were churning, physically twisting in fear at the consequence of his severe lapse in judgement. He had taken money from the hand of a demon.

"I don't believe you. There's more to this, and you know more than you are telling me. What is it? Talk to me, help me understand." Kim lunged at him, gripping desperately at his shirt, wanting to get inside his head, find out the truth. She was terrified for the children, for all of them.

Steve shifted awkwardly. "There isn't anything. I've already told you, we were just the unlucky ones, and I have to go to work and try and solve this shit, and I don't need more here at home. I've got to go. There are cops outside as I told you. You'll be safe. They won't be back, I promise!" He gently removed her outstretched hands, desperate to tell her the truth, but Kim was not overly forgiving when it came to anything that endangered her children.

Steve reached to kiss Kim's cheek again. This time she let him kiss her goodbye. He kissed Maisy too. She was happily playing with some toys, aware that something wasn't right at the moment, but too young to care. Steve's heart was racing, his cheeks flushed. He avoided eye contact with Kim as he left, his despair almost overwhelming him.

Kim knew there was more to this. She knew Steven, and he was hiding something. He wasn't a bad man, but didn't always make the best decisions,. The only person who could tell her what was going on was like a closed vault. What had he done?

Steve left quickly, shutting the door firmly behind him, hoping she wouldn't follow. He felt sick to the pit of his stomach. He had made a decision. He would give the information to them, whoever they were, but not Sorina; he would feed them McNare, the one causing them all their trouble. Then, hopefully, he'd be able to kill two birds with one stone, or so he thought.

Chapter 24
DNA Confirmed

Michelle was pulling her hair out up on the sixth floor of Fettes in the Public Protection Unit. She was at a dead end with Sorina, who just wouldn't open up. Michelle had tried to speak to her almost daily but, other than general small talk, nothing of importance was forthcoming, and she knew there was so much more. Sorina held a lot more important information than she was telling, but she was tight-lipped and frightened.

It had been months since Sorina had last seen Nicu, with his beautiful, innocent, little face and soulful brown eyes that oozed love for his mummy as they looked up at her. Their bond was a true gift, a love mothers share with their sons, an unbreakable thread that seemed to be stitched between them, a lifeline invisible to the eye that only death could break. He was a gift from a heavenly place when he came into her life, but since they had taken him from her, she had felt that her heart had been torn from her chest. The memory of him being so cruelly ripped out of her arms tormented her daily, crippling her ability to feel. Her face still bore scars from the fight she had put up to try and stop them taking him. She was still unaware of his fate and was frightened for her son's life, if indeed he was still alive to lose it, but she held onto the hope that he was still living.

Sorina still cried every day as she thought about Nicu, his smile, his giggles, his playful spirit, her heart both weak and strong from her loss. Weak through intense sadness from not knowing where her precious little boy was, and whether he was still alive. But an inner strength also burned deep inside, breathing life through her veins, giving her hope that he was still alive. She would never jeopardise the chance of his survival so, in her mind, if that meant protecting the bastards that had taken him then her silence was guaranteed without a word being said or a threat being made.

Michelle called Taylor at the Major Investigation Team, their chat initially light-hearted before getting down to business.

"Well, how is she, any change yet?" Taylor questioned enthusiastically.

"Nope, afraid not. Her lips are sealed. If we can't find her child, we don't have a hope in hell. If they still have him, she knows they'll kill him if she says anything."

"Does she think he'll be alive? How would she know? It's pretty rare to ever find children like that, alive or dead! We've checked all the databases, no names are coming up," Taylor reminded her.

"There are several hundred children throughout the UK, living a lost life in the care system, with untraced parents," Michelle replied, her knowledge of the facts better through her work in her chosen specialism.

"Shit, that many? What about DNA? Has she given a sample yet?" Taylor quizzed.

Michelle stayed silent on the other end of the phone. She had broken the rules and sneaked a toothbrush of Sorina's away for analysis without her consent. She had acted in good faith, which made her feel a little better about what she had done. Michelle had never done anything like that before. She always did things by the book, but she had also seen unnecessary heartache before, which heightened her frustrations at the red tape that bound them tightly. After a long pause and obvious hesitation, she answered Taylor. "Yes, the DNA was taken."

"Wow, that's great! But I thought she was adamant that she wasn't doing anything for us and had refused to give her DNA to us?" Taylor said excitedly.

Aware it was a recorded line, Michelle just said, "Well, she must have had a change of heart." her voice tailing off suspiciously.

Taylor didn't question Michelle's response. She was just delighted they could now trawl the DNA stores for a match, but she did wonder what had changed Sorina's mind.

"Have they got back to you yet, have they given any timescales?" Taylor was impatient.

"Not yet, but they have guaranteed it will be within the week."

Taylor laughed. "I'll believe it when I see it, but let me know please," she emphasised.

Changing the topic and looking for more gossip, Taylor asked, "How's Pete?" She was genuinely interested in how they were getting on.

"He's doing really well, I mean really well," Michelle said with a giggle and a huge smile on her face, a slight flush appearing in her cheeks.

Although Taylor could not see her, she could sense the slight embarrassment in Michelle's tone, a certain satisfaction on how well their relationship was going, a realisation that there is such a thing as fate.

"That well then?" Taylor laughed. "I'll say no more then! You are both so lucky."

Michelle asked Taylor how she was. Taylor rolled her eyes and said, "Don't ask."

"Why, what's happened now?" Michelle wanted to hear details.

"Michelle, we need to go out for a drink some time. My head is so mixed up right now. I don't mean to hurt people, I don't understand why I do what I do. I really was ready to give it a go with Kay. She is beautiful, strong, just lovely really, and then she had her breakdown, and now that she is back and knows what I've done, she really doesn't want to know me just now and deservedly so. Then there's Fran. She's gorgeous, great fun, sexy, loving and I've hurt her too, but I need to try again with Kay." Taylor sounded exasperated as she talked, her normal untouchable strength clearly wavering as her voice gave her emotions away. Then she hesitated. Michelle noticed. "There's more isn't there? The firefighter, is it her?"

Taylor didn't answer her question. "I'll chat more when we go out for that drink?" she said.

"Bloody hell, you! You're deep, very deep! I'm free later this week. What about Thursday? You really do need to talk."

"Thursday it is. I'll let you know when the DNA results come back." Taylor came off the phone and looked up as Marcus was coming back to the desk, a slight glistening of tears in her eyes, emotions on show from the conversation. If anyone would notice, it would be her soulmate, Marcus.

"You all right?" he quizzed, a little worried. The last year had been a rollercoaster for both of them, personally and professionally. His troubles were forced upon him, but Taylor, unfortunately, brought all of hers upon herself.

"I'm fine, I just need to sort my life out. I can't keep hurting people. I need to distance myself a bit, I might even ask for a move."

"No way, Taylor. That's too drastic. Things will sort themselves in time, just let things settle!" Marcus gently gripped her hand, his expression intense.

Fran was over at the next pod of desks and was trying hard not to listen, but she heard the last sentence and couldn't help reacting with both painful emotion and a little anger, her feelings still alive with sadness and disappointment and, to her regret, for her continued attraction to Taylor.

She got up from her seat and walked towards Taylor and Marcus, their heads still close as they tried to talk privately, totally unaware their conversation had been overheard.

Fran stopped at Taylor's desk, her leg bumping Taylor's arm. Taylor looked up with a start. Fran had come from behind and she hadn't had a clue she was there.

"Don't bother, I've saved you the trouble. I've put in for a transfer back to CID. I go in four weeks." Her words came out with venom, but her eyes were hurt and filled with sadness.

"No, no Fran! You don't need to do that. It's my fault, not yours. I'm really sorry, so very sorry I hurt you. Don't go, please don't. We need you here. You're brilliant at what you do. Take back your transfer to go, please. Take more time to think about it." Taylor pleaded with her, her request heartfelt and genuine.

Fran sat down on the empty seat beside them. All the other heads in the office bobbed up like meerkats, aware that something was going on, heads close, whispering with animated facial features and hand gestures.

Fran moved closer to Taylor and whispered, "I can't bear to be near you. I love you too much and you're hurting me, Taylor. Every day, you tear another piece of my heart away."

Taylor's face contorted, a sickness in her stomach hearing these words. Words that should melt her heart were doing the exact opposite, because she felt the pain she was causing Fran. Taylor still had feelings for Fran, and possibly still loved her, her own heart broken in two, but the way she felt about Kay was just too powerful. She was drawn to Kay and felt she owed it to her to give it another go, but she was not ready for the pain she would cause to others in the process.

"Fran, I'm so sorry, I really am. Let's go somewhere a little more private to talk," Taylor asked with pleading eyes, hoping Fran would agree.

Fran got up slowly and started to walk towards the restrooms. Taylor followed, relieved that Fran had agreed, knowing that they needed to talk.

They encountered one of their colleagues in the restroom. One look at the two red faced detectives and she left quickly, aware her presence was unwelcome. Fran turned to Taylor abruptly, her eyes wide and clearly hurt, tears visible as she began to sob. Taylor hesitated before she approached her, unsure if her embrace would be welcome.

Taylor put her long arms around Fran's shoulders, and pulled her close to her, her embrace tight and indeed welcome. Two hearts that were once together were now so far apart, but the friendship, respect and fondness for each other still remained. Fran broke down in Taylor's arms. She pulled herself closer, her head resting on Taylor's chest, her scent familiar, her senses aching with the loss of their intimacy.

"We need to talk, Fran. I need to try and explain to you that my feelings for you haven't changed, but my circumstances unfortunately have. I'm torn, and I don't expect you to care or even try to understand. You are truly beautiful, a pleasure to be with, but my heart doesn't feel free to be with you, not truthfully and exclusively, and that is what you deserve, and for that I am truly sorry."

Fran was crying, tears in full flow, as she looked up at Taylor, her heart sore, her head spinning. She opened her mouth to speak, then closed it again.

"What were you about to say, Fran? Please say it, no matter what it is," Taylor said, craving an answer, her eyes imploring Fran to open up and share her thoughts.

Fran hesitated before she spoke. "The truth is, Taylor, I do understand. I expected this. I stole a little piece of you from Kay, which was wrong on both our parts. I didn't think it would go this far between us, but it did, and I stupidly thought you might be mine one day. I fell in love with you and that's my problem to deal with now."

Taylor stood watching this lovely person pouring out her heartfelt emotions, explaining her pain, baring her soul, speechless at how hard this was and how unhappy she was that she had made someone feel this bad.

Fran reached up to Taylor's face. As Taylor was about to speak, she gently kissed her mouth, soft, closed lips, but there was true emotion in it. "Sssshhh," she said. "I know you love me a little bit but explaining that isn't enough. I want all of your love, and sadly you don't have it to give me, do you?"

Taylor looked straight into Fran's eyes, both transfixed in the moment, love, sadness, even a little adoration for each other.

Taylor kissed her back, a familiar kiss, tender, loving, intimate, until it ended and Taylor spoke. "I do love you, and I wish I was free for things to be different." They kissed again, both feeling a little passion growing inside.

The kiss lingered longer than it should have, both knowing it might be their last, before Fran broke away. "Don't, please don't. Don't give me false hope if there isn't any to be had. We just have to let it go, and I mean let go, as I can't stand by and watch you fall back in love with Kay."

Her hand brushed Taylor's face gently, and she smiled at her as she left, her intention to go home early before the end of her shift, her cheeks flushed from their emotional liaison.

Chapter 25
New Lambs to the Slaughter

The heavy goods vehicle rumbled up the motorway, having left the port at Dover after clearing customs, bribe accepted with open arms. The cargo it carried was stowed away, hidden in plain sight, its legitimacy unquestioned due to the official livery on the sides of the truck. The secret customised compartment within the lorry was very cramped. The women's bodies were pressed against each other, flesh on flesh, four days of sweat and filth from unwashed bodies cruelly contained in inhumane conditions, the putrid stench of excrement and urine overpowering. Their journey had begun in Romania when they had had hope of a new life, work and opportunity. All had paid a heavy price for their ticket to hell, their hopes and dreams dashed as they were bound and gagged, drugged to ensure their silence, passports taken and any other identification or personal belongings removed, all done with violence and brutality, ensuring every one of them knew the consequence of non-compliance once released from their bonds.

The men in the cab of the lorry only opened the container twice a day at most, as little as necessary to keep their cargo alive, as little as possible to avoid having their nostrils filled with the grossly unpleasant smell that seemed to cling to their clothes like death. Neither guard was moved or bothered by the suffering of the women within the truck, their focus only on the handsome pay check they would receive on delivery and their fear, fear of the life imprisonment they would both receive if they were caught with their livestock. When they opened the doors, the women begged for food and water. The air they were forced to breath was thick and noxious, only adding to their plight and fear of what was to come, many of them terrified that they would suffocate and not even survive the journey, the space they shared was so tight, with little ventilation. Water was offered on both occasions, but minimal food was given once a day. This was to cut down the need for the women to defecate.

Burnett paced back and forward in his flat. He walked to the large bay window numerous times, views of the forth spanning for miles, the Berwick Law, the Bass Rock, Fife, Kirkaldy, all in view. Not that this wonderful view would ever register in his mind and thoughts. His hands were firmly on his hips when his phone gave a ring. He jumped a little as his mind was totally elsewhere.

"Aye, alright Davy, what is it? Is there a problem with the shipment?" Burnett growled down the line.

"Naw, nothing to do with that. They'll be half way up the M1 by now, and on schedule boss," Davy Strachan said, always pleased to pass on good news to the boss, rather than face his wrath.

"Just as well. I was worried that there would be issues with the shipment after the bother they had in Dover the last time. A bit of luck to get them through, eh? Obviously the money gave us a little helping hand! Thank fuck really, we'd have been screwed if the girls didn't get here. We've been totally fucked since that fire, and the other girls are totally fucked too, literally." Burnett gave a heartless laugh at his attempt to be funny. The issue was far from funny. His remaining girls were having to double their punters after the losses in the fire, which was taking its toll on them mentally and physically - not that he cared about them, he just cared about the profits he could make.

Davy hesitated before explaining his reason for calling. "It's about that bent cop, boss. He's saying he can't get the location for that Sorina, the one that survived the fire. She's in a safe house apparently and only a few know where it is. He said that it would be too risky to find out," Davy said with reserve in his voice, knowing the reaction that would follow.

"Eh? You're fucking shitting me! After what happened to his missus and the kids? What a fucking stupid little arsehole he is. He's fucked now, I'll make sure of it."

"Wait a minute though, boss. He did give us something. I actually believe him about the girl. He sounded pretty genuine!" Davy tried to get a word in edgeways before he was cut off again.

"Fuck genuine! We own that snivelling dodgy wee bent bastard, and he owes us big time," Nelson bellowed down the phone.

"LISTEN Nel, he gave us a name." Davy became more abrupt and assertive, raising his voice to get his boss's attention, hoping not to annoy him more than necessary.

"What fucking name? It better be worth his life." There was a pause as Davy hoped it would be enough to placate his boss. "C'mon, Davy, spit it out then." Nelson's impatience was growing.

"CRAIG MCNARE, the guy that used to deal for you a year or so back. Do you remember him?"

"Aye, that useless wee cunt. What about him? Is he back in Edinburgh? He's got some balls to show his face here again, after how much he fucking lost me, the little coward!" Burnett's face contorted as he remembered how close he himself had come to being caught up in the enquiry that followed. He had narrowly avoided being linked to the massive drug haul that had been confiscated, and going down for years.

"Yes! He is back, and he's apparently more than back, so our wee Stevie boy says anyway. He's the prime suspect for the fire at the warehouse, the shooting and the assault on Shaz," Davy said with a hint of triumph in his tone, enjoying the noticeable pause from his boss before anything else was said.

Burnett felt a fire burn deep in his belly, rage intensifying, his teeth grinding together as his fury boiled over. "That fucking snidey wee bastard. I'm going to rip that wee fucker's bollocks off and ram them down his throat, then kick the living shit out of him while he chokes on his own baws, no word of a lie. How fucking dare he, the gallous wee prick! He's dead, he's so fucking dead, or ma name's no Burnett."

Burnett thought back to when the police had intercepted the drugs and McNare had run. He didn't normally reflect on the past. His attitude was what is done is done and things can't be undone, and he never showed any remorse, but he remembered his rage back then and his desire to make McNare suffer. His mind went back to the headlines in the Evening News: "Pregnant woman dies in house fire, enquiries ongoing to trace arsonist.

Such a fucking pity the bitch was pregnant. Nae wonder the wee fucker wants to get back at me. I didnae even mean fir her tae die or know that she was up the duff, but the wee twat got what was coming.

"Did Steve say where he was?' He said. "Is he working alone or what?"

"The polis don't even know where he is yet, 'cause he's certainly gone to ground. Nobody has come up with any info on him, no hostels, council, hotels, nothing yet, but he's been seen on CCTV near to both Sighthill and Cables Wynd at the right times."

"That'll do for me. I don't need it beyond reasonable doubt to prove it's him. He's gonna pay, the fucking wee arsehole. He'd better crawl right back under the rock he came out from, cause he has no idea what fucking pain is! Make sure Stevie is warned to let us know when they get a hit on where he is. We'll do the rest. He'll be much safer if the polis get him first."

The truck rumbled on. Inside one of the girls started to convulse, her eyes rolled back into her head, only the whites visible. Her whole body went rigid, and she began to froth at the mouth. The other girls tried to give her space. Bernadette pushed forward to kneel beside her. Initially, she thought it was just a fit, but as the convulsions continued, and the girl's face started to change from reddy purple to a paler colour, her lips showing signs of cyanosis, Bernadette knew it was worse. The girl had seemed to be suffering more than the others recently. She was underweight to begin with and had a fever when the gruelling journey began. She didn't seem as fit as the rest. Some of the other girls started to bang loudly on the walls of their makeshift prison to try and get their captors to notice, but their efforts fell on deaf ears, their loud pounding in vain. The truck didn't slow down. They were simply wasting their precious energy. Many had tried this ploy at the beginning of the trip when their claustrophobia took hold.

Bernadette managed to get enough space to lie the girl flat on her back, and she could tell by just looking at her that this was a major medical emergency. The girl stopped breathing. Bernadette tried to find a pulse but, even though her neck was very slim, she couldn't find one. Nobody knew of each other before they were forced together in these tragic circumstances but, over the last few days in such close proximity, they had formed a bond, a tight one, one that they wouldn't have thought possible beforehand, one of unity. The collective spirit and desperate need to survive through their ordeal was evident, and nobody wanted to lose anyone.

Her ribs crunched with each chest thrust as they made a desperate attempt to save her life. Her body was still, no longer convulsing, no longer alive, but Bernadette was determined to try to save her. Her mouth met hers, one mouth surrounding the other, the seal made as she blew her own air in to try and save the girl. Cycle after cycle of CPR seemed to go on forever, each woman taking their turn as the others became exhausted. Without medical intervention, there was little or no chance of saving her. None of them wanted to give up. They didn't want her to die, they themselves didn't want to die, but the possibility was now very real. Their worst nightmares could be becoming a reality. Eventually, a firm but gentle hand squeezed Bernadette's shoulder. "She's gone," Leanne said. "You'll have to stop. You can't keep going or you'll collapse. We tried, we did our best. I'm so sorry."

The women sat close together. Standing in the moving truck only led to them falling over. They stared at the lifeless corpse of what used to be a young woman, disbelief that one of them was now gone. There was no guarantee that it wouldn't happen to them too. Their situation was even more terrifying than before, their own mortality questionable, their fate still unknown, but as they looked down at their companion, they noticed that there was peace in the dead woman's face. Her body would remain her own, her death saving her from the vile acts that lay before the rest of them.

Chapter 26
Never Lose Hope

Januk sat playing in his room. He sat in silence; he had not spoken since he had said goodbye to the other little boy David. The police had been really nice to him, but he just couldn't speak. He tried, but every time he opened his mouth something inside stopped him. He remembered the words of the men that took him. He remembered them saying that they would kill his mummy if he told anyone anything about her or him, anything. He was beaten until he learned his new name, Januk. Januk, Januk, Januk, Januk. He remembered every punch, kick, slap, bite, cigarette burn, his skin being twisted cruelly as they taunted him to keep saying his new name over and over.

The carer, Pauline, came through from the kitchen. She was carrying his lunch - cheese on toast and a yoghurt. She put the tray down on the little table near to the telly where he sat day after day, watching in silence, tears regularly glistening on his cherubic face. She knelt down beside him as she had done daily. She was very fond of this silent little boy. She had tried and tried to get through to him, her endless display of patience and kindness never-ending, but he had never once spoke back to her, his love for his mum, and his fear for her life was enough to bind his lips shut. Until now.

Pauline was sitting beside Januk, his perfect features, his innocent gaze fixed upon the telly. Pauline couldn't even begin to imagine what the little boy had witnessed, what had made him so petrified to speak. Her heart ached for him. She wanted him to open up, let them help him. She had seen the marks and scars on his body, evidence of the violence suffered and witnessed, something nobody should ever have to endure.

He looked up at her as she put her arm around his shoulders. He was rigid at first, always wary of human touch. Even though he had been there for months, every touch sent electricity to the ends of his body, prickling away with an unpleasant sensation, terror striking his heart, waiting for the change to violence and torture, but it never came. All he ever experienced here was love and kindness. The police people came every week. They were nice and kind too and kept asking him questions, but he never answered. Pauline felt his rigid shoulders slowly relax, more noticeably than ever before, and he leant towards her. For the first time he cuddled into her and allowed her to embrace him. He started to cry, his shoulders moved up and down, and for the first time he let go of all his emotions, those that had been forcibly buried deep inside. His self-created isolation had to stop. His very young mind had made a decision; he did not want to live alone within himself anymore. He did not want these horrible people to win. He wanted these nice people to help him, as they promised they would. They said he was safe and that they could protect other people if he would just tell them who the nasty people were.

Pauline held him. She let him cry and cry without asking anything. This was a first, a breakthrough, the seal broken, emotions previously hidden now on show. Januk turned and put his arms round her neck and hugged her back and then turned away again. She felt his body stiffen and feared that he would disappear back into himself once more, but he didn't. He opened his mouth, and closed it again, looked straight into Pauline's eyes. She daren't drop his gaze as she silently tried to encourage him to say what he so clearly wanted to say.

The stare seemed to go on for an eternity, but neither dropped their eyes, the boy searching hers for any badness there, his heart wanting to trust her, his recently learned fear preventing him.

Suddenly, he sat bolt upright, pulled away from Pauline's arms and stood up. He looked away from the television that had become his life recently, and this time, he spoke.

"My name is Nicu Costea. They said they would kill my mummy if I told you, but the police said they can protect people. Can they protect my mummy and all of the other ladies?"

"They can, they can, I promise you they can," said Pauline.

Little did Pauline realise the importance of the information she had been given. She quickly took a note of Nicu's real name, in case he clammed up and stopped speaking again.

He didn't. He started talking. The floodgates had opened. Nicu began going through everything that had happened to him. Pauline had the foresight to discretely turn her phone on to record, because she knew the things that were being said had great significance, and most were also likely to have evidential value. It seemed there were scores of women and children being trafficked, and Nicu was now one of the luckier ones.

Her heart felt heavy as she wondered if his mother was still alive. She hoped for a miracle for the woman and the little boy.

Pauline took her time listening to him for as long as he wanted to keep talking. She made a point of using his true name, over and over to install it safely back where it belonged, showing him he should not fear using it anymore, because he was safe there.

Eventually another carer came in, and Pauline told Nicu that she would be back as soon as she could, and she meant it.

The other carer took over the chat, and Nicu joined in when she pulled out some toys, toys he had never ventured near in his time there, his tortured soul not allowing him to play, to smile, to live, his inner fear had been so powerful, his love for his mummy unyielding, but now he was beginning to believe the police could save her.

Pauline quickly phoned the Major Investigation Team at Fettes. She was hoping to speak with Taylor Nicks as she thought the boy's real name was of great significance. The phone rang for a while. It was eventually answered, and Pauline was a little disappointed when another detective answered, a man's voice, which she didn't recognise, but she knew she needed to pass on the new information to the team as soon as possible. They were the leading department in the initial incident when the little boy had been rescued.

Pauline recounted what the boy had said. She explained that she had a recording of most of her conversation. Then she said his name, "Nicu Costea." There was silence at the end of the phone. Pauline thought that the line had gone dead, and she was about to redial when the detective spoke again, giving reason for his hesitation within their conversation. Pauline thought this was a little odd but carried on anyway.

The detective made arrangements to secure all of the recordings of what the boy had said and assured her that they would send someone to come and speak with Nicu in due course. He also made it clear that they didn't want to rush things to avoid Nicu retreating back into himself again.

Pauline listened carefully to the instructions given, and assured the detective that she would not tell any other departments in the meantime for security reasons. The detective said he would deal with those who needed to know personally.

When the call ended, Pauline felt an emptiness. A cold shiver trickled down her back, an unspoken uneasiness, an unexplained sensation of something not being quite right, but what? She made a mental note to phone DS Nicks about this later, but at that moment she had to get back to little Nicu. He needed her and she needed to be with him right now, he was the most important thing. She wrote down the detective's name on her notepad – DC Steven Shack.

His hands were sweating and his stomach had twisted into a painful knot,.His heart was pumping so hard he thought it would be noticeable to those around him. It skipped a beat when Taylor strode into the room just as he was moving away from her desk, far enough away to avoid any questions.

She looked up, her face a little puzzled and said, "Are you alright Steve? You look a bit worried."

"No, no I'm fine Serg, just busy, that's all." Steve moved back to his desk, his head aching with the enormity of what he had just heard and what he should do. Should he do the right thing or save his own skin? His problem now was that it wasn't just his skin he needed to save. He felt physically sick. How could he have been so stupid to get involved with Burnett's lot and actually think the bastard would forget about it and leave him alone. He was a dead man one way or would end up in prison the other. His choices were limited and his heart heavy. His motivation to take the money had been to help his ill child. Marcus appeared behind him and asked him a question, and he nearly jumped out of his skin. It felt as if his thoughts were visible to the others. Marcus laughed at the reaction and made a joke about Steve's massive overreaction. Even he, mild-mannered Marcus, wasn't too sure of the new addition to the team but, like some of his colleagues, had no logical reason to feel that way, other than Steve was a bit nervous and awkward sometimes.

Chapter 27
What Next?

McNare was sitting on the promenade wall at Silverknowes Beach, hood up and a scarf over his face. He was looking over at Fife, endless thoughts swirling round in his mind - love, loss, what might have been. Then the sadness was engulfed by an unstoppable rage, a rage that he thought would never go away until he took his revenge on Burnett. He could almost see where Burnett lived from where he sat just down from the old Marine Hotel, which was nowadays some kind of backpackers' hostel. Muirhouse Mansions, a grand stone-built building, now offered temporary accommodation for many, including McNare, who had managed to secrete himself away in an unused outbuilding amongst a path in the trees. He made a point of coming and going discreetly at all times and, until then, had managed to do so unnoticed.

He took a deep breath and his mind went back to Lynne, his true love, her gentle heart, her belief in him as a person, her kindness, the person that had given him hope and had encouraged him to break free from his criminal ties. His face crumpled as his thoughts of her were cruelly interrupted by vivid screams of terror, screams that he had caused as he blindly took his revenge on his adversary. He threw up at his feet, his stomach in knots as the anonymous screams turned into

Lynne's. He could see her face, terror in her eyes and her hands reaching up to be saved and then down onto her stomach before she succumbed to their fate, her heart broken for her unborn child. He stood up and screamed maniacally out to the sea, the promenade stretching away from him on both sides, distant dog walkers stopping in their tracks at the eerie wail coming from the man near the beach. He clenched his fists and walked quickly up towards the trees, heart heavy with his loss, his mind tormented at what he had done. He had believed the warehouse was Burnett's drug factory where massive amounts of drugs were prepared and packaged. He had had no idea that that was where Burnett kept his trafficked girls. McNare had read the news in the paper and could not believe that he had inflicted the same fate as Lynne had suffered on so many others.

His mind was made up. He would find a way to get to Burnett in person. He had to stop him, hurt him. Burnett didn't care about those around him. All he did was use people, believing everyone and anyone could be replaced without a second thought. McNare knew that only too well. When he had been stopped by the police, Burnett instantly turned his back on him, disconnecting any ties and ultimately wanted to cause him harm for his failure. He had murdered those closest to him, with no rhyme or reason and certainly no loyalty to those that were taking the risk to do his bidding. McNare's eyes narrowed and darkened as he formed a plan.

Chapter 28
A Chance to Escape

Bernadette sat with her arms wrapped round her legs, her head resting on her knees, fear and anger burning inside like hell's fire with her ever-growing will to survive, to escape, to find a way to get out of this. She stood up and the other women looked up at her, wondering what she was thinking. Her posture had changed, her eyes were focused and there was a slightly crazed look in her eyes.

"We need to get out of here. We need to do something. We're just sitting here accepting this shit. I'm not prepared to die or for anyone else to die for that matter! Let's search everything we can get into, look for anything we can use as a weapon. Look for tools, tools that can help us get out of here. These guys don't give a shit if we live or die, and I am not going to die like this. C'mon, it's now or never. We're in Britain. The police here will help us if we can get to them."

The women were all weak and hungry, but they too were determined to survive ever since they had watched one of their own die, a fate that could meet them all a lot sooner than any of them wanted. Everyone was now fully aware that the jobs promised to them would not be anything like they had been told, and sexual slavery was a terrifying and real prospect for them all. They knew they could make as much noise as they wanted as everything they had done so far had fallen on deaf ears. Screams or shouts for help had been ignored. They put their remaining strength into their chance of escape. They knew it wasn't a solid refrigerated container, otherwise they would have suffocated already. They needed to try and get to the outer skeleton of their prison. Each helped the other to clamber on top of the cargo and over the hundreds of crates to the outer shell. The space between the last crate and what seemed to be the side of the lorry was practically non-existent. Bernadette reached down to help Leanne and Elena up to where she sat perched on the top. They could feel the lorry was still travelling at speed and they swayed with the motion. They could feel every bump in the road, and their balance was tested several times to avoid falling the twelve feet or so drop back to where the rest of the women were. Bernadette kicked the side of the lorry, expecting something more substantial than the noise that returned suggested. To their joy and surprise, the outer shell felt like some sort of plywood. The framework containing the now enraged and desperate cargo was not very substantial at all. Together they leant back and began to kick with all their might to see if the outer shell would give. At first it barely moved, but after several kicks there was a bowing, the wood giving slightly and offering potential if they were more selective in their choosing a site to damage. They could all see there was a chance.

Chapter 29
Loose Ends and Dead Ends

"Any more positive sightings of McNare?" Taylor quizzed the team as she strode back into the office after her meeting with DCI Sommerville. Fran, Steve and Marcus looked up from their computers and shook their heads.

"Afraid not. He's totally gone to ground," Marcus followed up, noticing that Fran had not answered and wanting to avoid an awkward silence. Fran had put her head back down almost as soon as she had looked up and did her best not to look at Taylor, her heart still sore but not wanting Taylor to see her pain, not wanting to draw any sympathy. Fran wasn't that type of person. She was sad but not in a needy desperate way. Fran had known where she stood right from the start. She was the extra person. Kay had been there first. Fran knew that Taylor really liked her, and they had only had the chance to be together because of the hideous and brutal intervention of Brennan. Kay was back now and, just when Fran had thought there might have been a chance for her and Taylor to have a proper relationship, Taylor's heart strings had been pulled in the opposite direction, torn away from Fran, her affections redirected back to Kay.

Taylor was looking strained these days - from the pressure at work, Kay being back off sick and DCI Brooke Sommerville's frostiness towards her. DI Findlay was the same useless pig he had always been, making the usual negative comments towards Taylor as he tried to assert some control and dominance over her. She thought his manner and approach to her were both adolescent and childish. He was an insecure, insignificant jumped-up little irk, whom Taylor barely acknowledged. She wasn't going to rise to the bait and give him any sort of satisfaction. In her view, he lacked intelligence and maturity and was a weak-minded fat little prick at best. He was also a jealous wee bastard, and a lard-ass, wee dumpling into the bargain. DI Findlay stared at Taylor so she just looked back at him, gave no verbal response and a glance of pure disgust, which was all he deserved.

Steve was also aware of the pressure mounting for Taylor. She depended on her team to feed back to her, all of the information they had gathered out there on enquiry, so she could push the investigation forward, guiding the teams on their next tasks as the leads came in. He could feel his stomach knotting. He was the only one on the team that knew the connection between Sorina and Nicu. He was struggling with his own problems and the ever-mounting pressure he faced to keep his family safe. The new information could be a huge benefit to those that were threatening his family, a bargaining tool to keep Sorina from testifying and speaking out against the organised crime lords, but the boy had been through one terrifying ordeal, and Steve didn't know if he could serve him up for another. He felt sick over the mess he was in, but if he could get those threatening him to pay him some big money for this information, he and his family could just leave, disappear. His decision would need to be made sooner rather than later though, as it was only a matter of hours at most until this window would close. Those caring for the boy would call again wondering what was to happen with the child.

Taylor looked at Fran, her head still down, giving the appearance she was hard at work. Taylor could feel her active avoidance of her and was sad that she had hurt her, and herself for that matter, because she did have feelings for Fran.

"Fran, I need you and Marcus to head down and speak with Sorina again. We need to get a statement from her. We need more information about where the women were kept, who they saw, where they worked, how they got there, how the girls were controlled, what threats were made to stop them escaping. We need anything we can get, even the type of transport used. Once we know that we can try and intercept their vehicles. You are scheduled for a shift at the safe house so use this time wisely. Don't be too obvious but get her talking, get her to trust you."

Fran looked up, her face a little flushed. "No problem. Do you think she will speak to us this time? Nothing has changed. She hasn't said a word, she's too frightened they still have her boy."

Taylor smiled kindly at her, acknowledging the blush and the awkward working environment she had caused between them.

"Do what you are good at, Fran. Convince her, convince her that by talking to us we will be able to do more to find and protect her son. This will give us more avenues to investigate and stop them getting to her and her boy, if he is actually still alive. The surveillance on Burnett has come up with sod all. He knows what we are doing, and the phones we are monitoring are clearly burners. He's a clever bastard and knows how we work. He always seems to be one step ahead."

Marcus nodded in agreement. "Do you think he's getting tipped off?" he said jokingly, not even considering it as a possibility.

Steve squirmed. Although he knew his actions to date were enough for him to go to jail, and for his family to be in danger, he also knew that he would be found out at some point soon. It was just a matter of time. With this thought in mind, he had to put his own family before that of Sorina and her son. In his nonsensical, crazy thought process, his mind once undecided was now made up. He had to find a way to speak to Sorina, get the boy and get them to back off and leave his family alone.

Marcus looked down at his schedule for the day. He had something arranged for the main part of the day, an urgent interview from another case. He looked up at Taylor and apologised.

"Sorry, boss. I can't really reschedule this interview. Is there anyone else that can go along with Fran?" he pleaded. "This meeting has taken ages to arrange; this guy's been actively avoiding the police for weeks and we've finally tracked him down. I'm really sorry."

"Like who, Marcus? Who would you replace you with? Give me a name. The list has to be kept to a minimum, you know that! Can you not get someone else to do your interview?" Taylor exclaimed.

"Not really. I know this case inside out. The stand-in wouldn't get the results that I can. I know how to get him to trip himself up! Surely one more on the list wouldn't hurt, boss, as long as they are cleared. We've all been vetted, some are just better than others though," he said, with a sarcastic expression on his face.

Steve tried not to look overenthusiastic or transparent in any way. This was his opportunity, so he spoke out casually. "I could do it, boss, I've not got anything on today. I left it free in case you wanted anything specific done. Really, it's not a problem."

Taylor's instant thought was, *No way, not you!* She had a gut feeling about Steve. There was something that wasn't quite right about him, but, other than a hunch, she didn't have any reason to mistrust him. He always seemed to be jumpy, a little on edge but there was nothing concrete. She swithered, not wanting her feelings to be too obvious, and Marcus wouldn't have asked if what he was doing wasn't important. Taylor had a situation here. She needed someone to fill in and Steve was offering the solution. He had been vetted the same as all the other detectives. There had been no issues with him reported, and he had come onto the team with glowing references. He was just a little insular for her liking.

Fran's face was a picture. She would much prefer to be with Marcus, at least he had some banter. She thought Steve was a bit dull and odd for that matter, and the thought of spending twelve hours with him was torture.

"Okay, okay, Stevie. You'll need to go through to the DCI and get her to put you on the list for Team 2. This will mean you might get called upon again at short notice and have to do very long hours, but you volunteered so serves you right," she said with a smile on her face.

Stevie could feel the goosebumps rising under his skin at the enormity of this opportunity, what it meant to him and what he would do next. Of course, there would be no turning back, but he knew his life was already fucked, the clock was already ticking. He would try to get more for his family, then at least his daughter would get the specialised treatment she needed.

Chapter 30
Keep Your Mouth Shut!

Taylor swivelled round on her seat, and then again, and again, smiling to herself at how childish she had just been with the chair, also hoping she hadn't been noticed. But she had been spotted. Brooke was watching from her office. She smiled, her thoughts trailing back to the one night they had shared, knowing it wasn't on the cards again any time soon, if ever, but she enjoyed the view. Her thoughts quickly changed back to the task at hand. The investigation seemed to be going nowhere fast.

"Taylor!" the DCI called from her office. "Can you come in here for a moment please?"

Taylor walked in slowly. "Ma'am?"

"Steve! What is the reason you never came to speak to me in person about him and you left it up to him to let me know the change of personnel? That's not very professional, is it? I can hardly ask him if he's up to it, how important the secrecy of the location is, all those things and more," Sommerville snapped at her.

Taylor shrunk a little. She knew she should have run this by her boss, but she was under pressure and had taken the easy option, which she was about to regret. She replied sheepishly, "I didn't think it was that much of a problem. He's passed all the clearances to be here with us, and Marcus had something on, something he couldn't reschedule again. Sorry, ma'am."

DCI Sommerville's brow curled up into an incredulous scowl. "Listen Taylor, there are certain things I expect the Sergeant to deal with and this is one of them. It's not for you to palm off onto somebody else. You should know that."

Taylor could feel her temper rising. She had never liked being blamed for things but, on this occasion, she had been lapse in her judgement. She should have run the change in personnel by Sommerville first, and she knew it.

She squeezed her thighs and looked up at her boss, hoping for a little slack. "I'm sorry, boss. I was a bit harassed, I never gave it too much thought really. I was just so busy and it seemed the easiest thing to do. Steve's alright though. There wasn't anyone else that could fill in anyway. It was a needs must but, you're right, I shouldn't have done it without running it by you first."

The DCI was annoyed with Taylor, who was normally one hundred per cent reliable. "That's not the point, Taylor. There are protocols in place and they are there to be followed to prevent any embarrassing moments, moments like this. You left me with very little choice but to use him."

"You could still have said no," Taylor said, her face flushing with annoyance as she tried to offload a portion of the blame. She felt like Brooke was making too much of this and possibly enjoying it a little.

Brooke was angry. Taylor may not have followed protocols, but she was correct with her last statement - ultimately, the final decision was hers. She could still withdraw Steve and change personnel. If questions were asked later, or something went wrong that would be something she would have to deal with!

"Are you sure there is no one else that can do this. It's such an important job. Steve is new with us and, frankly, he's been a bit up and down lately, but I just can't put my finger on why. Do you trust him?" Brooke asked.

Taylor shrugged her shoulders. She couldn't really answer that. "I trust Fran, and she will be there with him. I trust

Marcus, but he can't do it, so I needed someone else, and the extra name on the list will ease the burden on the others. It is round the clock and there are never enough cops to do it, ma'am."

Brooke sighed and smiled at Taylor. "He just makes me uneasy. He's a bit guarded. I just can't work him out, and that doesn't sit right with me."

"I wanted to give him a break, what with his family issues and the incident. I wanted to give him a little more responsibility, try and get him on board, become more of a team player." Taylor grimaced. "I hope I don't live to regret it."

Brooke clasped her hands together. "This is a one off. We'll move Sorina soon. It's the time factor, and I get your point about the pressure on the officers selected for this, but until we get McNare and nail Burnett, the smaller the group involved, the better right now. Do you agree?"

Taylor sat upright and replied frankly, "Actually, I do agree. I think I was wrong to make that decision about Steve. Do we just stop it now, recall him? I could do half a shift there."

"It's too late now. I need you here and we definitely need two there. There is nobody else so, although you should have run it by me, there was no other option at the time other than cancelling Marcus's appointment. I checked out what that was and the fiscal won't wait any longer for it! So, Taylor, let's arrange to move the safe house, hand pick the officers next time and allow a bit extra for resilience. We can give Steve something else important to do to avoid him feeling like he's been dropped, more like he's been hand-picked again. And, Taylor, watch him. Keep a closer eye on him. See if you can get him to open up a bit." Brooke gestured with her head for Taylor to get on with it. She could see that Taylor was stressed, a little broken but still strong.

"I'm on it, I'll get it sorted asap. I'm sorry, really I am." Taylor stood up, and looked at Brooke. Their eyes locked. Taylor, shoulders hanging, turned and left the office with her head lowered, disappointment twisting in her stomach.

Fran pushed the Peugeot into third and revved the engine as they drove quickly up towards their destination, Cluny Gardens, an affluent area of Edinburgh next to Blackford Hill, one of Edinburgh's seven hills. The stone built houses, many three storeys high and more were all over the million-pound price mark, the roadway wide and luxurious. It was a lovely place to live.

Fran didn't hang around. She was a bit of a rally driver at the best of times, but always aware of her surroundings and pedestrian traffic, taking precautions when necessary. She was pissed with Taylor and Marcus - she couldn't think of anything worse than having to sit with Steve for twelve hours. She thought he was odd, not a people person, and she didn't really trust him. He made himself hard to like, and that was down to the way he was with the rest of the team, never opening up, a real closed book, even appearing a bit shifty at times. They pulled into the driveway of a nondescript house, numerous bushes and shrubbery in the garden, ivy on the walls. It looked rundown, certainly not eye-catching or anything that would command a second look. Fran's tyres scrunched to a halt on the gravel, leaving deep rivets behind her as she had come into the driveway a little fast and had to alter her position at the last minute to avoid hitting a low wall and blocking their colleagues' vehicle in.

They walked round to the rear of the premises and down the steps to the basement, which was a self-contained, two-bedroom apartment with one public room, a bathroom and kitchen. They had to knock and wait for the door to be unbolted and answered by a tall muscular officer from the previous shift. He looked weary, bags under his eyes from his fourteen-hour shift because they were so late with the personnel change – over two hours late. They were working twelve on twelve off, not ideal for those who had a life outwith the force, but it was the only way to reduce the numbers. In Edinburgh it was very rare for anyone to be in protective custody. The officers were unarmed, although there was an armed response unit in the area. This was hardly ideal if anyone with real intent arrived with the desire to do harm, but there was no specific intelligence, and no direct threat had been made to Sorina, so they hadn't been granted authorisation for arms.

Once inside they took off their jackets, and Fran went over to Sorina who was sitting in the corner. She looked meek, withdrawn and nervous, deep sadness etched on her face. Fran knelt down in front of her, offering her hand warmly to introduce herself, genuinely wanting to help and gain Sorina's trust.

Steve, on the other hand, spoke from behind Fran and smiled Sorina's way, his mind racing as if mice were spinning round their wheel in his head. He had to act now. He had calls to make, and he needed to get Sorina on her own. It would only be a matter of time before Fran needed to use the toilet. He also needed to get money, a lot of money, and put it in his wife's bank account before the end of this tour of duty, a massive task and a huge risk. Then he would disappear off the face of the earth and try and make it look like he had been abducted so he could avoid jail.

"Coffee, tea? Does anyone want anything?" Steve said coolly as he moved round the apartment and headed to the kitchen. He checked out every window, the door, and to his fortune, there was a rear door too, a requirement for fire safety. He smiled to himself. This would make things even easier for someone to enter unnoticed and stop Fran getting a call out for help. The only thing going for this place was its location, the secrecy of where it was and the lack of knowledge of its importance, but with Steve on the inside, these positive features would not help. He knew now that he could pull this off, the abduction of Sorina and the boy, that's if another call hadn't already been made to the team about Nicu's real name. There was nothing he could check without drawing attention to himself, but that was a risk he would have to take.

***

Burnett was drinking beer, more aware than ever that the Feds were closing in on him. There were too many big mouths out there that could fuck him right up; they could identify him and he would go down for life this time. His missus, Irene, was busy in the kitchen sorting something for him to eat. His phone beeped. Is was Davy. At first Burnett was of the opinion, *What the fuck now you annoying little prick,* but when he read on, he realised that there may be an out, a way to silence all but one of the loose ends. Still, he knew McNare would come to him eventually. He'd just have to wait - that little prick could die later.

Burnett read on - locations for the boy and the woman, the bent cop too, and another feisty little copper into the bargain. A lot to get on with in the next eleven and a half hours, but at least he might not be going to jail, which at present seemed pretty inevitable.

He read on, *250 Grand, today, you devious little prick, and you think you're gonna live!* The message continued: *She can ID you, down to the shoes you wear and the tattoo above your dick, you twisted fuck. You should never touch the merchandise, the girls, the drugs, murder, torture, life imprisonment for sure - you choose, because even you will find jail is shit. You might even get a taste of your own medicine. Money now or you are fucked big man, and I'll make sure of it. I'm fucked anyway, so it doesn't really matter to me, but you could change your fate. This is your last chance to save your skin and PS, keep the fuck away from my family!* Steve was bluffing. He had not even spoken to Sorina yet, but he had looked Burnett up and notes on his tattoos were on their systems along with the designer clothing he wore. The rest he had imagined reading between the lines.

Burnett was raging. In the bigger picture, the money was not a problem. He had plenty of it, and he couldn't use it in jail the way he could use it normally. He knew he could shift that amount of cash quickly. It was a drop in the ocean for him. He'd been laundering money for years and had legitimate bank accounts and stashes of cash. He couldn't threaten to do Steve

Shack in, because the witnesses would still be there. The wee bastard had him by the short and curlies, and he would have to play along with him if he wanted to avoid prison. He decided that he would transfer the money, but had no intention of letting Shack get the chance to enjoy it. Shack would feel his wrath although the money would be gone, but he could live with that.

Chapter 31
Escape from Hell

Bernadette felt the truck slow down to a halt. She looked at the others, all of them squeezed tightly in the small gap between the legitimate cargo and the outer skin of the cargo hold. It was time for action, now or never, all taking the risk to escape, not knowing where they were or the dangers they faced when they dropped down from the truck.

The driver in the car behind could not believe what she was seeing as she waited at the traffic lights - legs, multiple sets of legs, coming down from the truck in front. Then whole bodies. The first out remained upright, the next few falling down onto their knees, and they just kept coming.

She gasped in terror as the truck started to move off. It was heading north, down Easter Road, a tight street with old four and five storey tenements on either side, their outer walls blackened with the volume and constant flow of the traffic below. There was not a lot of room for an articulated lorry to manoeuvre, but it was heading down to an industrial unit at Leith Docks, which would be used as a transit hide for the women until they were formally housed in the brothels and other holding venues around the city, where they would be transported to and from to work.

She hurriedly scrawled down the vehicle's registration, make and colour as she knew there was something very wrong with what she was witnessing. The final few women dropped down from the truck, but the very last one hesitated, and with the truck starting to rumble on, she lost her footing, landing awkwardly as she fell to the ground. She rolled half under the truck. The woman in the car behind gasped in horror as the rear wheels of the lorry crunched heavily over the woman's legs, her screams audible from within the car, even with the windows shut and radio on. The truck kept moving. Most of the women had run away in all directions as fast as they could, anywhere but remain there. They were frantic and desperate to escape, dazed by the sunshine, fearful of being recaptured, unnecessary fears as the men in the cab of the truck were unaware the women were free and hadn't even checked their mirrors. They were totally oblivious of the loss of their precious cargo, sealing their own fate by inadvertently running over one of their captives in front of scores of witnesses, most of whom were now thumbing their phones to call the police and ambulance services.

Bernadette, Leanne and Elena, who had jumped out in the group first to leave, all heard the screaming and stopped dead in their tracks, none of them prepared to leave anyone behind.

They turned and ran back to where the truck had been. As they came round the corner, they were horrified to see one of the girls lying on the road. There were other people already trying to help and comfort her. Her legs were crushed, her feet turned outwards at a disfigured angle. Her bones were clearly badly broken, open fractures visible, the skin on her lower legs torn horribly away from the bone, and there was a lot of blood.

A crowd was gathering. The traffic was now backed up to London Road, side roads also beginning to get congested. Bernadette managed to get through and kneel down beside the woman on the road. She looked at her injuries and felt physically sick, but that did not stop her from comforting her newly found acquaintance, their bonds stronger than many lifelong friends may share. She spoke softly, words of strength, support and hope, and tried to shield the horrific injuries with a coat passed to her by a bystander, the woman not yet realising the severity of her injuries, adrenaline pulsing to every part of her body masking the pain a little. Their hands locked together. A nurse, who had been in one of the vehicles further back, had brought medical supplies from her car. She was trying to apply indirect pressure to the femoral artery up near the groin to stem the flow of blood coming from the lower leg injuries. She searched her bag hoping to find a tourniquet that she knew was in there, the spurting flows of arterial blood indicating that a major artery had been severed. Tears shone in Bernadette's eyes as she moved closer to the woman on the ground. She was merely a girl, barely eighteen years of age by the look of her. Sadness and anger mixed like chemical toxins, Bernadette's heart breaking at the thought that another of their group might die.

"Look at me, listen to me, listen, please listen! Can you hear them coming? We're safe now, you're going to make it. They can sort this, they can save you. Then we'll be free and you'll be alright, I promise you. You have to fight now. Don't let them beat you, not now." Bernadette realised that she didn't even know the girl's name, and felt a great urge to find out. "What's your name?"

The girl was gasping in pain, her face white, blood draining away from the outer peripheries of her body. She looked up at Bernadette, and smiled. "My name is Juliani, Juliani Radu," she said with pride, before falling unconscious, but she was still breathing. Her fight for her life was not over yet.

Sirens rang out from all around, police heading from Leith, Gayfield and Craigmillar stations, and all over the city, roads policing vehicles were heading in from the trunk roads in order to trace and stop the truck.

A single paramedic arrived on scene first, police and an ambulance following shortly after, traffic sets on stand by for the fast escort hot on their heels, all the personnel in place to give her the best chance of survival possible.

As the medics got to work, the police began speaking to witnesses, ensuring they found out exactly what had happened and preventing anyone leaving the scene.

The driver that had been in the car behind was quick to approach the officers, shedding light on what had gone on minutes before. She pointed to the three women close to the injured woman on the ground, who was now being treated by several professionals. She told them that all four had come out of the lorry, and that there were, at least another twenty or so that had run away.

Realising immediately the enormity of what had happened, human trafficking on a large scale, the officers called for more units to attend, specialised resources that needed to be at the scene - MIT, CID, the PPU and anyone else who could help get to the bottom of this and secure all of the evidence available.

Taylor's phone buzzed. She answered it, quickly taking in what had been said. She ordered everyone that was in the office to get their kit on and get down to the scene. She popped her head round the DCI's door to let her know as well, deliberately avoiding talking to DI Findlay, knowing he'd hear what was said anyway. It was unlikely he would leave the office through fear of having to do any work for a living. Sommerville looked up, and she too grabbed for her stuff, practically ordering Findlay to join them. This was going to be a big operation with many witnesses. It could uncover a lot of high-profile criminals. Marcus was already in the car waiting for Taylor to join him, his interview successfully completed. He was eager to get to the scene and start working. The DCI arrived next. She opened the back door of the car. Marcus was taken aback that she was joining them. Her own vehicle had been left short of fuel, which she blamed on Findlay. She was leaving him to sort that out. Taylor came out, a little flustered and unprepared for Brooke to be sitting in their car. She climbed in the front and acknowledged her boss, asking her if she had enough room, a little sarcastically, because she had more than plenty in the front.

She nodded at Marcus and they made haste from Fettes on to Carrington Road and straight up to Ferry Road at high speed, blues swirling above their heads. They had to swerve through the traffic, people stopping in front of them, at islands, pulling out, not pulling in, sweat beading on Marcus's forehead . He swung down Newhaven Road, where he had to stop suddenly at the crossroads heading onto Pilrig Street as a wee wifey walked right out in front of them, the lights showing a green man. She was determined she was crossing that road, no matter how many blue lights and sirens there were. Marcus cursed loudly, not because she was walking across but because he had nearly hit her, his tyres marking the road as he came to an abrupt halt. Taylor swore loudly too when her face nearly hit the windscreen. She had been leaning forward, her seatbelt already stretched.

"Fuck's sake, Marcus, you complete fanny! I saw her halfway back up the road, and she was always going to cross. You could tell by the way she was standing, poised 'n' ready to go!"

"I saw her, but I didn't think she would be that bloody stupid!" he said a little sheepishly. He should have anticipated the woman's stubborn right to cross the road when it was her turn.

Brooke sat in the rear of the car shaking her head, the playful bickering in the front moderately amusing. There was no malice in it, just two adults ripping the piss out of one another, typical police humour, never any sympathy for the one in the firing line.

Marcus jammed the car back in gear and sped on. They crossed Leith Walk, the streets bustling with people, all stopped to watch as several police cars had already gone past, and it was a bit of a spectacle to see, so many emergency services converging on one place. The chicane was tight as the car swung onto Iona Street to cut through a tight built-up residential area to get to the scene of the accident.

They turned onto Easter Road to be confronted with a circus, the freelance press already there, plus fire trucks, several ambulances, scores of police cars, bystanders gathering in great numbers and people hanging out of their tenement windows, many with their phones out filming the action.

Taylor was quick to exit the car and went straight to the Police Incident Officer, prominent in his blue and white tabard worn on top of his uniform.

The officer quickly apprised them of what had happened. The injured female was being placed on a spinal board, her legs stabilised, the bleeding temporarily stopped. Roads police were on scene setting up road closures and cordons. Officers were dotted all over, heads down, writing up notes. Taylor and Marcus had the job of coordinating everything to ensure there were no lost opportunities. DCI Sommerville had listened to what had been said and went over to the press to give an explanatory statement - enough information to give them a headline but no details confirmed, not because she didn't want to tell them, but because clear details were yet to be established. Findlay had finally arrived and shuffled up awkwardly behind her, dishevelled and not a shining example of what an officer should look like. The DCI, on the other hand, was immaculate in her appearance, her suit fitted and smart, hair tied back neatly, her posture commanding attention.

Chapter 32
Who's There?

Fran was sitting beside Sorina, her natural warmth and humour clearly putting Sorina at ease. Her facial expressions had softened and she was starting to talk a little more. Sorina was still remarkably thin, still unable to eat well with her internal struggle to get over the loss of her son, Nicu.

Fran began to talk about Sorina's son – her liaison officer police training being put to good use. Sorina desperately wanted to talk about Nicu. It brought him back to life when she talked of his sweet innocent voice, his smile, his smell, her baby boy, although the loss continued to stab deep into her heart, ripping away at her guts, causing her constant nausea, forever hoping her little boy would return and she could hold him once again.

They had been chatting for some time when Steve came back into the living room, his face a little flushed and his posture shifty. Fran looked up at him and, not one for holding back, was quick to address how long he had been in the kitchen. Steve knew there would be questions. He had prepared some food for everyone, which was an adequate cover for the calls and texts he had been making, negating any further questions.

Fran was glad that there was food, but she still didn't trust the guy. There was something not right about him. He was always uncomfortable and awkward, his conversations short, minimalistic and never giving anything away. It was nothing personal. There just seemed to be an emptiness there, even a little sadness. He was a loner and not someone that had been welcomed by her or the rest of the team. He had come with high recommendation, sent over to the team as an asset and a very hard-working individual. She wondered what was going on in his private life that could have changed him so much before he came to their close-knit unit.

Fran made a mental note to try and get to know him better, to dig a little deeper and use the twelve-hour opportunity to try and speak to him, get him to open up a bit, let him see the fun side of her and that he could trust her. Once Sorina was asleep, she would have her moment, or so she thought.

Fran's phone pinged. It was Marcus sending her a quick text to say that something pretty big was happening in the city centre - human trafficking. Fran felt a pang of jealousy that she was stuck in the safe house while he was in town having all the fun, but that was the nature of the job, the luck of the draw. She let Steve know, and he just shrugged. Inside his guts were churning, knowing that this revelation could screw up everything for him. If it was one of Burnett's trucks, and more than likely it was, and Burnett got wind of it before this shit went down, then that might change things if more heat came Burnett's way.

Sorina went through to the bedroom. She was tired and her heart wasn't in the conversation anymore. It was firmly elsewhere. She thought she would never be able to focus on anything other than her son ever again, not until she knew if he was alive or dead. The same sadness tormented her daily. She lay down on the bed, her head filled with memories of her life before all of this, when she and Nicu had been blissfully happy together.

Fran followed her through to the bedroom and asked if she wanted anything else. Sorina looked up, sadness etched in her eyes. When she did manage to get some peaceful sleep it was a small respite from the reality of the constant pain she was in, her heart repeatedly broken as she longed to hold her little boy again. Her sleep was usually filled with nightmares and horror - rape, torture, the fire, her escape, thoughts of her most recent brush with death. Fran gently squeezed her shoulder, telling her not to give up hope. There was always a chance, and Sorina needed to keep her dreams alive. Fran returned to the living room where Steve was sitting in the chair nearest to the window.

It was getting darker outside now, but the shift was dragging and there were several hours left until handover. Fran had already run out of one-sided conversation with her rather odd and evasive colleague, who had become noticeably quieter since she had told him about the women intercepted on Easter Road.

Steve's phone pinged, and Fran watched as he nearly jumped off the seat. "What the fuck Steve! You nearly scared the living shit out of me, ya daft prick!" Fran was not happy with him. She already thought the safe house was a little spooky. It was also too isolated for her liking, which it was meant to be, but it was made worse having Steve for company, someone she didn't really know or trust. They had no common ground. He offered little or no comfort whatsoever to how she was feeling. In fact, he made her feel really uneasy.

Steve looked sheepish over his reaction to his phone pinging. He knew he had to give Fran something. She wasn't stupid, so he explained that his wife was just letting him know about his little girl, who was really ill. He explained she had had an episode earlier in the day, but she was alright now. Fran wasn't even aware that Steve's little girl was ill, he was such a private person, offering so little conversation at the best of times, but this revelation made her cut him a little slack. Maybe this was why he was so closed towards the others. All that heartache in his home life couldn't be easy. Perhaps he just didn't have the capacity to enjoy any banter with the team.

Steve knew that this was probably the only plausible and believable thing he could say to Fran, something that sounded truthful and that may make her more relaxed. He could sense she was suspicious of him. The text had actually said: *The money is there, and we are coming.*

Steve texted his wife and asked her to check their online bank account to see if a large sum had been deposited, following up the request with lies about a life insurance policy paying out in relation to medical expenses for their daughter, because there was no way that she would take drug money or become involved in anything illegal, no matter what it was for.

Fran started to ask him questions about his little girl and her illness, and why he hadn't said something to them, her thoughts now accepting why he seemed so distant all the time. He smiled at her and agreed that it was hard, tragically sad and that he felt desperately helpless to save her all the time. He found talking about it made it more real, and he didn't want to think about the prospect of ever losing Maisy. She was his brave little angel.

The next text seemed to take an age to come back. Kim said there was £250,000 in their account and could she phone him, to which he replied honestly that she couldn't due to protocol, knowing that she would believe him and take it as read.

"Coffee?" He lifted Fran's cup and waved it at her. She nodded in agreement and he went through to the kitchen. He felt sick to the stomach. This was getting far too real now. He really liked Fran, and he knew that what was about to happen might not turn out too well for them, but he had convinced himself that they would be okay. He typed in the address and explained the layout of the safe house, saying that he would unlock the back door. He could hear Fran heading through to the kitchen, so he quickly pressed send. There was no going back now, even if he wanted to.

"What's taking you so long? Are you away to Brazil to get the beans or something?" Fran said with a smile on her face as she poked her head round the kitchen door, her expression brighter and noticeably more responsive.

"The kettle is nearly as old as the house, Fran. It takes bloody ages," Steve lied badly. Fran just wanted a coffee. The kettle didn't look that shit to her. She glanced at Steve, who appeared even paler than he had been earlier.

"Are you alright?" she asked.

"Yes, I'm fine, just a bit worried about my little girl," he lied.

Fran went back through to the living room and was about to text Marcus to see how they were getting on when Steve came through and sat down right next to her, close enough to watch her. She shuffled sideways to give herself more room. She didn't like his closeness, and her feelings shifted back to awkward once again.

"For fuck's sake, Stevie! There's more than one couch in here!" She got up and moved away to the seat by the window, which for Steve was the worst place she could have chosen to sit. He was already regretting his intrusive choice of seat, which only made matters worse for him.

He could feel his insides churning, because deep down no matter how much he tried to convince himself of the opposite, he knew this could never end well. He had also sent the information about where the child was. Both things would have to be dealt with simultaneously or one or the other would be moved swiftly to a new safe house. He hoped for his sake that the connection between Sorina and the boy remained unknown to his colleagues.

Fran sent another text to Marcus. She had to check in anyway, and Steve knew that, so he tried to relax and hope that things would work out. He had to try and settle himself down a bit.

Marcus had explained that things were going well at Easter Road. The woman who had her legs trapped under the lorry was critical but in intensive care. Interpreters were getting statements from the other women. Ten women had been traced, and they believed that there was the same amount again still outstanding. He also said that Taylor was going to send him down to the safe house soon to relieve Steve, and that she had said that there was something else for him to do. He finished the text with another piece of news, one that sent Fran's heart racing. "The boy, Januk - apparently his name is Nicu. He finally opened up with the carer, and DNA had been checked against Sorina's. It was a match, confirming that he is her boy."

Fran could barely breathe with excitement. She typed back furiously, "When did they find this out?"

"Yesterday! Apparently, they spoke to a male within our department who said he would pass it on. They gave a name to Taylor, but I don't know who it was."

Marcus said that he had to cut the conversation short. He was nearly done in town and he would be with her in just over an hour.

Steve could see that Fran was buzzing, and her eyes were now questioning him.

Fran's guts were twisting. She wracked her brain for all of those who were around yesterday in the office, which were significant in their numbers. More than half were men, but she just knew it was Steve that had taken that call, no rhyme nor reason for her hunch, just gut instinct.

Steve tried to hide his discomfort and suspicion. "What was that all about then? What was all the excitement?" He tried to hold back the fear building inside him, worried about what she was going to say. She may be small in stature, but she certainly had a mouth on her and was able to hold her own if things took a turn for the worse.

"The boy, Januk - his name is actually Nicu, which means he is highly likely, unless the DNA is flawed, to be Sorina's little boy."

"Wow that's great news. When did they find that out?" he lied.

"Yesterday apparently, but whoever took the call failed to pass on the message," Fran said curtly, trying to get a reaction out of him.

Steve tried to stay calm. "Who took the call? I was in the office yesterday and never heard anyone mention it." He even managed to convince himself with his barefaced lie.

"They don't know yet, but they'll go through the recordings, because how the fuck do you forget to mention something as important as that? That poor bloody woman through there is at her wits end with sorrow for that boy, and every minute of every day her heart is broken. This news is very significant!"

Steve became more uncomfortable, hoping he had convinced her it wasn't him that had taken the call.

He hadn't. Fran rose abruptly, giving him a fright, and she marched through to the toilet, leaving her phone and her radio on the coffee table where she had been sitting.

Steve's bottle was crashing more and more. He was not sure he could go through with this. He was frightened for the boy, for all of them, his mind now racing. *Who's to say that Burnett won't just kill the lot of us and make us all disappear.* Now that he was thinking more sensibly, he could see that this was a real possibility.

Steve had managed to open all the locks at the back door and had closed the curtains. It was now fully dark.

When Fran came back through, she didn't notice that her radio was now on an obsolete channel, and her phone was switched off, as she popped one onto her belt and the other back in her inside pocket.

"I prefer the curtains open, Steve," she said with a frown on her face. "How the fuck are we supposed to see out if any fucker comes here?" She couldn't believe he had drawn the curtains. "This isn't a cozy wee night in, you know. We are here to protect her, and we need to see outside. What's wrong with you?"

Steve shrugged his shoulders. "It's my first one. I never even gave it a thought." He tried to play down her growing frustration with him.

His lies were failing to convince Fran. She said to him in an abrupt voice, "Marcus is coming soon to replace you anyway. Apparently you've to go and help the boss." Fran spoke deliberately and frankly to see how he would react. She was not comfortable here anymore and was about to call in her fears and ask for an instant change of personnel, even if it meant her having to stand down.

Steve felt his stomach fall to his feet. "Really, why's that then?" he said as calmly as he could. But his gestures and posture were a giveaway. Sweat beads had formed on his forehead and his speech was wavering. He stammered, something he had never done before.

Fran couldn't help herself. She was a feisty wee fire cracker and blurted out, "What the fuck's going on, Steve? What the fuck is up with you? It was you that took the phone call yesterday about the boy, wasn't it? I know it was you! How could you forget something like that?" She paused and stared right at him. "Or maybe you didn't forget, eh Steve?" She was now questioning his integrity, but she continued unperturbed and let rip, totally unaware of the situation playing out before her, not realising how cornered he already felt. He knew he couldn't let her get in the way, not now, although his intention was never to harm her.

She reached for her radio. He watched her without any attempt to stop her, not wanting to have to hurt her, holding back from any physical intervention. She tried to call out over the secure channel, but there was no response. The hairs on the back of her neck were now bristling and fear rose in her stomach. She looked at her radio and saw that the channel had been changed. As she looked up at him, he moved quickly towards her, his position and posture imposing and intimidating.

"What the fuck are you doing, Steve?" Then everything went dark.

Chapter 33
Not Again

Nicu was sitting on the floor with Pauline playing with Lego at the residential unit. He had really started to open up with her and would chat away to her about his life in Romania with his mummy. His eyes lit up when he talked about her, but then he would change and become sad and frightened as his mind went back to the day when they were taken away from their home, and later when he was wrenched away from his beloved mother, her tears, the screams of terror. He flinched every time he remembered seeing them hurt her as she tried to stop them taking him. Pauline could see his emotions were all over the place, and she was fearful that he would slip back inside himself. She put her arm comfortingly round his little shoulder and hugged him into her, and he moved into the hug, burying himself in the safety and warmth of her arms, allowing himself to be held.

The unit was small, providing one-to-one care, four members of staff to four very vulnerable children, each child damaged by their personal life experiences. The unit was cut into quarters, each corner self-contained, with a central communal room for the children to be together if they chose to.

Two men dressed in dark clothing, faces covered, moved quietly round the side of the building, careful not to be seen on

CCTV, which had good coverage of the outside of the building. Unfortunately, nobody monitored it constantly. It was only really used as an evidential tool following any incidents.

The men had been informed where the boy's room was situated, and they had downloaded a schematic layout of the unit to work with. Everything was on the same level, which served their purpose. They blended in with their surroundings in the darkness, their eyes the only visible part of them. There were some bushes near the fences, which also gave them cover. There would be only one chance to seize the boy. It had to be done now.

The rear fire exit they stood at opened onto a small corridor, which led to the boy's room. From what they could see through the window in the door, there were two people in the room, the boy and a carer.

The men looked at each other, nodded and then with one violent action, they wrenched the rear door open with a giant crowbar. They rushed in, burst into the room and made their way directly towards Pauline and the boy. Their intention was clear. Pauline instinctively scooped up Nicu into her arms, a primitive maternal action to protect the young.

She was metres away from the door and tried to run for it, her hand nearly reaching the alarm. Her wrist was grabbed viciously by one of the men, her other arm still wrapped round the boy. Franticly, she tried to free herself from the man's huge hand.

Eyes cruel and narrowed, his menacing voice rasped, "Give me the kid, lady or I will break your fucking arm!"

Pauline was not one to back down easily. She turned around quickly and head butted him, right on his nose, which made him take a step backwards and loosen his grip on her, but he didn't let go as he yelled out in pain and anger. She managed to get closer to the door, but the other male grabbed her hand that held the boy, and she felt her fingers being twisted backwards, the cracks loud and sickening,. Her hold on the boy loosened as her fingers were brutally broken. It was physically impossible to maintain her grip on Nicu and he snatched the boy forcefully from her. Nicu was screaming and scrabbling with all his might to get back to Pauline as he watched the man she had hurt raise his hand up above her and thump it down on her head, knocking her to the ground, forcing the wind out of her. Even though she was clearly injured, blood oozing from a cut above her eye, she still tried to grab for the man to try and stop him taking Nicu. His response was a donkey kick in her face. This time she fell still, unconscious and bleeding. The boy was violently sick, his head spinning in terror, his heart rate so high that he passed out onto the man's shoulder, every emotion alight with renewed terror. His little body couldn't take any more.

Silence fell upon the room, nobody any the wiser that they had been and gone. Only Pauline could raise the alarm, but she remained out cold on the floor.

The dark vehicle sped off, tinted windows, cloned plates, its destination untraceable. It was swapped for another at a pre-determined point, where there was no CCTV, no witnesses and no chance for the police to follow.

Chapter 34
Taken

Fran gulped hard as she heard footsteps come up behind her, lots of them. At least four people had entered the room from the back door area, a wisp of cold air following them. She lunged to where she thought Steve was standing, only to fall flat on her face on the floor. Steve had seen them behind her just before the lights went out and had moved to the side.

"Sorina, hide! Fight! Don't let them take you!" Fran screamed out into the darkness. She reached for her phone, only to find it was switched off, *You, sly little bastard,* she thought. *I was right, I knew it. The sneaky little shit. What the fuck is he up to?* "Steve, what have you done?" she said. Steve didn't answer.

The torch shone right into her eyes and she was temporarily blinded. Her phone was kicked out of her hand with force, sending a searing pain up her arm. She knew immediately that her wrist was broken. Fran was grabbed and lifted up by the scruff of her neck, her head held forward, her arms yanked behind her, the pain in her wrist intensifying as her hands were tied. She was furious at the situation that was unfolding. How could this have happened? What was Taylor thinking when she picked that dirty wee rat Steve for this detail? Why?

"Steve, you twisted little fuck! Why would you do this to her? Why? She has done nothing to you! She doesn't even know about her boy. What's fucking wrong with you? What about your little girl? You'll never get away with this. What were you thinking? They'll kill us all Steve, you do realise that don't you? You stupid little prick. They'll leave no loose ends. Think about it - you're more of a threat to them than her!"

Two men went into Sorina's room. She just stood there, resigned to whatever would be, very aware of what would happen to her if she tried to fight with them. She gave no resistance when they took her arms roughly and tied them behind her back.

Steve wasn't sure what he should do until the last of the men, six foot five tall, twenty-five stone, rushed forward, his face covered as he grabbed Steve. These guys weren't messing around.

"Take it easy. What are you doing? I'm the one who set this up." Steve tried to release himself but to no avail.

He was tied up along with the others, his heart now thumping through his chest, realising he too was a witness, Fran's words ringing loudly in his ears. He may just have sealed his own death warrant.

Hoods were placed over their heads. Fran yelled out loudly to Sorina, "Your boy's alive. We have him, he's safe!" She repeated the words until Sorina finally responded.

Sorina dropped to her knees, her legs unable to hold her up as the enormity of what she was hearing sent unseen love, like electricity to every tiny part of her body, the warmth helping her come back to life. "Really? Really? My boy, my sweet boy, he's alive?" The men holding her were not so amused. Both men had been pulled forward abruptly, their heads colliding viciously together, as her full weight dropped without warning.

"Get the fuck up, NOW! RIGHT NOW OR WE'LL FUCKING HURT YOU!" one of them raged, pain searing in his head, a cut appearing above his eye, with a little blood starting to trickle from it.

She hadn't meant to cause them any harm or inconvenience and was quick to struggle back to her feet, knowing what would come next if she didn't.

Fran was still yelling and fighting. Her hood was yanked back and a lump of material was rammed deep into her mouth, the dryness of it making her retch. She could barely breath. The gag smelt foul, her senses now very alert to everything. Her struggle now was to try and relax enough to avoid panic setting in, to breathe through her nose and try not to fall unconscious, or die.

The biggest man searched all of them. Phones, radios, earpieces - anything that could be traced was dumped on the table. GPS tracking and phone records were all means of tracing where they were. He ripped at their clothing up, crudely exposing them, ensuring nothing was missed, the search degrading und physically intrusive, deliberately exploring the intimate areas of the women more closely.

As all three of them were dragged outside, they heard a van reversing quickly towards them, the gravel lifting and dropping as the wheels went over it. The bushes surrounding the house gave cover for the kidnap, but the noise they were making must have drawn attention to their presence.

Sorina's heart was pounding but not with fear. It had been brought back to life with the news that her precious child was alive, erasing any fear she should have felt. An inner strength was growing inside her, the desperate desire to be reunited with her boy superseding all of her other emotions. She would play the weak victim to her advantage from now on, looking for any opportunity to escape.

Fran was fuming, her rage now without boundary. However, she was also struggling to relax enough to get much needed air into her lungs. Her nose felt like two narrowed straws had been inserted into it, her struggle to survive now very real as so little air was getting through to her lungs. Her attempts to stay calm had failed. This very experience was something she had always feared as she had watched it many times in movies.

Mind racing and senses dulling, she wondered if she would survive this. She'd been lucky once. Her colleagues had been there to save her that time, but this time nobody was coming. She struggled violently, her desperation to live spilling over in a frantic scramble to free her hands and take the cloth from her mouth, but her fight was short-lived as her legs gave way and she collapsed on the ground.

One of the men tried to get her to stand, but she was now floppy and listless. He gave her a boot in the ribs to check if she was faking it, but there was no response from Fran, not even a groan.

"Fuck's sake, the stupid bitch is unconscious."

"Fucking pick her up then, ya div. She's bloody tiny. Just get her in the fucking van, and hurry up. We need to move, now!"

His words were stressed as they needed to leave, all of them aware that the filth would be on them soon.

The men dragged Steve and Sorina roughly towards the back of the van, the doors making more unwanted noise as they opened it. The captives were bundled in and unceremoniously dumped onto the unclean metal floor, Steve grunting as he landed. Fran was thrown in, without even a check to see if she was still alive. Sorina sat quietly, her newfound inner strength escalating within her. A beacon of hope was now alight and, when the door closed, she was quick to go to help Fran. She turned round and, with her hands tied tightly behind her, struggled to get purchase on Fran's hood, but she managed to tuck her fingers under it and yanked at it, tumbling sideways as the van roared to life, the tyres spinning as the driver accelerated out of the driveway, soon to be lost to sight by anyone watching.

The van pulling away helped Sorina remove the hood from Fran, as she was flung to the side, her finger still tucked under it. Fran's face was a reddish purple colour and blotchy, with a tinge of blue round her mouth and nose. Sorina gathered herself and shuffled over to Fran again, scraping her knees as she knelt over her to pull the rag from Fran's mouth with her teeth. Fran's mouth closed over naturally and Sorina tried to blow air in through her nose, her bound hands preventing her creating a seal, but anything was worth a try to get a little more air into Fran, her balance tested with every turn and jolt the van made.

Steve just sat there, sick to the stomach. He had lost all sense of reality, in too deep to free himself. The police would screw him into the ground if he survived this. What had he been thinking? His captors were never going to let him go. They were clearly willing to spend a lot of money to stay out of jail and to clear up all of the witnesses. He had made it too easy for them to get him too. He was a free bonus, another witness who had to disappear as Fran had so bluntly pointed out to him not that long ago. He watched Sorina trying to save Fran, his colleague, a truly decent person. He had done this to her. He scrabbled over to them pushing down heavily with his head on her chest, over and over, hoping to save her.

Chapter 35
Too Late

Marcus put his pen in his pocket, took a couple of extra batteries for his radio, picked up his note book and went to let the DCI know that he was off to the safe house to take over from Steve.

DCI Sommerville looked up from her desk, relieved that the swap was taking place, still annoyed that Taylor had let it happen in the first place, despite the decision having been made in good faith because Marcus was needed elsewhere.

"Thanks, Marcus. Next time make sure you sort your shit out and prioritise. You were picked because we bloody trust you. Now hurry up and get up there!"

Marcus lowered his head, unaccustomed to being told off, but nodded in agreement to her request. He said, "I will. I'm sorry ma'am, I didn't realise."

Taylor came into the main office just as Marcus was leaving. "What's wrong with you," he said. "You look a bit flustered. What is it?"

Intrigued, the DCI and those in the main office also watched as Taylor strode towards the boss's open door.

"I've been trying to get in touch with Fran, and then Stevie. No answer on their radios. I've tried their mobiles too - no response there either. I've also tried calling Sorina." Taylor looked up at the DCI uncomfortably.

Brooke's face dropped. Trying not to show any worry, she said, "There will be an explanation, a low area of connectivity, something like that. Have you tried GPS?"

"Yes. They are all in situ, still at the safe house, but no one is getting back to us. I was going to send a set there straight away but, being a safe house, I thought I'd better check with you first. I didn't want more trouble," Taylor replied, a little sheepishly.

"You're right. You two get up there, and make sure there is a firearms set in the area too, just in case," Brooke ordered as she turned away, trying not to show what she was feeling.

Marcus and Taylor hot footed it out of the office, Taylor's neck flushing with embarrassment and anticipation. She was worried. Something wasn't right.

Marcus also had a concerned look on his face. Just as they reached the door, Brooke shouted at them to wait. She had just received a call from the unit where Nicu was being kept, and the news was not good.

She relayed the information to Taylor and Marcus. Taylor's heart sank to her feet, the news confirming that they were not going to be met with a good situation at the safe house.

"I'll arrange back up. The safe house cover is guaranteed to be blown, so let's get numbers up there now and see what is happening!" Brooke bellowed. She had already made up her mind about what they would see and started putting roadblocks on the routes leaving the city, just in case there was a chance of intercepting those involved.

"Who is involved though?" she muttered to herself. "Who the fuck are they? Shit, we don't know anything. Who? Why? What are they driving or how long ago were they taken, if they have been taken? Nothing's confirmed yet." She hoped everything would turn out to be alright, but her heart told her the opposite.

Marcus raced through the streets, the cobbles bouncing their car, the rumble beneath them loud and uncomfortable, their presence overt as they dodged through the traffic. Their small blue light and wailing siren let the public know that they were coming through, straight up through Stockbridge, up Lothian road and out up past Bruntsfield Links into Morningside and through the less busy streets to arrive at the safe house. They screeched to a halt a little further up the street, and ran towards it, keeping tight in to the hedges, climbing through to the house from the garden next door.

They looked on at the property, their eyes drawn to the gravel and the deep grooves ripped into it, the ones left by the vehicle that had been there minutes before, clearly in a hurry, the displaced stones evident. They sat tight for a few moments, but from where they stood, the place lay ominously still. There was no movement.

Decision made that there was nobody there, they made their way to the back of the house, the open door confirming their worst fears. They shouted in through the door, batons and spray drawn, but there was no response. They cautiously moved inside. The rug on the floor was furled up, the coffee table upturned, but nobody was present. They checked every room, but there was nobody there. Radios and mobile phones had been dumped on the sofa, abandoned where they lay, all hope of tracing Fran, Steve and Sorina left behind, clearly removed by those that had taken them.

Taylor was quick to get on her radio. The city was on lock down. Scores of officers headed to the scene of the triple abduction, in the hope that there would be some clues to follow. She hoped that Fran and Sorina would be okay.

The DCI was now speeding to the scene with mixed feelings about this self-inflicted debacle. How could her career survive this? If Steve had anything to do with this, she would ensure he would take a massive fall for it. She would even write the report herself.

Chapter 36
Reunited

The van moved quickly through the city, invisible in plain sight to those surrounding it, nothing out of the ordinary, just a plain white van, its cargo the only thing that was untoward. It stopped short of the Bush Industrial Estate and drove up an inconspicuous single-track road, pulling up at a security gate that lead to the empty car park of an isolated multi-storey industrial unit in sprawling grounds.

The van drove in to a large open garage area and the doors were closed behind them. Another van was already there. It was empty, rear doors ajar, its cargo already delivered.

A couple of men came to meet the van and help get the captives out. Both were taken aback when they saw the three people inside. There was vomit all over the floor. The smallest of the three looked in a shocking condition. Her face was visibly marked, her skin mottled and bruised. She did not look well at all. She appeared to be barely alive, hands tied tightly behind her back and her breathing clearly restricted.

"Fuck's sake, Dave! What the fuck's going on here? This one's half dead. C'mon, let's move her and get the ties off her!"

"Eh, the boss will go fuckin' mad!" Dave rasped back at him, not bothered about the state of the captives, fully aware of what was going to go down later that day.

"So fuckin' what! She's half fucking dead man! We have to do something!" the panicked young apprentice Dan Duthie pleaded.

"And?" Davy said, irked that the lad had no idea of what this was all about.

"Really, I cannae just watch her die. What the fuck are you on?" Duthie stood his ground, still wanting to help Fran.

"I think she's one of the pigs?" Davy told him, his lip curled up like a rabid dog, his hatred apparent.

"And? That makes it all right does it? Are you fuckin' mad? If you kill one of theirs, they'll find you and then you're fucked, Davy!" Duthie argued again.

"What do you think they are here for ya daft wee cunt? None of them are walking out of here. You know that don't you, eh?"

Duthie stood, his mouth agape, "No fuckin' way, Dave. Who agreed to that?"

"Naebody, but think about it. The reason they're here is to secure all the witnesses, ensuring their silence, and there's only one way to be sure of that. He's done it before."

Young Dan Duthie felt sick. Sorina sat there inwardly raging. Fran was still unconscious, but thankfully still breathing, their efforts to save her had paid off.

Duthie, leant forward and untied Fran and carefully moved her arms round to her front where he retied them loosely. He was not happy at all. He picked her up and put her over his shoulder, being careful not to hurt her any more. His bottle was crashing. This shit was too real. He didn't want to be involved in stuff like this. He knew the woman he was carrying was in desperate need of medical care.

Davy grabbed Stevie by the shoulder and dragged him roughly to his feet. Their eyes met and the recognition was there, Steve knew this guy, a well-known dealer in the city and this made him feel even worse. Davy was a very violent individual. His face uncovered, another aspect of the situation to fear.

Steve's thoughts turned to his wife and family and his profound love for them. Why had he been so dumb? He now realised they were all going to be killed, all of them, including the boy. He dropped heavily to his knees, his heart broken for Sorina, Nicu, Fran and his own beautiful family, his regret instant, but it was too late.

They were rushed into the building and up the stairwell, floor after floor of what felt like hundreds of stairs, to a room at the top of the building. An oppressive derelict open planned office space lay before them. The windows were painted over, their disorientation unabated by the lack of any views. They had no idea where they were.

Sorina was last out of the van. She stood up boldly and did not want to be carried. She allowed one of the men to grip her tightly by the inner arm. She knew they were in trouble, but all she wanted was to be reunited with her boy.

She looked the man straight in the eyes, her mouth turned up slightly at the side, which made him feel uncomfortable, her strength and lack of fear disconcerting.

He felt the need to try and suppress the feeling. "Who the fuck are you staring at? Get your fucking eyes off of me, bitch!" He raised his hand as if to strike her and stopped short.

Her wince was enough to empower him, to make him believe he could dominate her. She'd met him before at the brothel. She had been held by these people before, and knew what they were capable of - rape, beatings and torture - showing no respect for the women they controlled.

She knew the score. She knew what they needed, and she would play along. She did not care if he hit her. Pain was only physical, nothing like the painful emotional torture she had endured for all of these months, but the torn strings of her heart were soon to be healed. She believed that she would be reunited with her boy sometime in the future, and now that she knew he was alive, her fight to survive was a priority.

She scurried meekly along with him, allowing his dominance to control her, letting him feet like the oppressor. She counted every one of the stairs, he took her up, making a mental note of every turn, how many doors they passed, every little detail. Her blindfold had been left in the van, a big mistake on the part of her captors.

They got to the top of five floors, enough to kill you if there was going to be an opportunity to jump. Sorina was pulled along the corridor after the others to the office at the end. It had a sturdy door with several strong locks on it. She looked around the room, ever-hopeful that her boy might have been brought there too. Her heart sank as she surveyed the run down office space, tears rolling down her cheeks, her stomach aching with pain. Another sense of tremendous loss washed over her, but suddenly her ears came alive, pricking up to the tiniest sound coming from the far corner. There was a noise coming from behind a desk there. Every fibre of her body was electrified with excitement. Her heart was pounding out through her chest as she made her way towards the desk. A huge rat came scurrying out from under it. She stopped in her tracks and nearly broke down, screaming at the top of her voice, disappointment searing through her like a bolt of lightning.

"Noooooo!" She felt like she was going mad. What made her think he would be there anyway.

She fell to her knees sobbing uncontrollably, her heart so broken she could barely breathe. She was gasping for breath loudly and was trying to get control of herself when she heard it. She focused once again towards the desk. There it was again, the softest little voice coming from beneath it.

"Mama?"

Heart thumping, Sorina ran to the desk, skidding down onto her knees and round to the other side, and there he was, her gorgeous little boy, Nicu, curled up in the corner, his arms wrapped round his knees for protection. He had a cut above his eye and a bruise on his face. He didn't move, his eyes fixed with terror as he cowered there in disbelief that this moment had finally arrived. His beautiful dark eyes filled with tears as he focused intently on his mummy. Sorina crawled under the desk and reached her arms out to her trembling son.

"Come, Nicu, come. You are safe now!" She spoke softly to him, her voice tender and honest, her words filled with love for the terrified little boy.

Sorina took hold of one of his lovely familiar little hands and felt his fingers curl round hers as he let her pull him forward. Carefully and slowly, he crawled towards her, coming out from his hiding place and into the safest place in the world, the arms of his mother. She engulfed him, and he seemed to disappear into her as she surrounded him with all of her being. After months of separation, they were finally reunited, a moment she feared would never come.

Steve just stood there, motionless, watching the moment unfold, tears in his eyes and fear in his heart, knowing what was ahead of them all. Only a miracle would see them walk out of here alive.

Sorina, on the other hand, had been revitalised. She had no intention of dying any time soon, and was not going to let anything come between her and her son ever again.

Chapter 37
Where to Start?

Taylor was still at the safe house when DCI Sommerville arrived, her face flushed with a mixture of embarrassment and anger at this total disaster of a situation, a real-life nightmare that she hoped she'd wake up from, but no such luck.

"What have we got then? Any of the neighbours see anything?" Sommerville asked whilst breathing out hard, exasperation in her voice, clear for Taylor and Marcus to see and hear.

"We have exact timings, boss. There was a white Ford Transit. It sped out of here about 18.30 hours, two up in the front, lower half of their faces covered, both had a muscular build, big shoulders, one blond, one dark, both short haired and white. That's it, I'm afraid."

"Better than nothing though. Have you secured the CCTV with the timings and descriptions?" the DCI quizzed, already thinking she had the answer.

"Yessss." Taylor dragged out her reply and looked right at Sommerville, hoping her boss would give her a break after offering this positive response.

None came. The DCI remained as cold as ice. Clearly, she was personally affected by the situation. She was totally stressed out, fearful of the consequences for those missing, and for herself and Taylor for this monumental fuck up. The Superintendent was on his way down to the scene, and he was not happy. In fact, from his tone on the phone, he was seething. He would be the one doing the explaining to the Area Commander.

SOCO arrived further up the street. They donned their white suits, plastic overshoes and made their way to the scene, hopeful in their quest of finding anything of evidential value, even the tiniest clue.

***

Burnett paced back and forward in his flat. He'd just heard that the transport containing the new batch of women had been intercepted. His fist was cut and bruised from punching the wall. The truck had been stopped in Leith Docks and the drivers were now in custody. Things seemed to be falling apart all around him, but his arrogance never abated. He would ensure he didn't go down with this sinking ship. Others would take the fall for him. He would dump phones and anything else that linked him to those caught. He would make sure he would survive this. He smiled, already in the process of tying up all the loose ends. He paced round his flat, unaware that he had an unwanted visitor downstairs.

McNare stared up at Burnett's window. He was standing outside the block of flats down at Waterfront. He had been watching Nelson come and go for a while, but he had never seen him alone. He was always with someone, and there had never been an opportunity to get near to him, not without a witness.

***

Kay was at home, alone, very alone, her thoughts consuming her, her heart wounded. Her head was still trying to forgive Taylor for her obvious failings. In her heart she knew that they had something special between them, a true connection, but Taylor seemed to have a self-destruct button and had crashed in, spoiling things more than once with her impulsive actions. Kay knew what Taylor was like when they had first got together and didn't think they would have a relationship, but now that things had developed, she hoped in her heart that Taylor could change. Kay believed, despite all Taylor's failings, she did have genuine feelings for her. She had watched Fran fall in love with Taylor too, and this had hurt her, so she had pushed Taylor away when she had been ill. She had needed space to recover. When she had been in the office the other day, she couldn't help but notice that Taylor's eyes had been fully focused on her. Kay could feel that there was still something there.

One of the team had sent Kay a text at home to keep her in the loop, and she sat there feeling numb when she read the news about Fran, Steve, Sorina, and the poor little boy. She felt guilty that she had gone off sick again, even more so with all of this happening. Her technical skills were being wasted while she sat in her house. She should be using them to help her colleagues. Making the decision there and then to leave her personal issues behind, she got ready for work. The investigation team needed her to assist with the search. Kay knew deep down that she wanted to go back. She couldn't let her friends and colleagues down, especially Taylor, who would be pulling her hair out with something like this, taking it personally.

***

Michelle Smith from the PPU was at the hospital with Pauline from the children's unit, taking statements and DNA swabs. Michelle was genuinely distraught that the little boy she had dealt with earlier that year, and had a connection with, had been taken again. The poor wee soul had been through so much already. Why would they take him? Every action leaves a trace, and she was meticulous when she combed and swabbed Pauline for trace evidence, hoping that some form of DNA had been deposited on her that was still viable. Pauline was a strong woman and tried not to show her emotions, but Michelle could see she was deeply shaken up by what had happened and disturbed by the loss of the boy. She was blaming herself for

Nicu's abduction, despite having fought with everything she had to prevent him being taken. There was no way she could have stopped them. They would have killed her if they had to.

***

The Roads Policing vehicles were now strategically placed around the city, but so far there nothing had come from the numerous vehicles they had stopped and searched. Pete was with PS Blair. He had been recently promoted but was still willing to get stuck in with the troops. They were positioned at the roundabout that lead onto the A1 just up from Musselburgh. They were frustrated with the lack of results, realising they were too late, the horse had already bolted. Pete knew Fran from the last major incident they had been involved in. That was when he had been seriously injured. Fran had visited him in the hospital numerous times, all his colleagues had, and he would never forget what they had done for him when he needed them most. There was a bond there and he was desperate to do the same for her now. He, more than anyone else, knew just how lucky he had been to survive, when everyone thought he might not make it. He was gutted for Fran and the others. He hoped that they were all okay. The conversation turned to Steve. There had been gossip about him, some negative chat was going around about him, the finger already being pointed in his direction, and in the police force, mud sticks. Cops believed there was no smoke without fire. Guilty or not, there would be speculation about him for ever more. He would always be talked about, whatever the outcome.

***

Burnett grabbed his keys from the table. He needed to make calls from somewhere other than here. He looked around for Irene, worried that he had gone at it a bit too far this time.

"Irene! Irene, get here now, will ye?" No response came back. *Where the fuck is she, the daft wee cow?* He was ready to go and get her for disrespecting him. He was annoyed that she hadn't come when he'd called, something he wasn't used to. He marched through to the room. There was blood on the carpet. It trailed into the bathroom, where she stood staring into the mirror. She didn't flinch as she watched him come up behind her.

"When I call, you fucking come, right. What the fuck's wrong with you anyway! Why did ye no come when I shouted?" There was only silence. Tears, smeared with blood, rolled down her face, her expression blank and empty. She was broken with nothing left to give, and was no longer fearful of the consequences of not responding, her senses dead.

Burnett was a little taken aback. He had expected her to plead with him or scurry away to avoid another beating, something that would put him back in control, but there was nothing. She saw him raise his hand to strike her head, but she did not wince. She stood strong. She was no longer willing to cower away. She stood tall and braced herself, waiting for his hand to strike her, her eyes fixed on her own reflection in the mirror. She could not believe what she had become. Her blood clouded eyes looked away from her own and met his. She looked like Carrie from the 1976 horror movie, but there was something else there, hatred, and something new - strength.

Burnett was a bit repulsed at what he'd done this time and put his hand back down. He stormed out of the flat, his mind racing, hate filled and ready to put things to bed, whatever that took. He would sort her out when he got back.

He strode out into the early evening. He would head to the brothel and get Dave to meet him there, but first he'd go down to the beach to make his calls. He hoped that the two stooges from the truck would keep their fucking mouths shut, and that they hadn't said anything in front of the girls. He paid them good money to keep quiet. He looked in his offside mirror and noticed a motor bike pull out when he did. The rider wore a full faced helmet with a shaded visor. Burnett's smile was nasty. This was a bonus for him. *Whoever you are, bring it on!*

Chapter 38
Enquiry

Up at the cells complex at St Leonard's the two drivers of the lorry were being detained, both sitting in their individual cells, bare walls, concrete bench with blue mat, steel toilet in the corner and a blanket used for the thousandth time, a place where all you could do was think. They had been apprehended less than 10 minutes after the incident in Leith. The main driver's mind was racing. He felt trapped, claustrophobic, and helpless, like a caged animal. He stood up and rang the buzzer to see if he could speak with a lawyer soon. The steel hatch clanked heavily down, making a loud bang as it landed. The cells officer looked in. Their faces were less than a foot from each other. The officer, whose name was Ali, was accompanied by Gill to corroborate anything that was said. They knew why the man was in the cells and didn't like the shit he was involved in so Ali's conversation was short and to the point. He knew the man could speak very good English, as he had heard him when he came in, and knew he understood everything that was being said to him. The false pretence of lack of understanding was beginning to grate on Ali, but he remained professional and asked politely what the man wanted. The response in pidgin English made him sigh and repeat what he'd said more slowly, playing along with the continued pretence of not understanding. After several attempts,

Ali whispered to him, "Listen mate, just fucking say what you want. You'll still get your interpreter anyway, and if you stop talking shit, you'll get a cup of tea and a biscuit as well and, if yer really good, I'll flush yer lavvy too."

Sergeant McVay was on the phone in her office, listening to DCI Sommerville reel off what was to happen with the two drivers. Detectives would be arriving soon to interview them. Lawyers and interpreters were also on their way and immigration officers had been contacted. There was a buzz about the station. There was so much happening around the city just now and everything had to be done right. There could be no mistakes. These guys could not walk for a minor procedural error.

Taylor and Brooke were going to personally take on the interview and were on their way to St Leonard's. They had settled their differences for the time being and were discussing how to proceed next. They would have to tread carefully and try and get on side with these guys in some way, offer them something to make them burst, so that they would start talking. Their briefs would tell them that they were being charged with human trafficking, and possibly manslaughter with regard to the girl who had been found dead in their truck. Things were bad for them one way or another. Other serious charges were also being looked at as it appeared the truck had been purposely altered to create a secreted living space for its live cargo. There was no way the drivers couldn't have known about the women they were carrying. The journey from Romania alone would have taken several days. Without someone supplying them with water, they would have all died.

Prior to their statements being taken, each and every one of the women had been checked thoroughly by the nurse stationed at St Leonard's. Despite being a long-serving employee at the cells, Vicki had never experienced anything like this before, and certainly not on this scale, but she was determined to help the women as much as she could and make sure they received any treatment they needed, her kind and caring manner apparent as she spoke to them.

DC's Noble and Lomond of the Major Investigation Team had been speaking with the girls from the truck, noting their detailed statements. Their stories were harrowing, filled with the inhuman and vulgar treatment they were forced to endure, sexual assault and beatings if they spoke out. They explained the method of their entrapment, the way they had been duped into travelling with the men. There had been promises of work opportunities. All of the women were educated, and clearly not stupid. The men were kind and plausible initially. On their first meeting with them, their drinks had been spiked, even before the conversation turned to transport, money, and what was supposed to happen. The next thing they knew they were trapped in a confined space, all practically sitting on top of each other, no toilets, no food, just water every twelve hours or so. It had been terrifying.

DC Noble listened intently, not wanting to miss a single detail. She was kind and persuasive. One of her many skills was patience. She was a comfort to the women, giving them time to open up and talk. She put their minds at ease and was prepared to work hard to gain their trust. The women had been hard to convince at first, due to their lack of trust in their own police force, which was known for extortion, corruption and bribery. All of the women were fearful that it would be the same in Britain, and that they had jumped out of the frying pan into the fire, all assuming that their ordeal was not yet over. Bernadette and Leanne were both confident, clearly the natural leaders within the group thrown together in the lorry, both survivors. DC Noble discovered they had been the ones that instigated the escape, both totally unaware of just how close they had been to their final destination and a life of forced drug addiction and prostitution that would have become their living nightmare.

After interviewing all of the women at length, the officers were able to piece together little bits of evidence and the route taken from the stops made. They also had a couple of names and one name overheard when one of the men had been on the phone. It was only a first name, 'Davy', but it was better than nothing. The name had been used on more than one occasion and at different times, suggesting he was the main contact.

DCs Noble and Lomond knew that Nelson Burnett's right-hand man was Davy Strachan, but proving Burnett was involved beyond reasonable doubt was another matter. There were millions of Davys, and it was just a name! Everyone knew Burnett controlled things in Edinburgh, the drugs, the brothels, but getting people to speak out against him and live long enough to testify was another thing. The whole thing reeked of Burnett's foul stench, and everyone was worried about how it would pan out.

Taylor and Brooke had been preparing the interview plan for nearly two hours in relation to the drivers of the lorry, making sure they had their trump cards ready to contradict anything they said, make them feel cornered and make them think that their only choice was to reveal their resources, payments and contacts. They would offer them anonymity and a reduction in their sentence for worthwhile information they might provide, because it was clear that they were minnows in the bigger picture. However, their deliberate and unnecessary cruelty would not go unpunished. Their phones had already been taken to the Cycomms unit to be investigated, and their vehicle was being stripped right back and searched. It was a fairly new truck. It might contain a unit similar to a black box, a very useful tool, which could potentially reveal their every movement,.

Chapter 39
Connections

Kim sat looking at her phone, the text from Steve and the vast amount of money showing in their bank account, her heart sore with how stupid Steve had been. He wasn't a bad man, his heart was in the right place, but what was he thinking? Had he gone mad? Her mind was racing at the consequences for their family.

She looked over at her precious daughter, her heart broken at how ill she was, but she trusted the NHS to find the correct treatment for her somehow. Everything took time, but taking dishonest money was not what she wanted for her daughter.

She had been watching the news, and she was surprised nobody had been to speak to her, unaware that there were plans to do so, but there were only so many detectives available at this extremely busy time.

She got her mum to come over and look after Maisy, before she made her way to Fettes where her husband worked, or used to anyway. She had her phone with her, and was ready to tell everything. She knew it was only a matter of time anyway. There was no way things like this would go unnoticed. She stopped for a moment, just outside the grand building of Fettes College, one of Edinburgh's finest private schools. Tears rolled down her face, onto her lip and into her mouth, her sobs loud and audible to the passers-by, who looked and walked on by, none stopping to comfort her or check she was okay. She could not believe that Steve had lost all sense of reality and loyalty to the force. What had happened to him?

Kay was heading up to the reception area when she noticed Kim standing there, tears in her eyes. She quickly offered comfort and held Kim as she wept. Kay guided her down the stairs and into a small room where she told Kim she would arrange for a detective to come and speak to her, offering her a coffee in the meantime. Kay was warm and friendly. Kim knew of her but had never met her. It was only through general office chat that her name had been mentioned. Steve had talked freely of Taylor and Kay's tumultuous relationship, and that Kay had stormed out a couple of weeks ago, so Kim had a little sympathy for this stranger who sat kindly before her, clearly with her own troubles in life.

Kay tried to contact Taylor, but her phone was not being answered. She left a message informing her of Kim's presence at the station.

Taylor was in full flow in the interview and felt the vibration in her pocket. She managed to take a peek and nudged Brooke to look too. The text stated that Steve's wife had arrived at the station and mentioned a large sum of money in their account and Kim's own suspicions about Steve recently. Things seemed to be becoming a little clearer, at least the motives were there anyway. Both knew Steve had a daughter that was very ill, and although his actions were unforgivable and beyond comprehension to a sane and focused mind, they were made through desperation and love.

Taylor had to settle herself down again. The fact that Kay had texted her with information suggested that she was back at work. She had left several days ago, following the revelation about Taylor and the DCI. The text was a relief for Taylor. It meant Kay's anger and dissatisfaction were abating.

Burnett was out of his car and heading down to the beach, fully aware of the bike that was following him and now a car had joined him too. He could tell the car was the Feds. He laughed to himself as he thought about how their stench gave them away. *Oink, oink, little piggies.* The guy on the motorbike was a little more disconcerting. *Who the fuck is he?* He thought through the list of options, and there were plenty of them. He consoled himself that McNare wouldn't have the balls to try anything, and he was confident of his own ability when it came to any of his other enemies. Unless they came right up to him and shot him, he'd be fine.

McNare stayed back, but was positioned just in front of the cops. He too had spotted them a mile away, they just had that look. His brow was sweating. Hatred boiled within his guts, revulsion at how arrogant this prick actually was, Burnett truly believing he was invincible. McNare's heart quickened as he thought of wiping the smile off Burnett's face right there and then, or even broadening it, permanently. The knife he carried was secreted down the crack of his arse, which at times was uncomfortable when riding his recently acquired motorbike. He was surprised it hadn't been flagged up on the cops' database yet, as they surely must have checked him out. Maybe a stolen bike was not worthy of their attention these days, or was it because they had their eyes on the main prize. McNare worried that they might have contacted the traffic police about him and that they would be arriving shortly, but he knew this bike was like shit off a shovel and they'd have no chance of capturing him. They wouldn't even get near him. He rode up closer to Burnett, and carried on down to the foreshore, which was a pedestrian area, his stance menacing, revving the engine deliberately to draw the attention he desired. He then pulled back on the throttle and sped straight towards Burnett. Burnett instinctively ran, jumping onto the low wall that separated the promenade from the beach to get out of the way. He yelled out a tirade of expletives as the biker sped off, his rage and embarrassment obvious for the cops to see. A silent mirth passed between them as they enjoyed a little summary justice, but it was their duty to keep him safe and offer to help and they headed down to see if Burnett was okay.

"What the fuck are youse clowns gonnae dae aboot that little fucker then, eh? Fuck all probably, just like yis normally do!" The words rattled out of Burnett's mouth, straight into the cop's face that stood before him. They knew their cover had been blown but there were replacements on their way, so they knew they had to try and placate him meantime and offer a forced friendly ear to listen to his painfully annoying rant.

After his repeated shouts of injustice, swathed in every swear word possible, Burnett calmed a little. His momentary silence allowed one cop to ask, "Do you know who that was Mr Burnett?" His question was said with genuine curiosity as there were very few people ballsy enough to have a go at Nel Burnett.

"How the fuck would I know ya daft wee prick? It's your fucking job to find that out, so get after the cunt, and stop yer fannying about wi me. What the fuck are ye following me around fir anyway? Yer wasting yer fuckin' time. Now if you're not fuckin' arresting me, then fuck off, please!"

The two officers struggled to remain civil amidst the tirade of abuse. They had to walk away, annoyed that he thought he had the upper hand. They were under strict instructions not to arrest him, just follow, observe and report.

Chapter 40
Trapped

Sorina was pacing up and down in their prison, trying to work out how they could escape. Little Nicu was curled up on some cushions in the corner of the sprawling office, a couple of abandoned coats covering him. She looked down at him, and her heart felt sore once more. She felt helplessness as she thought about their fate. She was finding it hard to see how they could get out of there alive.

Fran was still unconscious and was lying close to Nicu, her face badly swollen. Steve was worried for her. He had seen how hard she was punched, and suspected she could have a bleed on the brain or other serious injury. He had never wanted his colleague to get hurt, anyone for that matter. He just hadn't thought about the consequences. He had felt trapped and desperate after his first mistake. He was going down anyway, so felt he had to get something out of this mess for his family, before he was caught, as he should have known he would be.

He sat down beside Fran and put a hand on her shoulder, hoping for some reaction. Sorina had already tried, but there was still no response. None of their captors had looked in on them, checked to see if they were still alive. Their lack of care and interest in their wellbeing was disconcerting, especially as they knew Fran was critically injured. They didn't even seem to care that one of their captives was a very young boy. No food or fresh water had been offered. Steve was troubled. He knew this set of circumstances did not bode well for them. Whoever was behind this had gone to a lot of trouble to get them there. Steve had his ideas of who they were dealing with, and he did not like it one bit.

"Sorina, come here a minute will you, please?" Steve asked kindly.

Sorina stared over at Steve, her loathing for him oozing openly from her. She knew it was his fault they were all here after hearing him talking to their abductors as they entered the safe house. She had already decided what type of person he was - greedy, selfish and not to be trusted - although she was well aware he was now in the same shitty mess as the rest of them.

"Why?" she scowled.

"I need to ask you something," he pleaded.

"Why would I know anything and why would I tell you anyway," she said, her tone curt and scathing.

"I need to know what you know, why have they brought you here, why both of you? There must be a reason."

She just stared straight through him, her mind going over what she did actually know and the importance of it. The police officers had seemed very interested in her. She herself wasn't really sure that she knew anything of any real evidential value.

She wracked her brains and thought back to her time working from the warehouse, who would come and go. Sometimes she had been coherent and other times totally junked up and unaware of anything. It all depended on how the drugs were administered to her. She always tried to discard them, but sometimes they had injected everyone by force. Since she had been brought to Scotland, she had been forced to sleep with many of her captors and really didn't know who was who. However, there was one guy that had taken a shine to her, her body, her eyes. He seemed mesmerised by her, smitten even! He liked what she did for him, and he was always well dressed. He was rough with her, and didn't like that she had a child. It was as if he was jealous of her attention to the boy, the fondness for her own child. He wanted her full attention, so he had sorted that.

Once Nicu was ripped out of her arms and taken away from her, he came around a few more times, but Sorina was never the same, the opposite of what he had wanted. She was cold as ice and refused his demands. Everything was forced, her heart broken, her open resentment so outwardly rippling that it was almost intimidating. She did not care anymore. This caused him to beat her badly, his rage violent and uncontrollable, but still she didn't respond or give in to his demands. He made sure the other men kept a closer eye on her after that, almost like a punishment for disobeying him.

"Did you ever meet someone called Nelson Burnett?" Steve continued, refusing to give up.

"Who's he? Should I know him?" she questioned.

"The police have been after him for ages but he's slippery, always on the periphery of so many busts, never too close when the police come to call. No one is ever willing to speak out against him. They are too scared of what would happen to them and their families. He's been remanded several times, linked to huge drug hauls, serious assaults and unexplained deaths, but he always gets released due to insufficient evidence by the time the trial comes around."

"What does he look like?" Sorina quizzed.

"Big man, tall, six foot at least, maybe more, muscular, no neck, bald, shaved head, always a growl on his face, nice clothes, mean temper, gold fillings, a scar on his right cheek."

Sorina's blood ran cold. She had run her fingers over that scar once and he had nearly broken her wrist when he took hold of her hand to stop her, the force so brutal it terrified her. He was like a wild animal. He had snapped, teeth clenched, rage in his face, as he relived how the scar came to be there. He had slapped her face so hard with the back of his hand, she too had a scar above her eye now where his sovereign ring had cut into her skin. He had held her face up to his and rasping through his teeth had told her never to touch the scar again.

She had thought he was going to kill her. After the outburst he had continued as if nothing had happened, taking what he wanted sexually, even more forcefully and viciously, teaching her a lesson for being too familiar with him.

Sorina snapped out of it and looked at Steve. "Yes," she said.

"Yes! What, have you met him?" Steve looked excited.

"Yes, I have met him, many, many times. I know every little detail about him. He even has a mole on his dick."

"You're fucking kidding me? Nel, you've met Nel?"

"Who is Nel?"

"That's what his associates call him, Big Nel."

"He's not big," she said with a satisfied look on her face, her way of bringing him down in her mind.

Stevie laughed a bit, thinking how the other cops would rip into him when he recounted this little quote, forgetting that he would never be one of them again.

"Wow! Why you, surely there were loads of girls?" he quizzed.

Sorina glared at him, his last comment a little insulting. "There were! But he had his favourites, the younger ones, innocent and impressionable, easily controlled, and one or two of the other women with nice eyes. He had a thing about eyes. A bit of an odd guy really, considering his own eyes were hard and cruel, shark like, emotionless and empty, not a man you would cross. He looks evil and his actions prove it! I have seen him beat one of his men. He wouldn't stop, stamping, kicking, biting. It was horrible,. The man wasn't moving when he'd finished. I never saw the man again. Who knows, he's probably dead, same as some of the women. One or two of them never came back to the unit either."

Steve just sat there on one of the revolving office chairs, looking at her. "They're going to kill us, you know, all of us. You can identify him, maybe even the boy can, 'cause it's clear that Nel Burnett had something to do with his disappearance too."

"What do you mean?"

"He didn't just have him taken away, Sorina. Nicu was sold to a paedophile ring, and from reading the reports on where he was rescued from, he wasn't meant to live."

"No, no. Was he hurt? What did they do to him? The filthy, vile bastards. My poor, beautiful little boy." She began to cry and started pacing the room again, her anger at boiling point.

"Nothing, they didn't do anything to him. Listen, Sorina, he was medically examined and he was unharmed. Really. Some vigilante got there first and the man that had him was found dead, trussed up like a chicken. She rescued the boys. She saved them both."

"A woman, a woman saved them and murdered that guy? I need to meet her. You said boys - what happened to the other one?"

"The other one was a cop's son. He was saved too. He looked out for your lad. If we ever get out of here, I'll introduce you to him. I'm sure Nicu would want to see him again. Meeting Amy, the woman who rescued them, might be more difficult, but not impossible. She's in prison. I'll get someone to help you with that, although I don't think I'll have much clout anymore," he said with remorse in his eyes.

Sorina looked directly at him. "We will get out of here, Steve. My boy has a future. We are not going to die in here!"

Steve just looked at her, impressed with her positive spirit and strength, but he was less optimistic. Being realistic, he couldn't see how they could escape this. They were too high up to jump and live, and they would not be able to fight their captors, who would easily overpower them.

Sorina suddenly uttered, "Why?"

Steve covered his face with his hands. When he removed them, he was crying. Sorina was taken aback. She hadn't expect tears from him, she had thought she already had him sussed.

Steve began to talk about his daughter and her plight, her illness, the cost of specialist treatment available abroad. He talked and talked, pouring his heart out to her, his sadness open and truthful. His regret was genuine and his remorse obvious, the desire to turn back the clock overwhelming.

Sorina wanted to keep hating him, but on hearing why he had faltered and taken a bribe and his tormentors' coercion after that, it was clear he hadn't done it out of greed and selfishness. It was desperation and selflessness. He had thought he could save his daughter and believed there would be no repercussions from his actions or a repeat of his stupidity. He hadn't realised he would be held to account by them forever, blackmailed into more corruption and desperate acts to save his skin and that of his family.

Reality was crushing him inside. His poor judgement would leave his family fatherless and worse off than before, let alone the dire situation they were all in now.

Chapter 41
Despair

Taylor drove slowly back to the office from St Leonard's, her mind troubled with what ifs. She cut down through The Meadows, a large open area of greenbelt in the centre of the city overlooked by the Old Royal Infirmary, now transformed into state-of-the-art apartments. She then cut down through Lothian Road, the Sheraton Grand Hotel on one side and the famous Usher Hall, a prestigious dome-shaped concert venue, on the other. The new one-way system, brought about by the new tram lines, skirted round Charlotte Square and down onto Dean Bridge. As she crossed the bridge, she thought back to the year before when she had attended to a suicide. A man had chosen to jump into the shallow waters below, feeling that there had been no option other than to end it all, his existence finally over and his tortured soul set free. She thought about his background, his elderly mother, who had been left to cope on her own, the poor soul in disbelief that her son had felt so desperate and alone. Taylor refocused and made her way along Queensferry Road, down towards Stockbridge, her tyres bouncing over the cobbles, the sound similar to a train on the tracks, a sound she normally enjoyed, but not today. Finally, she came round by Inverleith Park and back to Fettes.

She paused at the security gate and had to raise up from her seat to free the pass from deep in her pocket, getting cramp in her thigh for her troubles, her frustration obvious when the gate opened just before she removed it and reached out, her efforts and contortion wasted. She muttered, "Thanks," while under her breath thinking, *for nothing, you're too bloody slow!* She felt her world was falling apart. Her judgement was being questioned, Fran was missing, Kay hated her and her boss wasn't happy with her either. She felt that she was losing control. Everything that she cared about was slipping through her fingers, fingers and hands that were so used to being in control. She used to trust her own judgement, but now there was more hesitation, and doubt. She took a deep breath and decided it was best to face her problems head on.

She parked her car and clambered out, her blouse not tucked in properly, her hair unbrushed for several hours. She looked dishevelled, which for her was out of character. Her heeled boots clacked loudly as she walked, her stride wide and a little aggressive, almost marching. She pulled the door to the open plan office with more force than she had meant and it swung back, banging loudly against the wall, causing everyone in the office to look up and stare at her. Marcus rose up from his desk and went quickly to meet her. He knew the pressure she was under and that she would be crumbling inside and, more recently, outwardly too. The finger pointing and blame culture was already rumbling in the department's daily discussions. He had overheard the gossip several times as he walked by certain officers' desks. The operation was the talk of the station, the topic on everyone's lips and a free for all for everyone's opinions, good or bad. He moved quickly to her side and, as a loyal friend, quickly pointed out her hair and blouse, guiding her through to the small kitchen area to allow her the privacy she needed to sort herself out.

She looked up at him, and he could see the tears building in her eyes. Reaching out his arms, he pulled her in for a hug. She had stood still, reluctant to move to him, trying to refrain from needing support, but every other fibre of her being longed to be held and comforted. She wanted to bury her head in the sand and run away from everything. Everything seemed so broken, and she felt helpless to fix it.

After a minute or so he felt she had had enough time to be freed from his embrace. Her eyes were bloodshot and her light eye makeup had run down her cheeks. He wiped her face kindly and smiled at her. Clasping her face with his strong hands, he spoke gently to her. His words were reassuring, carefully chosen and inspirationally motivating, he too accepting of his part in the shit hitting the fan. If he hadn't had that urgent enquiry, the change of personnel would never have happened at the safe house and the window of opportunity less accessible for them to carry out their plan, although they might have found themselves as captives instead, or worse, dead. Taylor took a piece of kitchen roll and wiped round her eyes. She drank some water and stood up straight. Then she looked at Marcus and smiled, the best she could muster, and whispered, "Thank you, I needed that. I really thought I was losing it there."

They strode out of the kitchen, every head seeming to turn towards them as they reappeared. It was obvious that Taylor had been crying. Many were concerned for her, glad it was not them in her shoes. They quickly turned back and put their heads down and at least gave off the impression they were working. All but one of them. Kay's head remained up looking straight at Taylor and Marcus, her expression one of concern and distress. She was worried about Taylor, who looked awful, tortured, a little gaunt, with dark rings round her eyes. It was clear she hadn't been sleeping. It took a while before Taylor looked up and scanned the room, instantly spotting the familiar face, a face she had longed to see. She looked for any hostility or dislike, but there was none. All she saw was a face of concern, and something else, something she never thought she would see again - affection. Kay's eyes showed that she still cared. Kay longed to go to her, to hold her, but she stayed put in her seat, knowing that this was the last thing Taylor needed, fuel for the office gossips.

Taylor smiled at her and raised a hand in greeting, but she could not go and speak with her just now. The boss wanted to see her as soon as possible, and she wouldn't take kindly to any further delay. The DCI had seen Taylor come in. It had been ten minutes and still nobody had reported to her office. Sommerville stood up in her office as she saw Taylor and Marcus walking towards her. DI Findlay was there too but he remained at his desk, with a smug look on his pudgy little face, revelling in Taylor's very public fall from grace, hoping that this would end her promising career, his deep resentment feeding off her demise.

DCI Sommerville swung open the door, her formidable presence making them both instinctively straighten up in tandem, like a couple of school kids sent to the head's office. They acknowledged her politely out of respect and sat down once offered a seat. Sommerville noticed Findlay staring at Taylor. She knew there was animosity between the two and thought it only fair to give Taylor some privacy for the discussion that was to come. Handing Findlay some papers, she asked if he could take them to the superintendent and give a briefing of progress to date. She knew the super would grill him for every little detail, so he would be there for at least an hour.

Sommerville felt sorry for Taylor. Her decision to send Steve to the safe house had been made in good faith and within required guidelines. It had just been a lapse of judgement with the personnel chosen due to a set of unfortunate unforeseen circumstances, which were beyond her control. Taylor had flagged up Steve's behaviour previously, but was unable to say why she felt wary of him and couldn't openly act on her suspicions without concrete facts to back them up, or he would have put in a complaint.

The DCI sat behind her desk, dominating her private space, guarded by the solid wooden desk, a barrier between them and her, giving protection from any hostility that came her way. She tapped some papers on the desk and looked up at them, both eagerly awaiting what she had to say.

"We have some better news," Brooke smiled. "A little progress a least. We have a hair from the murder at Cables Wynd, and a footprint confirmation from both Sighthill and Cables Wynd crime scenes. The hair is confirmed as Craig McNare's, a drug courier, an old associate of Burnett's.

"We think he was the one that managed to kick one of the cops in the bollocks a year or so back and make good his escape." She said this with a smile and an incredulous look on her face, an expression that acknowledged that they should never have let him get away, aching balls or not! Unfortunately in the job, things like that did occasionally happen. The cops on the receiving end of any failure would have the piss taken out of them for ever more.

Taylor smiled at this. Even amongst everything going on, there was always time to rip into their colleague's failings at a level that all cops understood. There was no malice, just a lifetime's worth of office banter.

"That's good news. But why now, what's the connection here?" Taylor quizzed.

Brooke, smiled again, her ace still to play. "Revenge, I believe. We did a lot of digging, stuff that ought to have been uncovered first time round, but it was never common knowledge. They were together but people just didn't talk to us back then through fear of repercussions."

"Who was together, c'mon spill?" Taylor pleaded with her eyes, expectation starting to annoy her a bit.

"It was McNare's partner who was killed in that unsolved arson attack a couple of years back, the one at Wardieburn, and to top that, she was several months pregnant at the time she died, reason enough for him to want payback," Brooke said triumphantly.

"Can we link them though?" Taylor exclaimed.

"What do you think? Not a bloody chance in hell, just like the drugs haul. Burnett's sweaty little hands are all over it, everything, the drugs, the trafficking, the abductions, but we have diddly squat to bring him in again! We can see if we can close the net on McNare though. He might be the link we need to get Burnett. He might even be prepared to talk - he's got nothing to lose now. Surely this time we can make something stick."

"I don't think McNare will be planning to hand himself in any time soon. He's not that stupid, is he? He's trying to deal with this his own way, he's just taking too long," Taylor expressed.

The radio went and they all heard the update from the cops that had been carrying out surveillance on Burnett. Their cover had been blown and someone on a motorbike had tried to mow down Burnett.

All three of them were a little disappointed that whoever it was had missed, and all of them now had a good idea who it might have been.

Brooke lifted the radio and asked for clarification about the bike. The response was as suspected, it was stolen.

"What about Davy Strachan? Have we managed to track him down yet? He is always there or thereabouts when Burnett is concerned," Brooke asked, ever hopeful.

Marcus cleared his throat and said, "There is a lot of phone work being done in relation to him. His phone was last pinged near to one of the sauna's in the New Town, the one Burnett owns, and the apple never falls far from the tree."

Taylor's eyes lit up. "Do we bring him in? There is enough to link him to the shipment of trafficked women we intercepted, and who knows he might spill his guts if we push him?"

"I doubt it. He's never grassed on Burnett before and he's done time for him a few times, after his no comment stance," Brooke was quick to point out.

"What about the white van? There must be CCTV that we can follow up on," Marcus added.

"We have a whole squad on it. We have followed up on so many white vans, all traced with a negative result, so sweet FA really, which is so frustrating. Where the fuck did they go? They can't just disappear," Brooke said, her frustration and fear for her officers and the other captives clear in her facial expression.

"They might have ditched the original van and had another legitimate one waiting, and if it was checked out without its cargo, all would look pretty normal, don't you think?" Marcus suggested.

"What are you saying - that we might have checked it out already and it was legit?"

"Who knows? It's not impossible though, is it?" Marcus said with disappointment.

"Even still, it could be one of so many. How do we find which one if that is what's happened. There are no reports about any recovered burn-outs either?"

Both Taylor and Marcus looked at her in despair, the magnitude of their task daunting.

"Someone will make a move soon, a call, a text, an instruction, something, and let's hope we're not too late!" Taylor said with sadness in her eyes, her thoughts going to Fran. "Fran had said to me that there was something odd about Steve. She thought he was always on edge and uptight, a bit jumpy and secretive, but nothing anyone could act upon, to have him removed from the squad."

"Well, we know now why he was on edge. He was being blackmailed and is up to his neck in shit. His wife has come forward and confessed his sins to us, but she truly believes his motivation was for good intentions, and he's just been outrageously narrow-minded and stupid."

Brooke was nearly done. "What about this guy Davy? Strachan isn't it? The one the women had talked about when they intercepted the truck."

"It's not confirmed that it is one and the same, but they have made numerous enquiries into his whereabouts, he's not been seen by anyone lately, he has no up to date phone, nothing linked directly to him, no vehicle, nothing, he's like a ghost, nobody knows where he is, where he is staying, not even his lady friend ma'am. Who know's if he's even alive. If he's in that deep, then maybe he's outlived his usefulness," Taylor said. "Who says he's not just collateral damage now, too dangerous for the boss to have around anymore, with the amount he knows."

"Nobody just disappears, there must be someone who knows something." Brooke looked totally defeated.

"Not necessarily. Their tight-lipped loyalty is unflinching. Even the usual grasses don't seem to have anything to say."

Sommerville stood up and, without any further words, they were dismissed.

As they left, they heard her say quietly, "Please find them!"

Taylor and Marcus went straight back to work at their adjoining desks, heads together, deep in conversation, desperate for a breakthrough lead.

Taylor sat up suddenly, excitement in her eyes. "His wife!" she exclaimed

"Who's wife?" Marcus looked impatiently at her.

"Who do you think?" she paused momentarily. "Burnett's wife of course, ya dafty. She will know what premises he has, and plead stupidity to what goes on in them."

"What makes you think she'll talk? She's been with him for a while and she's never uttered a word against him," Marcus mentioned a little sarcastically.

"Did you see her face the last time? Maybe now is the time. Maybe she's getting fed up of being his punchbag all the time. Everyone has their limit."

He smiled. "Worth a try, I suppose, but what's in it for her. We can't offer her anything. This isn't a movie you know."

Taylor smiled. "Her freedom."

Both rose from their seats, and moved towards the door. Taylor remembered Kay was back and looked over expectantly, but she was not at her desk. Her heart sank with disappointment. *I'll call her later. I need to make things right between us. Even if we can't be together, I want her friendship more than anything else.* Taylor was trying to fool herself that friendship was enough. Her heart came alive when Kay was around, and Taylor realised she was still deeply in love with her.

Chapter 42
Hope

The knock on the door was loud and intimidating. Irene sat bolt upright, as still as a rock on her sofa. She was still shaken from the vicious assault earlier. She put her hands over her ears and hoped whoever it was would go away. The knocks on the door got louder, and there was the sound of a hard object being used, enhancing the volume. Irene began to shake and started to rock back and forward, wondering if it was someone reaping their revenge on Nel. It wouldn't be the first time he'd been out when his foes came calling for him. She had the scars to prove it. Eventually she took her hands away from her ears and heard a strong female voice through the door, the word "Police" clearly audible. Unlike Nel, she was not overly bothered by the police. She knew they were a necessary evil in life and had come to her rescue many times before, but Nel hated them. He totally despised them and would assault and injure officers at every opportunity and tried to instil this hatred in all those around him.

"Irene, I know you're in there. We're only here to ask you a few questions. There's nothing to worry about." Taylor and Marcus waited silently outside for several minutes, hoping she would give herself away as neither of them had heard anyone within. Marcus had lodged his baton in the letter box, pushing the bristles aside to leave a small gap that allowed him a clear view up the hallway. They weren't entirely sure if Irene was actually in there, but were ever hopeful. They were chancing their luck a bit, and were delighted that Burnett wasn't there. He would have been out like a shot, shouting and bawling at them. Taylor poked Marcus, who was still crouched down peering through the letter box, and shrugged her shoulders. They were about to give up when their patience paid off. Light footsteps could be heard coming from the living room. Marcus saw Irene come into the hallway, her tiny frame now visible and heading meekly towards the kitchen, her arms wrapped protectively round herself, believing that they had gone.

Marcus spoke softly to her and she stopped dead in her tracks, startled that they were still there, her shoulders visibly slumping even further. Marcus could see her face was swollen and bruised, and it was obvious that she had suffered some sort of assault recently. Instantly he knew they would have leverage to get her to come to the door and to get her on side. Legally, they could now put the door in if necessary, in order to check Irene's wellbeing, to ensure she was okay, as all officers have a duty of care to everyone they deal with.

"What do you want? Stop hassling us. Nel's not in anyway, clearly." Irene ended her statement with a huge dose of sarcasm, which Marcus got, because he'd already sussed that from the lack of verbal abuse and violence coming from the property.

"Please, just come to the door, Irene! We need to speak to you, and we need to see if you're alright. It won't take long. Come on, help us out here." Marcus used his most pleasant tone. He genuinely wanted to check her over, knowing that Burnett had an uncontrollable temper and liked to hit women.

"Why should I? I'll just get more of the same, or worse," she said as she spun round and pointed to her bruised and battered face. Her face was contorted with exasperation, desperation and despair, but for the first time, Marcus also saw something different in Irene's demeanour, defeat. He didn't want to be too obvious in his approach, but this was their best shot at getting her on side and maybe giving her an escape from the prison Burnett had created for her.

Taylor spoke next. She was matter-of-fact, probably because she was a woman and could not understand how some women allowed themselves to be dominated like this, beaten repeatedly, staying there for more. Her tone was kind and honest, a truth about her desire to help her. Both detectives needed Irene more than ever before.

Irene came to the door, hands shaking. When the door opened, both officers were taken aback when they saw her broken frame. Her face was a mess, tears leaving trails through the dried blood, swelling under both eyes, her cheek clearly broken. There were grip marks on her wrists and throat, and she was bent over a bit, suggesting her ribs might be broken too.

"Bloody hell, Irene! This has to stop. He's going to kill you one day. No matter how much you dislike us, you know we're right. We can help you, we can make you safe," Taylor pleaded with her.

"Nobody can make me safe, and you both bloody know it. He'll hunt me down, and he'll find me, and you know what he'll do then! You can't protect me 24/7. He wouldn't give up you know. He'd get me. I'm his and he won't let me go until the day one of us dies - til death do us part and all that," she said as she walked them through to the living room and gestured for them to sit, openly wincing in pain when she sat down.

The living room was large and luxurious, the corner suite engulfing the room, cushions of all shapes and sizes covering it, all coordinated, fixtures and fittings too, a room created with the help of an expert. Burnett was known to have taste and an expensive eye for things and was never slow to spend his wealth. The circular multi-panelled windows and balcony gave breath-taking views over Fife, the Firth of Forth and beyond in one direction and a view of West Pilton in the other - a total contrast, an area with a lot of poverty, a place where good and bad lived alongside one another, a place filled with many willing to follow Burnett. They were paid well for their loyalty and protection.

"Look at yourself, Irene. Look at what he's done to you. What was this for? Something you hadn't done right, or were you not quick enough to answer him, something trivial, I bet?" Taylor asked, trying her best to get Irene to see that it didn't matter how much she did for Burnett, or how hard she tried, she would never be good enough. She needed to get out of this poisonous and dangerous situation before it was too late.

Irene just seemed to shrink further into herself, a woman beaten into submission, a shell of what she had once been. She used to be a strong, confident, outspoken woman, and a very pretty lady in her day, but Nel had taken all of that from her. With control, oppression and violence, he had gradually dominated her every breath, her confidence and her personality. He had beaten the very essence of her being out of her.

Irene looked at Taylor. Their eyes locked, and Taylor saw a glimmer of Irene's old self deep inside her, and Irene saw an honesty coming back. Irene wanted to speak out, scream out loud, tell them everything she knew, but that would mean sealing her own death warrant if she grassed on him, and that epitaph would be etched on her headstone.

"Listen, Irene, we don't want you to grass on him. We know what he'd do to you, but there are people missing - two of our colleagues, and a mother and her little boy. We need to find them before something terrible happens to them. Do you understand that? All we want is information on his premises, anything you know of what he owns, where he has lets. We don't even want to know what happens in them, just where they are. We need a place to start, the rest is up to us. With a little luck and timing, none of it would be traced back to you. How would he know how we got there? We have other sources, we have ways, but what we don't have is time. If Nel has something to do with this, which we think he does, he has a motive, and I don't think this is going to end well. Do you? We all know Nel is a no loose ends kind of guy. He will do anything to achieve that, so help us out here. Wrack your brains. You don't want the death of a child on your conscience, or another should I say." Taylor deliberately added the last few words.

"What do you mean, another? He hasn't, has he?" Irene looked up, disgust in her eyes.

"We believe he had a pregnant woman killed a while back, exterminated to be precise. It was an act of revenge, two innocent souls, not involved in anything. The woman's only crime was to love a man who failed your husband. We stopped his car over a year ago, and he lost Nel's haul of drugs to us. Of course, that's enough to sign your death warrant isn't it? Isn't it, Irene?"

"Listen, he doesn't tell me anything like that. I only hear what is said on the streets. I don't want to know what he does. I don't want to become a loose end too. The less I know, the better," Irene said honestly.

"I hear you Irene and believe you. I agree not knowing is definitely better. Anyway, this man wasn't available. We reckon he did a runner to avoid what Nel would do to him. When Nel couldn't get him, he got to him through his heart, where it would hurt him the most, with no care or thought for the suffering of this innocent woman and her unborn baby. Irene, don't let the next child to die be on your conscience. You're better than that, I know you are. I know you don't normally have any influence on what goes on, or have any power to change anything, but this time you do! You can actually do something here. Help us, please, help us save them." Taylor had barely taken a breath, her passionate plea was genuine and desperate.

Irene looked down at her hands and took a deep sigh, before reeling off building after building linked to Burnett. It was like a fast flowing waterfall, information spouting from Irene's mouth. As she spoke, her voice gained volume and strength, empowered by what she was doing, and the power she yielded. Taylor was taken aback at just how many properties there were, Burnett's empire spiralling deep into the heart of the city.

Chapter 43
Watching

McNare sat astride his borrowed motorbike, full helmet on, dark visor down, affording him anonymity and disguise. He sat one street further up from one of Nel's saunas, the one close to Scotland Street. He had no idea if anyone would come, but he knew the cops were now tailing Burnett, and he couldn't risk following him again, not just now anyway. He had no intention of getting caught.

He watched for over an hour, long enough to see the large framed, stout masculine woman came out onto the step and light up a fag. She took a deep draw and her pleasure showed. McNare remembered her from their previous meeting. He could just see the scar he had made on her face, even from where he sat. He knew her as Shaz, the madam of this so-called sauna, but everyone knew it was a knocking shop. He'd met some of the girls there years back and had felt sorry for them, all of them caught up in an inescapable hell, all futureless sex slaves for the pleasure of men and to line the pockets of Nelson Burnett. McNare now realised that back then he too was a pawn for Burnett and was caught up in his inescapable web of control, but he could not help the women without bringing retribution on himself. He had always felt uncomfortable with what was going on there and for their plight, not realising he too was owned.

His mind went sharply back to the women he had killed, trapped in the fire that he had started to get revenge on Burnett. His sadness and deep regret ate away at him daily, but as he thought of what future they had faced, a lifetime of hell and the depraved acts that would be carried out upon them, his remorse eased a little. He allowed himself a little forgiveness, letting himself believe that he had saved them from their hopeless future. He knew these girls were drugged daily to keep them in line, forced into obedience and compliance, threats to have their families killed if they didn't do Burnett's bidding. McNare tried to convince himself that most of them wouldn't have felt anything anyway in their drugged-up stupor. Ultimately, he had set them free from their prison.

McNare's senses came alive, his wait paying off, when a very familiar face came out of the building and stood alongside Shaz on the front step. Davy adjusted his belt and reached in his pocket for his cigarettes, shoving one in his mouth. He leaned over towards Shaz for a light. They chatted for a bit, enjoying the hit of nicotine, before flicking their fag butts on to the road. Shaz turned to go back in. Davy reached into his pocket and pulled out a phone. Looking down at it, he gave a shrug and then stuffed if back into his pocket.

He walked briskly to his car parked further up the road. McNare watched Davy closely. He looked around as he opened the car door. *Probably checking for the Feds, McNare thought.* He turned over his bike in anticipation of Davy moving off at speed.

McNare also checked for unwanted company before moving off. He didn't want the Feds catching up with him either.

Davy drove carefully up through the town. He could hear the sloshing of liquid in the canisters in the boot. His car was a non-descript hire car with a large boot, dark in colour, a car that would not draw any attention. Speeding was out of the question today. Davy drove efficiently up through town, up over the North Bridge, which straddled Waverley Train Station, giving a view of Edinburgh Castle and Princes Street, then up through South Bridge. Davy didn't realise his brow was sweating and his pulse racing, or that he was being followed.

He went up Nicholson Street, which became Clerk Street, passed the old Odeon Cinema, a building in need of refurbishment, before heading down Minto Street and out towards Mortonhall Crematorium. He drove by Howdenhall Police Station, smiling as he passed, and whispering, "Night night, ya pig bastards," as he did so. This was a big deal, and he was shitting himself, but his loyalty and fear of Nel superseded his apprehension. Nel could be very persuasive with his methods of control. Davy had questioned whether he could get away with this, but Nel convinced him that there wouldn't be an issue and told him to lie low for a couple of years. Nel had given him plane tickets and a six figure sum to disappear for a while, which Davy took, the risk worth two years of living the high life. His intention was never to come back, which Nel wasn't aware of. Nel trusted him, and he didn't trust many.

Davy went under the city bypass, past Straiton Retail Park and out towards the Bush Industrial Estate. Numerous metal framed units sprawling over a large acreage came into view, some with office blocks by their sides, businesses tucked away from the main thoroughfare, unseen and unvisited by anyone without a specific purpose for being there. Each was surrounded by substantial grounds, ten foot high fencing laced with barbed wire and cameras strategically placed, most to avoid unauthorised entry, but the one Davy was going into was to ensure unauthorised exit.

Davy stopped at the entry system and keyed in a six-digit code. The screen in front of him lit up. It was one of the younger lads, Duthie, who came over the intercom. He asked Davy for the security code. Davy, who was second to Burnett, just growled at him and rasped, "Open the fuckin' door, ya daft wee cunt. It's me, Davy! Fucking little prick. I'll fuckin' boot you right in the baws, ya cheeky wee bastard," he muttered, raging at the audacity of the wee twat. He carried on talking to himself, "Impudent little fucker." Davy was getting impatient to get things moving and get the fuck out of there. The heat was rising, and he knew the police would find this place sooner or later.

McNare had stopped a fair bit back to avoid being clocked. He had no idea what Nel had to do with this place. He had never heard him mention it when he was working for him, but it was pretty similar to the drug lab he had torched in Sighthill, the one that turned out to be filled with trafficked women and girls. He wondered if Nel had a new basement here too, filled with more unfortunate imprisoned women.

McNare's heart was racing. He had read the news on his phone yesterday and was aware of the incident in Morningside. It was top news, the abduction of two police officers and two civilians who still remained untraced. Not a lot more had been said, just pleas for information about the getaway vehicle.

McNare thought Davy was a bit dumb and too willing to do the dirty work for his boss. Nel knew this, which was why he paid him so well. This made McNare wonder what was going down here, Davy's reckless loyalty to that man would be the end of him, but he was just too thick to see it.

McNare watched on from afar, the distance making their movements difficult to see. He saw several guys come towards the car and help lift unmarked boxes from the boot. He had no idea what it was they were unloading. He didn't like what he was seeing though. With the gathering of Nel's cronies, he knew something sinister was about to happen.

Chapter 44
Desperate Times

Sorina had heard the vehicle drive up outside, the gravel making a distinctive and unsettling noise. All visitors made her skin tingle with fear and sometimes a little hope, hope that the police would find them and that they would be rescued, but so far, there had been no such luck.

Why could the police not find them? How difficult could it be? Her thoughts were turning to anger and despair. She watched through the dirty, cracked window. There were at least five or more men carrying boxes into what she assumed were the delivery bays as she could see the road sloping downwards.

She squinted her eyes as she looked at the man that had been driving. She recognised him from the brothel. He was a regular, just like Nel, another that couldn't help himself from testing out the merchandise. The girls talked about him back at the warehouse, and he was one that certainly got around, a different girl most nights. He'd do them all, but she smiled a wry smile to herself. All the girls said he never took long. He was always quick, even she had had to service him once or twice. She wondered, now that she knew that Nel was the boss, how well he'd take it, if he knew one of his men had been savouring his favourite girl. Not too well she thought.

Steve came over beside her, banging his leg on one of the desks, moving it forward causing a loud scraping noise and waking up little Nicu.

Sorina glared at Steve. At least when the boy was asleep, he wasn't scared and hungry.

"Sorry, I didn't see it." Steve moved up right beside her, straining to see through the filth. "What's going on down there?" He wiped another circle on the glass in front of him.

"Something is. They just brought in lots of stuff," Sorina told him.

"Maybe our dinner?" Steve smiled, trying to lighten the mood but failing miserably. Sorina didn't understand cop humour, which made light of the worst situations. She was openly worried about their plight, but she was also not ready to die.

She looked down at Fran, who was desperately unwell. It was possibly already too late to save her and she knew if a chance to escape came, her body would be difficult to carry with them. Fran would slow them down a lot. Sorina had no intention of leaving her, but Nicu was her first priority.

Sorina looked down at her son. He had gone back to sleep. She smiled at this. Children never ceased to amaze her, their ability to adapt and, of course, sleep. She looked over at Fran again, her breathing now slower and more laboured than before. Sorina's fear was growing that Fran wouldn't make it. This disturbed her immensely. She liked this vibrant, caring little woman, who had taken the time to talk to her and also actually listen. She was a genuinely decent person, who had only ever shown kindness and professionalism towards Sorina. The fact Fran was so critically ill seemed brutally unfair, with the cause of everything standing hovering over her shoulder. The irony and unfairness of it all enraged Sorina.

She looked straight at Steve, her anger rising once again. She was finding it harder and harder to contain the inner volcano from erupting, trying hard to stop her pent-up fury from escaping. He felt her stare and looked back at her, questioning her expression. Her eyes gestured towards Fran. Steve felt physically sick, his own inner despair twisting deep into his soul.

"I'm sorry, so sorry, sorrier than you can ever imagine. If we get out of here, I'll try and make amends, although I'll be banged up for years. The reason I did all of this was for my precious little girl, and now she will be taken away from me too," Steve said sullenly.

"God, I want to scream at you, hurt you, shake you. How could you have been so damned stupid. I want you to feel my pain, anything just to make myself feel better." She stopped talking and looked around. "Look at what you've done, look at where we are, look at this place in the middle of nowhere. Why here, a rundown derelict warehouse? Why would they bring us here? Have you thought why? I have!" She was now screaming in his face.

Sorina had become frantic. She was losing it. Her heart raced as she remembered the men had been carrying something heavy due to their speed and posture. She hoped it was supplies, but her worst fear was that they were going to start a fire. She had been in a fire before and did not want to experience another. This place would offer the same enclosed crematorium as before, but this time they were at the top of the building. There were no drains to escape through. If you tried to squeeze through the window, you'd cut yourself to ribbons trying to get out and then fall to the ground smashing your skull to pieces, or shatter your legs. Either way death was highly likely.

"Calm down! Try and keep calm. The police will find us. They will have every person available working on this, I promise you!" Steve said trying to convince her, hoping his words were true.

"When? When will they find us?" she screamed at him. "When it's too bloody late. I think this is it. You know they are going to kill us! Don't try and appease me. You and I both know it. Will they see us when the smoke starts rising? Police work methodically and that takes time, and we don't have any time left. Fire seems the obvious choice. Why would they wait? I'm surprised they haven't done it already!" All Sorina's patience had gone, the harsh reality sinking it.

She looked out of the clear piece of window she had wiped with her sleeve and stared out, craning her neck to see as far as she could in all directions, the height of the building giving decent views and an elevated view of all the surrounding properties. It was too far to shout for help. She couldn't quite work out where they were. She hoped to see a landmark of some sort, but they were just a little too far out of Edinburgh for that.

She looked at the windows of the neighbouring units, but there were no lights on in any, no people to be seen, nothing. She then moved her eyes round the fence line, scanning the area, hoping for a dog walker, anyone around that could offer help. She looked for breaks in the fence, hoping that if there was a chance to break free, the fence wouldn't get in their way. Her eyes followed it right round. Just over a hundred metres from the entrance she saw a lone figure. He was slim, wearing jeans, a dark jacket and a helmet. Her heart sprang to life, her pulse now pounding through her neck. She watched the man. From the way he stood, his posture and the direction of his head, she knew he was looking straight at their building. She did not know why, but she felt that this was a good sign.

A new lease of hope stirred within Sorina. This man was going to be their saviour. She turned to Steve, who had seen her posture change and a flush of red rise in her cheeks. She ordered him to find something to break the window so she could see more clearly and try and get the man's attention somehow. He was still a fair distance away. It would be difficult.

Steve looked at her, irked at the way she had spoken to him, telling him what to do, but he knew she would never be well mannered towards him again. He understood why, and he thought she hated him.

He looked around, knowing that breaking an industrial pane of glass like that would need a heavy-duty implement.

He managed to dismantle a swivel chair and brought over the legs and stalk. It was heavy and the edge of the stalk had a sharp metal circular edge to it, which he hoped would allow all of the weight and force to go through that one point. In his mind, he thought she wanted to see, not bloody jump, so a small hole would suffice.

He brought it over and looked at her and then at the boy, who was stirring again from his noisy efforts. "This will definitely wake him up," he said, remembering her hostility when he had woken Nicu the last time.

She just rolled her eyes at him. "He will need woken up to give us a chance to escape so this time it's okay." The sarcasm in her voice was cutting and deserved.

Steve went to hand the chair stalk to her, and she just looked at him and then down at herself. She was a skelf of a woman, very slim and not obviously physically strong. Steve was a medium build, wiry and fit, with a well-formed upper torso, someone that took care of his physique when he could. He was clearly more capable of doing the job at hand.

He laughed nervously at how stupid he had just been. This window would take a lot of breaking and he was clearly the stronger of the two.

She peered back out. Her heart sank when she scanned the area where she had seen the man. He had disappeared. Common sense told her he couldn't have gone too far, and she was right. There he was, fifty-metres further round, and she could just see the tank of what she thought was a motorbike. He had taken off his helmet and rested it on the hand grip of the bike.

He looked young, light brown hair, slim build, not too tall, but to her he was like a dream come true.

"Where do you want me to hit? Which window?" Steve asked waiting for instructions, not wanting to get it wrong and face her wrath again.

Sorina was reluctant to take her eyes off the man again, so she pointed, flapping her hand impatiently towards the next window, fifteen feet away from Nicu and Fran. This allowed her to continue watching the man with the bike. She didn't want to lose sight of him.

The sound was deafening. Nicu sprang up from his makeshift bed, tears in his eyes, terror gripping his fragile little heart once more. It took three healthy strikes to create a small hole in the cracked strengthened glass. They worried that the noise would bring them some unwelcome attention. Hesitating, they listened, but they heard nothing. Nobody was coming, nobody cared what they did, which made them even more aware that there was little time left.

Steve used his makeshift implement to create a face-sized hole in the window, and Sorina squeezed her head carefully through, cutting the top of her head as she did do, causing blood to seep through into her hairline.

She looked towards the man, who was staring at the lower part of the building, where she assumed they had been brought in, and where she had seen Davy drive in and unload.

McNare turned and moved towards the bike, swinging his leg over it, squaring himself on the seat. He reached for the helmet. Sorina screamed out of the tight space as loudly as she could, no words, just a shrill scream, high pitched and deafening for Steve and Nicu, giving it everything she had, desperately wanting to be heard. She quickly took off her blouse, thrusting her arm out of the window to wave it about, carelessly scraping and cutting her arm as she did so, not caring about herself, just desperate for him to hear her or see her.

McNare tensed up when he heard the blood curdling and heart stopping scream. He stared intently at the building, scouring up and over all of the levels. Then he heard it again, and this time he looked up at the top floor, moving from window to window, but he didn't see anything untoward. He kept going, making sure he checked them all, because the sound of that scream was not one he wanted to ignore. It was the last window at the far end of the building where he saw an arm waving a bright coloured cloth. He strained his eyes to focus, heat rising inside him. He didn't know what was going on, but it wasn't good. He wanted to right the wrongs he had done, he wanted to do some good, he wanted to feel the way Lynne had made him feel. She had constantly told him he was a good man. She always wanted him to better himself. He needed to do the right thing now, to save his soul.

Sorina pulled her arm back in and poked her face back through the hole, her eyes focused on the man. She could see that he was definitely facing her way, and it appeared he was looking straight at her. She hoped he could see her. She was about to scream again when she saw him raise his hand up and wave at her. He was discreet and kept his arm low, clearly not wanting to draw any attention to himself either and give his position away.

McNare was bristling with anticipation at what to do next. He ducked down as he heard gravel rasping beneath the wheels of vehicles. Engines were being revved and he saw three vehicles heading for the gate at speed, two cars and a white van, His heart sank when he saw wisps of smoke coming out of the ground floor of the building. They seemed to be coming from the lower garage area of the unit, where the cars had come out.

There was now no option. Time had taken away any choice from him. He had to do something and do it now. He did not know how many people were in there, but if what he had stumbled upon was anything to do with the abductions on the news, there were four and one was a kid. This made his inner rage against Burnett flare up again, and his thoughts took him spinning back to Lynne, helplessly trying to save their unborn child, his heart aching for what might have been, his son or daughter, their life taken away so cruelly before it had even had a chance to begin. The force of the deep rooted sadness and despair within him still crushed him every day, constantly fuelling his desire to avenge the death of his loved ones.

McNare pulled his phone from his pocket and, for the first time in his life and against every fibre in his body, dialled 999. He wanted the police to come, fire and ambulance too, as he saw the first flames. His capture was the last thing on his mind. He knew they would track him down eventually, the death of twenty-seven people was a heavy burden to carry around for anyone.

The bike roared into action as he spun it round and headed quickly to the main gate. He had seen a bit of the fence where he could get over easily and laying his jacket on top of it, he threw his body skilfully over it, a well-practiced art he'd used many times to evade the police.

Chapter 45
Race Against Time

The call handler took the call from McNare, who had been succinct in his request, all three services requested or ordered to attend. His tone had been abrupt and straight to the point. He was unable to give the exact details of the unit and exact location, but the vicinity and destination were clear enough, and his parting comment, "Follow the smoke!" before he clicked off, made the call taker spring into action.

The caller had refused to give his details, but he had told her that he had seen at least one person trapped in the building. He thought it might be the missing officers from the news bulletin. The handler wasn't sure if this was a hoax call or not, but the man on the line had sounded convincing, not that she could choose not to respond whatever her opinion.

All three services were alerted and were getting ready to make their way to the location of the fire.

Taylor and Marcus were at Fettes. The list Irene had given them of buildings and warehouses linked to Burnett was spread out in front of them, officers already heading to some of the ones within the east side of the city as they had to start somewhere and then work their way through them methodically. They had chosen east to west. Ideally, they would want to go to them all simultaneously to avoid destruction of evidence, as anyone on the premises would warn the others about the raids, but there just weren't enough cops. Safety was paramount. They required the right resources, those with the specialist skills to carry out the raids, and these officers had to be mustered from all over Scotland. They needed numbers too in case significant numbers of assailants were encountered on entry. They would possibly be in possession of firearms, which would be problematic. The premises had to be turned over as safely as possible. They couldn't just send a couple of beat cops at random, possibly to their deaths.

The list of properties was impressive and they were surprised at how far reaching and well-connected Burnett had become over the past few years. He was a very rich, focused and intelligent man, his portfolio of untapped property a testament to his shrewdness.

The next move for them was to visit the two units on the outskirts of the city near to Bush Industrial Estate on the southern side of the city, the next buildings round on the compass. There was a communal radio sitting on one of the desks that all of the specialist resources were tuned into. It covered the whole country. "Any free specialist resources available," crackled over the airwaves. When the location for the request was relayed, Taylor's finger was virtually pointing to that address on the piece of paper in front of them.

They looked at each other, eyes filled with anticipation and fear as they heard that the fire service was already on the way and that there were persons trapped within. They grabbed their keys quickly and raced to their car, flipped the blue light on the roof and started to make their way through the city. Their journey would be no shorter than twenty minutes due to the location, but they both knew how quickly fires took hold.

Lana had been sitting at the break out area in the fire station, her team mates also filling their time there as they waited for a shout. On hearing the call, she responded and confirmed their attendance. She jumped into her kit, the legs of her fire resistant uniform already tucked neatly into her boots for speed. The rest of the crew were ready to go in minutes too, sitting in their engines impatiently waiting for the remote controlled door to open, moments feeling like an age, their hearts pumping, eyes bright and filled with anticipation and trepidation of what they may be faced with on arrival. Fear of seeing yet another charred and lifeless corpse if they arrived too late to save them was something they all dreaded.

Finally, they manoeuvred their cumbersome trucks out from the station on the Calder Road. Less than a thirty second wait felt like a lifetime. All three wagons and the turntable headed straight for the bypass. Their journey would hopefully be less than ten minutes to the location of the fire.

Lana drove with intent, heart racing, fearing what they might be up against. She did not mind the physical effort, the life-threatening situations they ended up in. She loved her job, but success was always easier to take than the opposite. Her heart and mind floated back to all of those that had lost their lives, the young and old, sadness pulsing through her in waves, something she hadn't quite learned to control and deal with, past shouts not yet fitting neatly into that box. Harrowing memories and visions kept creeping back into her mind every time she went out on a job. She could not help herself thinking back to the last unit they had attended in Sighthill, the sheer scale of that atrocity, the burnt shell and what it contained, numerous bodies trapped, charred burnt corpses, faces etched with desperation. She gave her head a shake as she pushed the pedal to the metal, squeezing every ounce of speed out of their bulky machine, chains clanking and sirens blaring as they raced to the scene. Lana had read the news, she had met two of the people who may be trapped in this fire, which made this all the more personal. Her colleagues in the back of the cab were also filled with anticipation of the unknown, all of them keen and ready to face whatever the situation brought with bravery, valour and selfless effort. They would do their best to save everyone.

Ambulance crews had also been scrambled from all over the city, the Specialist Operational Support team also heading from its base in Newbridge. They too had specialist equipment and training, all prepared for what was to come. Scotty Casement was driving his unit. His heart bristled with excitement. Young and fresh-faced, this was his first shout with the team. He was both exhilarated and terrified about what he might have to deal with, but he was ready to test his newly learned skills. He was frustrated at the lack of acceleration the ambulance had to offer as he tried to go faster. He had been partnered for the day with a long serving, skilled operator, who had more than twenty-five years' experience in the unit. Debbie was an old hand. Nothing fazed her. She thought back to her first job and knew how Scott must be feeling. She would assist him if the need arose, stop him making any mistakes or taking too many risks. The fire service would be taking primacy over the operation in the early stages. Their skills were the ones that could bring the situation under control, bringing hope for those that needed them, but this was not always guaranteed.

Police cars were beginning to arrive, all converging in the one spot, firearms units in their powerful four by fours, uniform and plain clothes officers, all of them with the same goal: to rescue their colleagues and the others trapped in the building. The caller had dropped a few names to the call handler - vehicle descriptions, one license number and more. Within seconds an all-points bulletin had been put in place. Airports, train stations, buses, ferry ports, every one of them had been put on full alert. Number plate recognition operators were tasked with intercepting the wanted vehicles. Everyone had their hands to the pump.

Taylor drove with haste through town, her frustration showing as she cursed loudly at the numerous cars stopping without leaving a gap for her to get through. Her heart was filled with sadness for Fran, Sorina and the boy, not so much for Steve, although she didn't want anyone to get hurt or worse die. Unfortunately, in her job, fairy-tales were few and far between. Happy every after was something she rarely experienced these days. Marcus was feeling it too. He was worried that they may be too late, both of them fearful for those trapped in the building.

McNare had jumped the fence, tearing his jeans at the thigh. The barbed wire had cut deep into his skin, blood oozing out from the jagged cut. He cursed and thought to himself that he was losing his touch. He ran at full pelt towards the building. There was a fire extinguisher in the loading area, but as he looked in through the glass partition of the door to the inner storage area, he could see the flames were already out of control. The insignificant extinguisher would not stop this fire. Flames were already licking the roof. Thick, black, acrid smoke billowed out from the ground floor near to the seat of the fire. He turned and ran around to the far end of the building and found a fire exit, carrying the extinguisher just in case it could give him some assistance. His decision to bring his compact bolt cutters from the bike had been a good one. He had used them to acquire the new wheels earlier that day. They were a thief's dream, dual purpose, one handle was even configured as a crowbar. He smiled - the designer had to have been an ex-con.

The double doors opened outwards and were chained on the outside. Applying the bolt cutters to the sturdy chain, McNare squeezed with force, contorting his body to offer maximum pressure. The link snapped and he was able to unthread the chain from the loops. He jammed the crowbar end of the handle into the central gap in the doors and started to jemmy them apart, conscious of the time he was taking to get in, with the fire already out of control. Unperturbed, he was focused on what he had to do, what he needed to do - he needed to try and make amends.

Once inside, he raced up floor after floor to what he thought was level five where he had seen the woman at the window. He counted the floors and steps as as he went, not knowing how long he would have a clear view for, although the smoke had not reached the stairwell yet. He groaned as he was met by yet another set of double doors, even more impressively sealed. His heart sank as he got the first light scent of smoke, acrid in taste. When he had looked in on the storage bay, he had recognised all too well the intense smell of accelerant, and that worried him, knowing the power of fire from first-hand experience. He banged loudly on the doors, shouting through them, hoping for a reply, but nothing came.

He did not give up, his shouts and continual banging continued, and finally his efforts succeeded. Sorina's voice came boldly through the doors. "Help us! We're trapped," she exclaimed.

"How many of you are in there? Are you all alright?" he questioned, hoping the answer would be yes. The smoke was now gathering a couple of floors below, snaking its way up the stairs more quickly than he had hoped. He knew time was running out - the fire had reached the second floor.

"There are four of us, including my son, three able and one unconscious and badly injured. Have you phoned for helped yet?" she questioned, hoping the answer was yes, her tone desperate.

"Aye, I have, but they're not here yet and that fire is raging like hell. We don't have much time and it's coming our way. Get something to cover your mouths. The smoke is in the stair here already. Keep low and I'll be in there to help you shortly. Get everyone close to the door." He said this as calmly as he could, but fully aware of his limited capabilities and the strength and speed of the fire below. *Hurry up, please hurry,* he urged himself, his heart heavy. They were all in mortal danger, himself included, from the intensifying blaze below. His chance to escape was also diminishing. It was now or never. He knew only too well what was coming for them all.

The first firearms set had arrived at the metal gates. They parked to one side and were flummoxed over how to breach the security gates, which were electrical with a mechanised, magnetic locking system. A bit of head scratching and a call to the control room for advice was needed to overcome the barrier, frustration and anger setting in at their unforeseen predicament. The fire was licking up the outside of the building now, and their thoughts were with the people inside.

The lead officer answered the controller, and the response was not good. As they took the unwelcome negative message, a large, bright red, brute of a fire appliance, twelve tons in weight, came hurtling towards them with no hint of stopping at the gates. The cops took a dive to the side as the wagon smashed through them, sending the gates flying open 180 degrees, hitting the other side of the fence with force. The windscreen of the lead wagon cracked, but the toughened glass held in place. Lana smiled to herself, thrilled at her entrance and looked back at the cheering lads and lass in the back of the cab, impressed at the way she had wellied the gate out of the way, a motivational start to the treacherous task ahead.

Lana was buzzing now, but she had seen the extent of the fire, and her stomach churned and twisted with an impending sense of doom, spiralling up inside her. She was frightened. This was a big one, and she knew they had to get in there as soon as possible to give the poor souls inside a chance. The ladder unit was the fourth vehicle in through the gates, its importance at the scene obvious. All of the lower floors were filled with fire and smoke now.

The cops also commented at the devastation of the gates. They were buckled, and there was significant damage to the front of the engine too, but there had been no other option available to get in there in time, and one thing they didn't have was time.

Hydrants were forced open, with heavy-duty drain lifters. Many were jammed shut with debris and rust, having never been used for years. Hoses were unravelled with speed and skill, each six-inch hose weighing approximately sixty-five kilos per hundred feet without water, their weight immense but handled with relative ease by the powerful firefighters. Numerous hoses stretched across the parking area like snakes entwined in one another, water gushing forcefully at the seat of the fire and up to the upper floors, some of which were not yet alight, but smoke was coming out of a hole in one of the windows on the top floor.

The watch manager issued instructions to the crews. One had equipment to perform window entries, the turntable ladder already extending up to the highest level, four crew on the platform, all eager to get up there and get in.

Police were setting up cordons a safe distance away, along with the ambulance service setting up their equipment in hope that they would receive viable casualties to tend to, the police frustrated that they were virtually helpless here at the scene with no suitable protective equipment, entry for them was a no, no, it would mean certain death.

McNare kept talking through the door, but Sorina was no longer responding. She was lying on the floor cuddling into her son, their faces covered with wet cloths, soaked from the toilet. She had also covered Fran's face. Her breathing was now virtually non-existent, but, in a twist of fate, her shallow breaths, would perhaps give her a better chance of survival. Steve had climbed up on a chair, panic taking over. He was screaming out of the window. He had failed to take heed of McNare's advice to get down on the floor, his thoughts simply to try and get some fresh air, but the smoke was congregating in the same place as his face and was now all being funnelled through the one space right beside him. After a few smoke filled breaths, Steve fell heavily to the floor, the poisonous fumes rendering him unconscious.

Finally, McNare managed to burst into the room where he was met with a wall of smoke. He tripped over Sorina and landed heavily on his face and hands. He had not yet had to endure the smoke and scrabbled frantically around on the floor. He shook Sorina hard, but she did not move. His heart sank a little more when his hands felt the shape of a child cradled into the body of his mother. He did not know what to do at first, his exertions making it difficult for him not to breath too deeply. His heart was pumping with fear, and he was struggling to make decisions, the stress building up. He didn't want to leave any of them behind. He wondered just how far down the stairs he could get with the boy before he would succumb to the smoke. Decision made, he grabbed the child, lifting him up into his arms, and scrabbled backwards, retracing his steps back to the door. He had never stopped counting. He turned at the door, bumping himself as he went, eyes burning and blinded with the smoke. He counted fourteen steps per floor, each turn to the next flight also counted. He felt like he was about to collapse , but something inside made him keep running, flight after flight, the child tucked under his arm. He held his breath and was starting to convulse as his body tried to overrule his mind. He had two flights left to go when he ran headlong into the fire crew heading up the stairs in full breathing apparatus, knocking one off his feet, the other managing to steady himself. The firefighter still standing was fully aware that this person was in dire need of fresh air, and only when he went to help McNare did he feel the body of the small child. The firefighter took hold of McNare's arm, checking on his colleague, who was now pulling himself back up off the floor. Together, they guided McNare and Nicu down the two remaining flights, their hoses left where they had stopped, their new goal to save the man and child in the stairwell.

All four of them burst out of the double doors and into the car park, McNare dropping to his knees, drawing in lungful's of fresh air. The child had been taken swiftly out of his arms, the curled up tiny frame hanging limply in the firefighter's arms, the lack of muscle control obvious to those now moving forward to render assistance to the boy.

McNare blurted out, "There are three more up there!" He coughed and spluttered, phlegm hanging in thick slimy strands from his mouth, black soot covering his face, his nostrils lined with carbon and totally discoloured. "The boy's mother is just inside the door at the top of those stairs," he wheezed again. He could barely talk, but he had to tell them what he knew. "There are two others in there too, one is in a bad way," he said. Then he stopped talking, coughed some more and threw up in front of those watching, his body trying desperately to excrete all of the unwanted toxins.

An oxygen mask was thrust onto his face where he sat, relief at last for his desperate lungs. The boy was being attended to in the nearest ambulance. Oxygen was being administered and a line inserted into his throat to ensure that the lining of his airway way was kept open and didn't swell up preventing oxygen getting through.

The crew that McNare had encountered in the stairwell had already re-entered the building, the smoke now thick, their vision down to practically zero. They too had to count steps and rely on their sense of touch as they carried on moving upwards. They retrieved their abandoned hoses and moved as quickly as their kit allowed, all the way up to the fifth floor where the others were believed to be. A floor to floor search was out of the question as the lower floors were now fully alight and out of bounds. They had very limited time to make this rescue before the building would collapse beneath them.

Medics had moved forward to give more assistance to McNare, Scotty Casement kneeling down by his side. Taylor and Marcus had watched the rescue unfold as the first two people exited the building with the firefighters. Both looked curiously at the man, who was now being treated, wondering who he could be. The bike at the entrance gates had been checked out and was confirmed as stolen. It was the same bike that had made off from the beach at Silverknowes after trying to run over Burnett earlier that day.

They walked briskly but casually towards McNare. They could see his face a bit better now. He had just had water poured over his eyes to try and clear them out, allowing him to see again, but his vision was still impaired, his face still pretty black, his features still disguised.

McNare on the other hand knew exactly who was coming. Those walking towards him were the Feds just by the way they walked. They would find out pretty quickly who he was and he knew he was going to jail, never to get out again, ever. He stood up from the trolley bed and stretched, almost theatrically, looking right at them. His chance to get revenge on Burnett was now gone, but he hoped he had given those inside a fighting chance, a little redemption for his mistakes, for everything he had done.

His thoughts filled with memories of Lynne and their unborn child. He just wanted to be with them, have an unbreakable reunion, one that death would seal. He smiled at Taylor and Marcus and shrugged his shoulders, lifting his hands upwards towards the sky, before turning away and sprinting back towards the open doors from where he had just come. Smoke now billowed out from them. He hesitated, because this was it, his last chance to change his mind. Tears filled his eyes as his mind was made up. In his heart this was right. He held his breath and ran. Using the hoses to guide him, he went as far up as he could before he was forced to take his first gulp of smoke filled air. This set off a fit of coughing, which in turn made him inhale another larger lungful of smoke, then another, and another. He wanted to get back in there and help if he could, before his life was over, to try and save one more life, but he knew now he couldn't, and his time was up. He had never intended to return. He had nothing to live for anymore. He knew he wasn't invincible, and the realisation sunk in that he wouldn't be able to save another person before dying himself. All there was to do now was wait for the inevitable. His lungs burned intensely and he could no longer breath. He sank to his knees, his thoughts racing, his human instinct to survive, to escape, fighting with his desire to be with his lost partner and child. His eyes bulged from the lack of air, and his veins popped out from his neck. His hands grasped at his throat, which was burning and damaged, and his eyes closed over. His mind filled with sorrow and regret, remorse for all that was lost. Resigned to his own death, he smiled as he slumped forward into an unsurvivable state of unconsciousness. The hoses by his side pulled harshly against him as they were dragged upwards. McNare's body lay still beside them, his torment finally over.

Taylor and Marcus just stood there dumbfounded. They had attempted to go after him, but he had the distance on them, and there was no chance of either of them reaching him, far less stopping him. They just had to stand there and watch him re-enter the building, knowing he was running to his own death.

The first crew reached the top of the stairs where the double doors were already ajar, saving them vital time having to break them down. It did not take long before they reached the first casualty, as their feet dunted into Sorina's lifeless body as they entered. They quickly fitted a lightweight oxygen mask to her face before turning in their tracks and heading straight back down the stairs, requesting an ETA for the ladder team as they went. This would be needed to approach via the windows, as they could see at first-hand just how dire the situation was. Their task there was complete, no-one else would be rescued through the doors. They were unable to search further, their priority was to get their casualty out. Another team was already heading up the stairs, but they had come across McNare's body and were dealing with him, unaware that they couldn't go any further up, as it was no longer safe to do so.

Taylor, Marcus and the other officers stood helplessly watching the carnage unfolding in front of them, their colleagues and others still trapped inside, along with the man that had run back into the building.

The identity of the boy brought out was believed to be that of Nicu, the unfortunate boy abducted for the third time in his short life. He had been rushed off to the Royal Hospital for Sick Children, hopefully with a chance of survival.

The fire crews in the stairs were working individually with their two casualties, carrying the bodies out of the building, flames on the lower floors spewing out from the windows below the top floor. They were lucky to be in the reinforced fire escape, which afforded them some protection and time, but it would not be long before it too was critically affected.

Simultaneously, Lana and her partner were high above on the platform, five storeys up. They used lethal looking entry equipment to smash through the plate glass, the metal spike making light work of the window as it was forced through the glass, ripping through it, as if it was a silk sheet. Their breathing apparatus and other cumbersome kit hindered their progress and agility, but they had created a large gap in the glass. They laid down the Kevlar blanket over the sharp shards on the bottom edge of the window, which stood up like rows of sharp teeth, waiting to cut and harm those entering. They sat down heavily on the blanket as they entered, trusting its strength to prevent injury, and climbed down carefully from their position. They could not see an inch in front of them. Once inside they used their feet and hands to guide them. As they entered, they stepped over Steve, missing his lifeless form completely. He was lying beneath the window where he had succumbed to the smoke, neither firefighter realising he was even there. They progressed further into the open space, unaware of the body just beside the window. The room was filled with smoke, layered thickly towards the roof and slightly lighter at floor level. There was a real threat of a flash over taking place. Lana's foot came up against something on the floor as she tentatively moved blindly forward. She crouched down and her hands felt the shape of a person who lay limp on the floor unmoving. Lana secured a mask round their face and oxygen flowed freely giving the lifeless form a vital chance to live. Lana knew this was the last chance to search the area. They had been told the fire would break through to their floor soon. There was a real chance the floor would collapse as they worked to get the casualty to safety. They didn't have any more time and were instructed to get out. It was now deemed too dangerous to remain. Their comms were starting to fail, faltering and crackling, making it difficult for them to receive messages. Lana spoke with her colleague, who helped lift Fran onto her shoulder. The other set was about to enter through the window when the message to retreat was received. All four of them did not want to hear this update, knowing that there was still someone outstanding, a police officer. Lana knew their part in the search was over. They had to take care of their casualty, the priority to get the person out. They turned and shuffled towards the window, their direction slightly deviated from their entry route. Lana's foot dug firmly into a soft but solid form on the floor. Was it another body? She told her colleague to crouch down and check and, when he did so, he confirmed that it was.

The crew that were half in the window and now heading back after the warning about the stability of the building heard the message from Lana's team. It was now up to them to decide what to do. Their supervisor would not tell them to re-enter the building knowing the risk to their lives. The decision would be theirs. They asked for information on the distance from the window, the size of the person, any obstacles in the way and the estimated time to facilitate an extraction. Lana relayed that the body was not far inside the window. It was a fluke and fate that she and her partner had missed it the first time. If they had found him first, the chances of a further search for the person they now had with them would not have taken place. Luck had been on Fran's side.

Marc and Nev, looked at each other and nodded, decision made. "We're going in!" was the message from the second unit on the platform. Those safe on the ground were fully aware of the increasing danger. The building was not far off from collapsing. Their hearts filled with anticipation and fear for everybody still in there.

Lana's partner clambered out first, fully aware of the mounting danger. She stood patiently, waiting for her turn to exit, although her apprehension was mounting, fear starting to twist her stomach, her nerves tingling with fear that they might not all get back out to safety. Lana brought Fran down from her shoulders and tried to hand a large portion of her to her partner on the platform. He dragged her through the window trying not to damage any more of her already broken frame, and trying not to dislodge her oxygen mask. With a bit of grunting, exertion and contortion, they managed to manhandle her onto the platform without further injury, still in one piece and with the mask still in place. Lana was aware of the flames just below her. Remaining there for much longer would be catastrophic for Fran who lay there without any fire-retardant protection. Lana was also reluctant to leave two of the team inside any longer than needed, but there was one casualty still in there.

The dilemma was over, and at last their luck was in as another turntable arrived, late to the party but very welcome all the same. This would allow them to pull back and get their casualty to safety and let it take over the urgent duties at the window, waiting precariously for those inside, but time was running out for everyone.

Taylor and Marcus watched as the first turntable reversed away, the platform still in the air to avoid injury from the explosions and bursts of flames that were happening below them. Loud crashing noises could also be heard from areas of the building that had started to collapse. They could barely see who or how many were up in the platforms as the thick smoke clung heavily around them. When the first platform finally pulled further away, two fire officers could be seen, one with a small body in their arms. Taylor strained her eyes and watched closely, trying to visually measure the size of the person they were bringing down, and then she saw the long brown matted hair. It hung down from the limply hanging head. She knew that a male and female had been brought out of the fire exit, the female confirmed as Sorina, the male's identity not yet confirmed but believed to be the man that had chosen to run back in. Sick to the pit of her stomach, Taylor's heart felt heavy. The casualty did not appear to be alive.

The platform was being lowered down to ground level. It seemed to take an age, and Taylor's desperation and impatience was starting to boil over. She could barely contain herself, although there would be little she could do to help. Other professionals were also eagerly awaiting the touch down so that they could start treatment and give the casualty a chance at life.

"Oh my God Marcus, it is Fran!" They both looked at her, her face badly injured and swollen, covered in black soot. She had blisters on her exposed skin and did not look good. Feelings of helplessness, guilt, affection and sheer terror rippled through Taylor, the serious nature of Fran's situation now very apparent. The paramedics and Medic One had cleared a space around Fran and were getting to work straight away. The firefighters that had brought her down and the police could only stand and watch, letting the experts get on with it, willing her to survive.

Their attention was taken away from Fran when the west side of the building began to collapse, creating a domino effect to the rest of the building. Hoses still aimed up at it, the waterlogged floors started to give way with the weight of the water and the fire damage to the walls and floors. The turntable driver looked back, falling debris dropping ominously close, worrying for his colleagues safety, their own personal dilemma now unfolding above. The huge fire officer Nev heard the screeching and moaning of the building surrounding them. It had started to crumble and give way beneath them. His partner, Marc, had already manoeuvred himself out of the window and onto the platform. He too was a big man and this was not an easy move for them. Both now feared for their lives, Marc yelled at Nev to throw the body out and jump for it. His mate just shouted back, "For fuck's sake man! Who do you think I am, fucking Superman?"

But his request was not a joke. Marc reached out desperately to try and break the fall when the body was indeed thrown out with every ounce of strength Nev could muster, the casualty's legs clunking heavily off the side of the window, his hands and upper torso just reaching Marc, who managed to secure them onto the platform. The dead weight was unceremoniously dragged further onto the platform. Marc laid him down like a sack of spuds as he was now needed urgently elsewhere. He looked back at Nev, who's eyes were wide with fear as a blast of fire, smoke and debris blew dangerously past his face, an explosion going off right behind him, so ominously close he felt his skin move beneath his suit. Luckily, he had made his decision moments before, and he was halfway out into the air, diving head first out of the window, his body catapulted forward with the pressure of the explosion behind him, but he fell short of his target, barely reaching the platform. His muscular arms grabbed for the safety rail and he managed to wrap them desperately round the bar, his legs left dangling heavily down towards the concrete below, flames now licking round all of them, the danger too close for comfort. The driver of the unit instinctively started to move it away from the crumbling building, lowering the platform in an attempt to save the dangling firefighter. Marc grabbed frantically at Nev's slipping hands, his gloves making it hard to hold on to him. Nev's face was just visible through his mask. His eyes were wide and terrified, pleading with Marc to save him. His grip was failing, the height he was at still enough to kill him. Marc forced all of his body weight down onto Nev's hands, almost crushing them against the bar, but it was that or watch his mate fall to his death, his own safety now at risk too as there was a chance he would overbalance and both of them would fall, Marc head first. The driver manoeuvred the platform away as quickly and safely as he could, heading towards a group of firefighters gathering together, already linking arms and preparing to catch their colleague if he fell. The platform was lowering slowly to a safer height. Marc couldn't hold on any longer. It was no slight on his ability, just that his mate was a big bloke. He yelled out in despair as he felt Nev finally slip from his grasp. He looked straight into his eyes with terror and sorrow as Nev fell backwards, his arms and legs scrabbling against air to climb back up. There was nothing Marc could do but watch and hope. He still threw himself forward instinctively, reaching down helplessly swiping his hands out to Nev, but he already knew it was too late. His heart screaming out for him to be saved. Only then did he see the sea of yellow helmets below. They surged violently forwards as Nev landed, helmets hitting off each other as the massive accelerated weight of the officer dropped, landed on them like a concrete block. Even with their collective strength, muscles and joints were wrenched out of their sockets, but all were willing to injure themselves to save their colleague.

A cheer went up as Nev was caught. He looked up at Marc leaning over the bar, clasping his hands together in praise of his friend and to whoever was looking out for him up there, and of course to his colleagues who had risked injury to save his life. The firefighters quickly pushed him up to his feet in a jovial way. Casual sarcastic comments about his weight were made as they could now relax and tease their colleague. They mentioned his laziness for lying about on the job, fun being poked at him in all directions moments after his death-defying experience, none of them allowing him any time to dwell on what had just happened. As expected, no sympathy was given as this was their way of helping him get over the experience. They all cared more than words could say, their team a second family, the strength in their bond unbreakable.

Medics rushed to the aid of the final body to be removed from the building, which was now an inferno, its structure and floors all collapsing to the ground. Bravery and tenacity had ensured that all those trapped inside had been brought out successfully, one unfortunately confirmed dead, and the four others classed as being in a critical condition.

Teams of detectives, and fire crews still fighting the blaze all remained. Sirens blared as the casualties were whisked off at high speed to the Royal Infirmary a short distance away. There was still work to be done at the crime scene. Marcus and Taylor left once their colleagues came to relieve them, their loyalty now with their fallen colleague and friend Fran. Both headed straight to the hospital.

Chapter 46
Fran

Taylor and Marcus arrived at the hospital where the hustle and bustle of everyday life continued, the entrance crowded with visitors and patients alike, unaware of their personal tragedy. People in wheelchairs still attached to their drips were outside sitting beneath the no smoking sign smoking cigarettes, probably the reason they were in there in the first place. A burly security guard sat at the main reception desk, flicking through the daily paper. Taylor leaned over and asked for directions to the intensive care unit where the casualties from the fire had been brought in. He looked up, scanned them both. He had been briefed about the fire. The casualties had been taken to a collective treatment area where the burns specialists could share their skills amongst them all as their injuries and needs were all similar, except one, who had other complications to add to their misery. Taylor and Marcus knew the one he was talking about would be Fran. They had seen her disfigured face, and both had a gut feeling, an instinct, so they decided that was where they wanted to go. They moved briskly through the hospital, nervously making conversation to avoid any silence, both actively avoiding facing the possibility that Fran might die, her condition unknown.

All those that had been rescued from the fire were being treated in ICU. There were some firefighters in the hospital too, most with minor injuries.

Taylor and Marcus were not allowed to enter the ICU and had to wait for instructions in relation to the most critical patient. The consultant came out, clearly stressed and very busy. He made a point of coming to speak with them, only allowing himself to leave the theatre momentarily. His time was needed there, which both detectives were very aware of.

His face said it all. Looking directly at them, he said, "Are you able to come through to the viewing area and verify the identity of this young woman, so we can confirm who we have here to allow us to check her medical records?" They went over to the window and stared with knowing apprehension. They looked on sadly at the recently cleaned face, the features now visible. The pixie-like face was most definitely that of Fran Andrews. It was badly swollen and bruised. Her identity confirmed, the consultant used her name when he gave her prognosis.

He spoke frankly in a kindly manner, fully aware of the situation and how the information would be received. "There is no easy was to say this. Fran has a fractured skull, which has been left untreated for many hours. The trauma suffered has caused a bleed on the brain and significant swelling, which may have caused damage to the brain cells, and it is unknown whether this will cause permanent damage. We are in the process of trying to relieve the pressure, and she is not in a stable condition yet, I'm afraid. The fire related injuries to the internal tissues in the larynx, trachea, bronchi and inner lung tissue have also been damaged, and that is why she is on a ventilator. We have put her in an induced coma to assist in her recovery. We believe she has suffered a stroke – CPR was administered by someone recently as they must have thought that her heart had stopped. She has recent damaged to her ribs, and on top of all of that she has facial fractures too. Whoever assaulted her used brutal, life-threatening force."

Taylor's face was crumbling. She could barely listen to him anymore.

"Will she survive? How will she be?" Taylor asked, not wanting to hear the answer.

The consultant clasped his hands, and answered, "Basically this young lady is lucky to be alive, and only time will tell. I wish I had all the answers for you. The stroke damage is unknown at present, and we won't know until she regains consciousness, but we will do everything we can for her." The consultant then gestured as if there may be more to follow, but he had to go back into theatre.

Taylor just stared blankly at the wall. Marcus was silenced too with what they had heard. They thanked the consultant before he moved quickly back into the ICU.

They knew they would be no use there, not for a while anyway. Their intention was to return daily until there was any noticeable progress or decline in her condition.

They looked at each other. Both could quite legitimately go home with the trauma they had been through that day, but their minds had already been made up to stay and fast forward progress of the enquiry. They wanted Burnett and as many of his associates as they could tie into this mess.

Chapter 47
So Close

Prestwick Airport on the Ayrshire coast seemed the right choice of airport to leave from, Edinburgh and Glasgow both too obvious and well policed. This was a far less busy place, out in the countryside, not a typical city airport, with police resources further away.

Davy smiled to himself, feeling smug. His journey through there had been peaceful and unchallenged, and he thought he was home free. He looked forward to the warmth of the sun on his face, and the freedom to do as he liked and not what he was told to do for a change. He thought back to the unit and the fire, those he had deliberately left trapped inside. He didn't allow himself a thought for their suffering. They needed to be silenced. They were simply disposable commodities to his boss, something that needed dealt with to save their skins. Both knew if they lived, their testimony would destroy the whole setup and they would get life behind bars, and Burnett wasn't having that. As always, if ending a life secured his freedom, he didn't give a fuck.

Davy was at the juice machine, digging in his pockets for change, the first time he noticed that there were police officers in the building. Two firearms officers were walking the floor. This startled him a bit, but he knew with the terrorist threat in

Britain that even in this small airport this was to be expected. He tried not to show his apprehension as they walked by casually taking in their surroundings.

The officers had the information from the All Points Bulletin, and whilst looking casual, they were actually studying everybody that they passed, both aware of the man at the juice machine, but neither could see his face clearly, so they would have to sweep back round for another look. The officers had thought they had seen the male fitting the description on three occasion already, all with a negative result, so this time they would play it cooler, as two of the other men had nearly shit themselves as they were pulled aside. They talked casually with each other and, once out of earshot, agreed their next move.

Davy watched them in the reflection of the machine and saw them move off, just far enough for him to walk the other way as casually as he could, but curiosity got the better of him, and he looked round to see where they had gone, which in turn gave the officers now walking back in his direction an opportunity to see his face properly. This time there were no doubts, and they both moved with purpose towards him.

Davy didn't want to take any chances and moved away more quickly, turning the corner to get out of sight. He then went straight out of the exit doors, abandoned his luggage and started to run.

A radio message was received, the direction and place last seen was passed over the radio as the two firearms officers were running to the door, their kit heavy and cumbersome, giving Davy an advantage but, little did he know, his time was running out.

"Stop right there, get on your knees!" boomed out from the dog handler outside. He was struggling to hold onto his Malinois general purpose dog, a breed known for their agility, athleticism and their ability to take down nearly anything.

Davy unwisely ignored the instruction and ran faster with no idea where he was going, his lack of understanding of his chance to escape without injury obvious to the dog handler, who smiled and unclipped the lead.

The force Davy was gripped with spun his full body weight round and he came crashing down to the ground full force, face first. Growls and the sound of teeth gnashing his wrist were indescribable. Pain seared through him as he felt the excruciating agony of his skin being pulled viciously from his wrist, exposing the flesh below. He could see his arm start to resemble a portion of chopped meat. Sinew tissues, bone, blood vessels and copious amount of blood spurted out as he tried to punch the dog in the face with his other hand. His futile attempts to release the grip with an assault on the dog just made the dog shake her head more viciously and in a more excited manner. She was enjoying her work a little more than she should until her handler eventually got there.

His command was strong and dominant, but Sky was a strong willed young lady, and she was going to have one last bite at Davy before she let go, so she released his wrist and then turned and snapped right at his face, catching him on the nose, his squeal loud and desperate, pain now displaced from the original site. He brought his good hand up to his face, and she bit down heavily on that one too, tugging at his fingers, knowing that this was the hand he had used to hit her in the face with moments before. She was determined to stop it happening it again. The tug on her lead was brutal, and she was given a kick in her ribs to get her back under control. The force used by the handler was necessary as the dog was not quite ready to stop, her inbuilt aggression and dominance needing to be checked and met with a higher level of dominance.

The handler couldn't help but enjoy his dog's bad behaviour, because the male they had apprehended was an evil bastard. His dunt in her ribs was not damaging, it was just a short sharp reminder that he was boss and she had to follow his instructions.

She took one more snap at Davy's face, cutting his forehead with her teeth before she stopped and sat back barking loudly in his face, wagging her tail, wishing he would run again, patiently waiting for her ball.

"Good girl!" The handler praised her, and she sat there with her ears pointing high in the air, a wide dog grin covering her face, her tongue hanging out as she panted heavily, with her paws shifting excitedly up and down, raising and lowering her bottom, in the hope the lead would be loosened.

The firearms officers moved forward with weapons drawn. Once secured, Davy was searched and cuffed on the ground. He was rolled back and forward to ensure there were no hidden surprises secreted into his clothing. He was lifted up and officially arrested for wilful fire raising, with many more charges to follow once sufficient evidence was obtained.

Davy shouted and swore in the arresting officers faces. "I'm going to fucking sue youse cunts. Look at ma fucking arm ya daft bastards, an ma face for fuck's sake. I've done fuck all. Stop fucking gripping onto me, ya prick. I'll rip yer fucking heart out and rape yer family. Do you know who the fuck I am? I know your faces!" he threatened continually.

The cops, now seven of them in total, just smiled at his futile attempts to threaten them and mocked his pathetic protests of innocence, knowing there were two officers in a critical condition. Most of the officers had their faces covered anyway, his threats and pure hatred towards them were common place when an innocent soul like him was caught for something they hadn't done.

They all knew of Davy. He was a well-known, violent individual, nearly as slippery as Burnett, and they hoped his days were numbered too.

The officers were fully aware of the new Criminal Justice rules, meaning his arrest time would not start until after his medical treatment and travel to the detention station, which for Davy would mean days, possibly weeks due to the damage to his arm. Plastic surgery would be necessary, so there was a mutual satisfaction among the officers, knowing he'd be even more unhappy.

Chapter 48
Closing In

Burnett was in his penthouse with Irene, He had seen the news, watched the casualties being brought out, and his rage was boiling over. His teeth were gritted, his speech rasping with anger. He was losing control, and Irene was terrified of him and what he might do.

"How the fuck did they find that place. These daft cunts can barely find their fucking feet, some fucker has tipped them off. They've raided over seven of ma places that they never even had a clue about before. Some loose-lipped fucking grass will find themselves six feet under. I'll do it personally, the silly cunt!" Burnett's face contorted angrily.

Irene stood still watching him pace the floor and out onto the balcony to smoke, not realising for a moment that it was her. She was visibly shaking, and her blood ran cold as he walked back in and stared right at her. "What the fuck is wrong wi' you. It's always you, you, you! Ya fucking useless bitch!" He raised his hand up and made to slap her but stopped when she pulled instinctively away from him to avoid the contact.

"This place is a fuckin' mess. What the fuck do you do here all day? Get me a beer and stop looking so pathetic, and put something nice on will ye! Oh, and run me a bath too. I need to relax and think. I need to fucking think. See if it was that silly cunt Davy, I'll rip his fucking baws off. Na, he wouldnae, too much to lose, lots more to gain." He was now talking to himself, rambling out loud, trying to figure out who knew about his places. Irene knew it was inevitable that he would hurt her tonight, physically and sexually, as this was the usual pattern when he was stressed and angry. She also feared that his thought process might eventually lead back to her, and that he would actually kill her if he found out the truth.

She scurried away out of the room, glad that he had failed to notice the sweat on her forehead and her shaking more than normal. He was buried too deep in thought, trying to work out how the Feds had managed to find the warehouse before the fire had done the job, which in his mind was not a coincidence.

She brought him a beer and handed it to him on the couch, hoping he wouldn't want her to sit with him. She knew him, she knew how and what he did, almost like a written list in order of occurrence - sex, anger, violence, blame, disgust and remorse.

"Don't go, sit," he said patting the sofa beside him.

Her insides twisted with anticipation, but she tried to relax and be as normal as she could pretend to be.

He took hold of her hair, a tight grip, meant to be passionate but brutish enough for her to wince in pain, which he liked. It turned him on, his kiss rasping over her lips, his tongue now deep inside her mouth, her disgust towards him making her feel sick. She could no longer switch on and off when he wanted her, something she used to be able to do, but it wasn't so easy now. He repulsed her, and she was screaming inside. His hands were all over her. Her breasts were groped, nipples pulled, hands gripping and pulling at her lower clothing, and she just had to let him, as no was not something he listened to, or adhered to. He had always taken what he wanted, when he wanted, raping her if she didn't want to have sex with him.

Irene sat bolt upright and exclaimed, "The bath!" genuinely worried it would overflow. Nelson didn't like mess, so he let her go and sort it, slapping her bare backside as she left, her jeans half down after Nelson's depraved advances, but she was given a little short-term relief from his unwanted desires.

She ran through just in time. The bubbles in the big luxury corner bath were sitting high, and the water level was already skimming down the overflow.

"Nel, the bath's ready. Let me give you a massage or something, to help you relax a little," Irene called looking for an easy way out, anything to avoid full sex with him.

Minutes passed, and Nel came swaggering through with his bare body on show, his manhood semi-aroused as he kissed her again and groped at her, his fingers finding where he wanted them to go. His arms reached round her, her heart racing as she thought he would just fuck her there and then on the floor. She wriggled in a playful manner and kissed him, moving her hips and freeing his fingers from inside her.

"I'll bring you a whisky too," she said pulling out of his arms, which she knew he liked in the bath.

He liked the heat of the whisky, the floaty head, which would help him chill, and he liked how it made him feel when he fucked her.

Irene walked through to the kitchen, the sensation of his intrusion making her feel uncomfortable and physically sick, and she had to stop herself from vomiting. Her mind was made up. She was leaving him that night, the minute he was asleep, no matter how damaged he left her. She hoped never to be found, and had some of his money stashed away already, for this very day.

"Phone, bring me the phone too will ye, Irene, and the charger. It's nearly out of juice. I need it to make some calls. I need to phone my lawyer. The filth will be calling here soon, 'cause these silly cunts think they have finally got something this time, NOT! Hurry up though," he said still wanting to carry on where he had left off, the hot water keeping him aroused.

Irene shouted through from the kitchen, "The charger won't reach the bathroom, Nel!" Nelson couldn't stand stupid shit like this. "For fuck's sake, ya daft bitch. It's no difficult, ya silly cow. Get the bloody extension. There's one in the cupboard there, and then get the rest of yer kit off and join me. I'm not finished wi' you!" he said with his hands under the water fondling his genitals.

Irene went to the cupboard, got the extension, plugged it in and slowly started to undress, her tiny frame already feeling the cold. She was nervous about what she was going to have to do, her body still bruised and sore from the last beating and rape, which he classed as just having sex.

She handed him the whisky and stood there patiently with the phone, waiting for him to take his hand off his dick. She recoiled at his vulgarity and lack of decency. He had never been chivalrous or a gentleman in any way. Her hatred for him had grown lately, the realisation of the monster he was could no longer be ignored for the finer things in life. What he was capable of was a daily reality for her. She would not be exempt from his wrath, especially if he found out what she had done.

She snapped out of her thoughts as his sharp and commanding words snarled viciously from his lips. "What are ye tryin' to do to me, fucking electrocute me ya dafty? Get a fuckin' towel to dry ma hands, ya silly bitch!"

She handed him the phone, and he just looked at it, his frustration at her stupidity growing. "It still needs charged for fuck's sake, put the thing in will ye."

She hated the way he spoke to her. He had changed so much in the time they had been together. He had always been rough and coarse, heavy handed, but he had shown her in his own foul way that he did like her. He no longer showed these fleeting glimpses of semi-human affection. He was now openly vile, cruel, brutally violent and his sexual depravity was more apparent and unrelenting. He was responsible for immeasurable suffering in the city, drugs, trafficking, prostitution, violence, money laundering and murder, and he seemed to be bringing his work home more often.

She stood with the phone in her hand, his hand back on his dick stroking it back and forth as he supped his whisky.

He looked back over his shoulder at her, his hand wet again, demanding the towel again and for her to hurry up. His head tilted to the side as he began to relax.

He could see her slightly behind him and was irked by her hesitation and delay to come to him. She was just standing still with his phone in both hands. Slowly she came round beside him and he pushed his hand up between her legs once more. Her face changed and she could no longer hide her disgust for him as his fingers invaded her without invitation. She knew she could never escape him. If she left, he would send people out to find her and deal with her permanently.

Unwittingly, he had given her an idea. Totally unaware, he rapped the side of the bath at her as she hesitated once again to hand over the phone, his other hand still violating her vigorously, getting her ready for his pleasure.

He turned towards her impatiently. She handed the phone towards his free hand as he looked up at her with his furrowed brow and curled lips and for once he looked at her face. He saw that her once loving eyes were dark, filled with hatred and now, fully focused on his, he saw what he thought was a hint of evil present.

She smiled at him with an odd expression on her face, "No! No more, Nel!"

"What the fuck dae ye mean, no fucking more? I decide what happens, ya silly bitch!" His manner was cocky and boorish as always.

Her hands were quick as she pulled the phone away from his outstretched hand, and smiled sweetly at him. His eyes remained focused intently on her, contorted with anger and impatience. She just shook her head, and whispered "No, Nel, I decide." Calm and determined, she pulled herself out of reach of his busy hand, her eyes on his, and in a comical gesture dropped the phone into the bath.

"Oops!" she said, her smile filled with a little madness.

The initial jolt was violent. His body straightened in a way where there was insufficient space for it to do so, contorting his limbs and joints awkwardly, causing Irene to jump back with fright. His eyes bulged grotesquely out of his head, steam rising as the current continued through him and the water steamed, wisps of smoke now coming out of every orifice of his face as the current pulsed lethally through his heart and central nervous system.

She looked at him with no remorse, no feelings, just a sense of relief, never thinking that she would ever have been free from him. *He just kept pushing and pushing, he left me no choice*, she thought to herself.

She made sure her bare feet kept away from the water and went to grab everything she could take from the flat, car keys, fake passport, and left the house. There were no lights on in the common stair. She was shaking all over, surprised that the electricity had not cut off. Nel would have killed her right there and then had he survived.

Once in her car, tears clouded her eyes, the realisation, of what she had done hitting home. She was still shaking intensely, her hands barely able to get the keys in the ignition. She paused, took a deep breath and turned the keys, and only then did her shoulders drop out of their tensed-up state, but she did not regret what she had done. Irene turned up towards Edinburgh College, her destination the airport. She would buy a ticket to the Canaries, change her name to the one on her fake passport and hope to just disappear and live a long and happy life in a more tranquil setting without fear and intimidation ever again.

.

Chapter 49
Too Late

Taylor and Marcus were back at Fettes. There was barely anyone there, their resources stretched to the wind. Kay was at her desk. She hadn't looked round when they came in. There had been a multitude of visitors that day, many people coming and going, and she had given up hoping that Taylor would walk in.

Taylor, on the other hand, noticed Kay straight away, her familiar upright posture, her beautiful hair strategically combed to hide the portions that remained shorter, the clumps that had been brutally torn out at the hands of Brennan. Taylor sighed. Everything was such a mess, and she couldn't see how it could be fixed, but her heart was warmed by just seeing Kay back at work, getting well again.

Brooke Sommerville had been waiting impatiently for their return. She had been at what they called a gold meeting, all of the bosses discussing the further plans in relation to the major incident ongoing - everything relating to what their raids had uncovered, the abduction and how that had been possible and, finally, the fire and the casualties. She herself had encountered endless questions from the Chief Superintendant, who was answering directly to the Chief Constable. Her squad was under fire and there was no escape this time. Heads would roll, most likely one would be hers, and this just added to her frustration and anger.

"My office, please!" Sommerville's voice was efficient and firm, but she was fully aware of the shit day, week and month they had all had and was not going to make that worse intentionally. Kay now looked up as they walked slowly to the DCI's office, heads bowed, but Taylor glanced back at her, and they looked at one another with kindness and sorrow.

The DCI offered them both a seat, Kay still watching through the glass, her heart fluttering a little, her affection for Taylor still there, even with all her failings.

Once seated, DCI Somerville asked how their colleagues were, and as they explained everything, she was deeply saddened at how everything had turned out. She shook her head, still in disbelief that this had happened. She said that action would be taken in relation to DC Shack, although what that would be had not yet been decided.

"He might not make it, ma'am," Taylor said with some venom in her tone.

"If he does," she retorted quickly, with similar angst, reiterating that he would be dealt with either way, a little annoyed at being interrupted with such a challenging tone.

Taylor too was a little frustrated and not in the mood for being lectured. She was not impressed with her boss's tone. "What about Burnett?" Taylor asked.

"What about him?" Brooke replied abruptly. "Nobody is bloody talking! We can't interview Davy any time soon, because the dog annihilated him. His arm is bloody mangled. We are exactly where we were before. We know it's him, but how can we bloody prove it? Right now anyway, and our witnesses, Sorina and the boy, are in no state to talk any time soon either, that's if and when they recover and assuming they are willing to do so after all the shit we've inadvertently put them through."

Taylor did not want to be beaten down. She too wanted Burnett. There was no way he could get away with his last atrocity. He had avoided any recourse from the previous incident as nothing from the drug lab could be traced back to him.

"I think Irene will talk. We can use her knowledge to connect him in some way. I think she's done - she wants out," Taylor said, convinced Irene would help them. She had seen it in her eyes at their last meeting, the fear and the increasing brutality from Burnett now overriding the good life she used to be accustomed to.

Kay knocked on the door, her face flushing as she entered the office, but her message was one she decided could not wait.

She blurted out, "A grade three call has come in - flooding coming from a flat above…," but, before she could finish, she was cut short by the DCI.

Sommerville glared at her because of the interruption and the triviality of the type of call she was bringing to their attention, and was about to comment rudely before Kay confidently continued.

Taylor and Marcus hoped there was more to it, as this could become embarrassing for Kay, but they knew her. She was no fool, and the DCI was being deliberately out of order.

Kay continued unperturbed, a little irked at the boss's presumption of her naivety. "Before you say it's not a police matter, the address is the reason for the significance. You didn't give me a chance to finish, ma'am. It's Burnett's address the water is coming from and officers are looking for assistance to gain entry," Kay finished a little triumphantly.

"Right, right, I see! Sorry, Kay, it's been a shit day for everyone. I should have let you finish."

She ended the meeting. "This can wait. We can catch up later. You're the only two cops available here. Join the uniform guys and take the ram to force entry. See what's going on down there - quickly, please!"

Marcus and Taylor rose and headed for the door, Kay leaving at the same time, head down, annoyed at her boss but aware of the tension and stress she was under. Her hand trailed behind on the door handle as Taylor's inadvertently joined it. It was only a slight touch, but it sent electricity to every inch of Taylor's body. Kay felt the sudden rush too. Their connection was still very much alive.

Taylor smiled, excusing herself, looking at Kay as she left. Kay just watched her. The flutter had returned within. Her feelings were back, a return to her old self now a possibility.

Marcus also smiled and bid farewell to Kay. He had watched her demise. Her mental breakdown had shocked them all. Everyone had been willing her to recover.

"Come on, let's see what this is all about. I hope his carpets are alright," Taylor said with a grin, patting Marcus's leg.

They sped down from Fettes to Waterfront in less than five minutes, arriving just as the uniform officers were smashing the front door down. They had brought their own equipment and were eager to destroy the door, knowing whose door it was and how annoyed he would be.

It took a lot of effort to break it down. The ram took the concrete surrounds away with the door frame due to the elaborate locking systems in place, all there to deter exactly what they were doing just now. The officers enjoyed the sight. It had been a long time coming, all involved in the entry revelling in this little bit of retribution against the bane of their lives. The stairwell was dim, only lit by the fading light coming through the windows. This was noted by all on the way up, their nerves tingling, unsure of what they were going to find.

As the door swung inwards, they were met with a strong smell of burning flesh. All with long enough service knew what it was. Marcus warned those entering to take care, as there were no lights on or working inside. There was clearly an electrical fault, with its own inherent dangers.

They lit their torches and walked through the large sprawling flat, searching each room in turn, aware that Burnett was a violent man, who openly hated the police, and could be in there waiting.

They came into a hallway where they saw the extension lead heading to what they believed to be the bathroom, the door closed, secreting what was hidden behind it.

Marcus went to the door. He was apprehensive and hesitantly careful as he entered, not sure what he would find inside. He checked at his feet for water and put rubber gloves on before gripping the handle as he wouldn't put it past Burnett to set a booby trap for them. Taylor was worried that they would find Irene dead inside and that Burnett had left.

Marcus raised up his torch, lighting up the bathroom ceiling, then down to the bath. A heavy arm lay out of it, fingers nearly reaching down to the floor, the wire from the phone stretching up and into the water. Marcus shone the torch onto Burnett's face. It was bloated, almost unrecognisable, his eyes bubbling grotesquely out of his skull with a melted consistency, both protruding in a death like stare, his skin charred and blistered, blood and fluids oozing from every orifice. Taylor peered over Marcus's shoulder. "Eeeugh, gruesome," she said, but as she reached over him leaning on his shoulder, both looked at each other with a smile, glad that it was Burnett and not Irene. This was the end of their troubles and that of a multitude of others.

"Couldn't have happened to a nicer bloke," the cop behind quipped, not bothered how unfeeling his comment sounded, knowing what Burnett had done to so many people.

Marcus had read about this before. An unsuspecting teenager had died in exactly the same way whilst listening to music on his phone in the bath, a failure of the home owner to have a power cut off mechanism in place. Burnett must have failed to have one installed, or had he altered it himself for other reasons?

Taylor flicked the switch in the hall, unsure if there was still a current flowing or not, wondering if it had blown everything.

Taylor went back over to the bath, checked Burnett lying there, his features altered with the blistering and scorch marks, but she confirmed it was definitely him. They would have to get Scottish Power to isolate the electricity and make the scene safe. They couldn't risk checking Burnett to see if there was a chance he was still alive, or have it confirmed anyway, as to them he was clearly dead, but that wasn't their call. They could only presume life extinct with either decapitation or severe decomposition, a little insulting, but there was always a chance he could still have signs of life.

She couldn't help but smile openly when she addressed the officers and asked them to secure the apartment and start a crime scene entry log, have the electricity made safe, call CID to attend, Scenes Examination Branch too, and other specialist resources. Taylor and Marcus could not commit to this enquiry at that moment, with all the other ongoing investigations they still had to deal with.

There had been a chance, even with everything that had happened, that Burnett could have slithered free once again, but not now. A sense of relief washed over Taylor, but it was short lived. She turned around, a lightbulb going on in her head.

She looked at Marcus. "Irene, where is she?"

Chapter 50
Free at Last

Irene had chosen Edinburgh Airport, the closest, and had headed straight to the checkout desk for Tui. She had used her phone to buy a flight to Gran Canaria, her car abandoned in the short stay car park. She had no intention of being back to pay the exorbitant fine that would be payable on return. She was sitting on the plane, the engines at full throttle as it hurtled towards the end of the runway, and as the wheels lifted off the ground, she finally allowed herself a sigh of relief.

She did not know how long it would be before they discovered Nel, but three hours had passed, and she started to believe she may actually get away.

Burnett had always insisted on having false documents and passports for them both for such an occasion, more for him than her, a necessity if they had to leave in a hurry, their identities untraceable, giving them sufficient time to leave the country unchallenged.

For that she would raise a glass to him. She knew the police would have an APB out within seconds and all of the flight manifests would be checked, but her new name, Sarah Long, would go right under the radar, and she would blend in unnoticed, her slight frame and the fact she had dressed down assisting her in her escape.

She was apprehensive. She had no friends, and she wouldn't be able to contact her family without giving her location away. She was alone now, alone but safe, and free from Nel's control and violence at last.

Her heart nearly stopped as she came out of her daydream when the air hostess asked what she would like to drink, the trolley pushing against her arm, her mind racing, believing she had been caught.

"Any drinks or snacks?" the hostess said kindly, a big broad smile on her face as she apologised for bumping Irene and clearly giving her a fright.

Irene hesitated, trying to calm herself enough to act normally and answer. "Yes please, two Bacardi's and a coke please." Nothing too fancy that would draw any attention to herself, although she would make a point of celebrating once she got to her destination. The hostess placed the drinks down in front of her. Irene smiled up at her, waiting until she was away before lifting the cup slightly into the air to give a quiet toast. "To new beginnings," she whispered.

Chapter 51
Life Goes On, or Not?

Kim sat at Steve's bedside, holding her husband's hand, tears pouring freely down her face. She had been there when he passed away, his burns and the smoke inhalation too damaging for him to survive. Her grief was devastating for all to see. She knew he wasn't perfect; he had clearly got caught up in something that was too big to get out of. He had made a mistake that he couldn't escape from, but he had done it for somebody he loved, his daughter. He had stupidly hoped he could make a difference for her, not thinking of the consequences, and had started to lose his sense of reality. He would be missed greatly by his family. He had always been their rock. Together they had fought to make things better, but they had come up against a brick wall lately, and he had been desperate, desperate to give his daughter a fighting chance to survive. He had just taken things too far in the wrong direction.

***

Sorina sat on the floor playing with Nicu in their new apartment. They were both still receiving treatment for the full thickness burns they had suffered. Skin grafts and painful surgery would be ongoing, a price they were willing to pay to be back together.

She pulled him close to her and whispered, "I love you", into his ear as she held him close.

He cuddled into her, his tiny arms reaching round her neck as he whispered back, "I love you too mummy", right in her ear. It tickled and as she curled her neck away from him laughing, he too giggled and did it again. Sorina looked to the sky and smiled. She had hoped and prayed for this, that she would find her son alive. She made a promise to herself never to leave his side again, and she meant it. It seemed a lifetime ago since they had been stolen from their homeland and brought to another country to be sold as slaves. They had been put forward for residence in the UK now and a chance to live peacefully.

***

One month later – Fran was finally out of her coma, and sitting up. The nurse offered to bring over the pile of get well cards, because Fran had not stepped out of bed yet and was not sure if she could actually manage it. She read the kind words, messages that were warm and caring, filled with friendship and love. She could feel the desperation in some of the cards, almost willing her to survive, not realising why. Only after speaking with the consultant did she understand just how close she had come to dying. Her head was shaved on one side where they had drilled into her skull to save her, her ribs still ached and burns were still visible on her face, neck and arms, but after all she had endured, she was still here. She had come through her ordeal alive, a miracle as the nurse had described it to her. Fran hesitated as she came to Taylor's card, sadness twisting inside her stomach although she had always known their relationship wouldn't last. She would have always been playing second fiddle to Kay. A tear rolled discreetly down her cheek, sad for her loss, but then she started smiling again as she read Marcus's card, his cheeky upbeat comments all meant to cheer her up, which they did. She opened another. It was signed 'Lana'. Her words were kind and filled with emotion, and as Fran read on, she realised why. She was the firefighter that had brought her out of the building, saving her life whilst risking her own. She leant her head back, her heart filled with gratitude for all of those involved in her rescue and saving her life, but this card seemed more personal. All of the other firefighters from the stations that had attended the scene had sent big collective cards.

Fran fell asleep sitting up, still exhausted and barely able to stay awake for long periods. Lana had entered the room unnoticed and sat silently on the visitor's chair, as she had done nearly every day since Fran had been admitted, willing her to get better, never wanting to disturb her. She had been there as often as she could since the incident, hoping and willing Fran to survive. She had been there for over an hour before Fran turned to her side and finally opened her eyes for the second time that day. She gave a little jump when she realised she was not alone and winced in pain as she sat up. She did not know who the visitor was sitting beside her.

"Hello! Sorry if I startled you. I didn't mean too. I'm Lana," she said in a calm and kind voice.

Fran took a little time to remember the card - the firefighter, which was highly likely, due to her frame and stature, strong and powerful shoulders, tall and fit looking.

"Sorry, you don't know me, but I was the one who helped get you out from the fire, and you were in such a bad way, I just wanted to make sure you recovered. I've actually become a wee bit obsessed with your recovery. Sorry, I just wanted you to live," she said apologetically.

Fran looked at her for a while. She could see a mixture of sadness and joy in Lana's expression. "Thank you, thank you so much for saving me, for caring. I don't remember anything. I don't remember a fire but, looking at my body, I was definitely in one," she said with a big hint of sarcasm and a smile, raising her arms out to her sides and looking down, again feeling the pain at the tightness of her skin.

"There's no need to thank me. You know we were just doing our jobs, like you were doing yours," Lana replied genuinely happy to serve.

Fran was sad as she looked down at her burnt hands. "I'm not sure if I can keep doing my job though Lana. Look at me! I don't know if I can do it anymore. I'm scared, so scared." She started to cry and cry, letting everything out. Lana didn't really know what to do, so she got up and sat on the side of the bed and held Fran as her tears kept flowing, her shoulders heaving painfully up and down as her emotions overflowed.

The nurse came rushing in as Fran's heart monitor had started sounding an alarm as her pulse rate rose significantly. Lana moved away to let her in to tend to Fran.

"It's okay, you can stay," the nurse said kindly to Lana. Fran looked up at the nurse apologetically and recognised Ann from their previous investigation. She was the nurse Brennan had assaulted, now fully recovered and back to what she did best.

"Hello you! I'm just covering in this ward for a bit. Long time, no see, although a wee visit would have been better for a catch up though!" Ann said smiling, trying to comfort Fran and relax her. Fran was happy that there was a familiar face looking after her. She had been feeling totally lost and alone, even though her parents had been in earlier that morning when she first came around, leaving just before Lana arrived.

Lana was now sitting back on the chair when she heard a familiar voice outside the door, which caused her to sit upright.

Taylor popped her head in the room. She had received a message from the hospital that Fran had regained consciousness. She had a huge bunch of flowers in her arms, and Marcus was just behind her with a massive cuddly toy, a red panda, Fran's favourite animal.

Fran gave a smile, one filled with mixed feelings. She was sad she had lost Taylor but she still had genuine affection for her. She was glad Taylor had come to visit her, and Marcus too of course.

Taylor was moving over towards Fran to hug her when she noticed Lana with a little sign of shocked recognition, but she didn't show it. She hugged Fran gently, taking in her very noticeable injuries, more so now that she was sitting up, revealing the true horror of her burns.

"Hi," Taylor said to Lana, their lack of contact after their brief liaison a telling sign it wasn't going to be continued.

"Hi! How are you?" Lana asked politely with no agenda or resentment.

Fran watched them, not overly interested that they knew each other. She was too broken to care right now.

Lana stood up. "Fran, I'll be off now. I'm so glad you're on the mend and truly blessed to have had the privilege to have been able to finally meet you awake," she said with fondness and humour before she turned to leave. She stopped as she reached the door, fully aware of her audience, and asked politely, "Do you mind if I visit again?" Her eyes suggested she hoped the answer would be yes.

Fran looked directly at her, also aware of her audience, and said, "Of course, I'd love to see you again. Come as often as you want, I need the company." She turned and looked at Taylor when she said it. She wasn't trying to be cruel, but she had to free herself from Taylor, and she knew deep down that Taylor wanted to be freed by her too.

Taylor balked a bit at this, but she saw the kindness in Fran and read between the lines. She knew what she wanted, but couldn't help but feel a little jealous and truly sad at her loss.

*****

When Marcus and Taylor got back to the office, Kay tried to meet their eyes, to warn them before the very familiar voice boomed out through the open plan office.

"You two in here! Quick smart, now!" Findlay bellowed with a very satisfied and sinister smirk on his face.

They were very aware how sparse the office looked now that the single desk had been moved back to its central position in the room.

Taylor's face went white at the realisation of the significance.

"Yep, she's gone, probably to the Sheltand Islands after that monumental fuck up she had," Findlay said with pleasure, smiling like a Cheshire Cat. "It's time to get back to how it used to be around here, how it should be." Findlay's pompous sense of superiority was renewed. "Where have you two been anyway? You've been away for ages and didn't answer your radios."

Taylor replied with a snake-like turn of her head, pure venom and rage in her voice as she answered him, her open disdain for the man oozing from every pore. "We were at the hospital Inspector. Fran's come out of her coma today, she's sitting up. We needed to go and see her. She's one of our team." Her words were filled with resentment.

"Not on my clock you don't. If you want to see her, do it in your own time in future. Do you understand? This is not up for debate," he said quickly as he saw that Taylor was about to argue, inwardly enjoying her anger.

"There's been a body of a male washed up on Longniddry Bents, a missing person from two weeks ago. See if you can offer a hand to our uniform colleagues," he continued with a smirk on his face. He wanted to assert his authority once again. It had been months since Sommeville had taken over his office, offering a fairer and more respectful leadership, and control. He was just sending them out to what he thought was a trivial job, because he could, unaware of what secrets the corpse would actually reveal.

"Oh, there's also been a road traffic collision I need you to go to as well," he ordered.

"Why would we attend that boss? That's not in our remit. Is there something special about it?" Marcus enquired with as much false respect and control as he could muster.

"And which of these uniformed enquiries would you like us to attend to first, Inspector?" Taylor interjected with open hostility and a questioning tone, not trying to hide her feelings for this vile man.

Findlay ignored her question, choosing to annoy her by answering Marcus's question first. He looked up like a cat that got the cream, and spoke triumphantly. "Nathan Sloan ring a bell?"

Taylor knew instantly who it was, but was still a little irked that they had been brought into it, until her boss said that the casualty had an entry on the Scottish intelligence database in relation to alleged offences relating to indecent images of children. He had never been charged though and was now a nursery assistant, disclosure only covering convictions.

Taylor and Marcus looked at each other. Both had wondered if he had had any involvement in their last case, and now their curiosity was resurrected. They hoped and believed he hadn't been and this was just an unfortunate coincidence.

They were dismissed in Findlay's usual ignorant fashion, both delighted to get away from him. His unkempt dishevelled appearance and lack of deodorant was a sight and scent neither of them wished to endure any longer than necessary, both happily leaving to go and do what they did best, their jobs.

Kay looked up and beckoned Taylor over to where she sat, Marcus going back to his desk to get printouts of the incidents they were about to attend, shaking his head at their return to Findlay's oppressive and old school ignorant reign, wondering how they could be in two places at once, and what they could do to oust him from his position. He had broken every rule in this new diverse world. His way of working was outdated and totally out of order.

Taylor already had a flushed face, her anger always causing her neck to become a little red among other things. She could not believe that Brooke had been emptied out that quickly without warning, brutal swift measures taken, but that was the way it worked sometimes. Someone had to take the fall, get the blame, carry the can, and on this occasion, DCI Sommerville was the scapegoat. Taylor knew Brooke was really good at her job, and whatever failings there had been, none were directly her fault, but she had taken the rap. Taylor would contact her later to offer her some small comfort and much needed support and listen to the reasons they gave her for her impromptu exit from the team, which would be an interesting conversation.

Taylor straightened her suit as she walked over to Kay, a little apprehensively, but her skin was tingling and alive, her heart racing as she approached, wondering what Kay had to say. She was also a little hopeful.

Taylor leant over the desk, gently laying her hands there. She could smell Kay's perfume, and she inhaled deeply, enjoying the memories that it brought back. Kay didn't hold back. She placed her hand openly on top of Taylor's. Both felt sparks of electricity flow through them, their long-forgotten desire flooding back. Kay's heart was finally alive once again after months of suffering, no emotion, no feelings, just emptiness, sadness, fear, an uncontrollable loss of ability to live and feel normally.

Taylor was taken aback, not expecting Kay to touch her, or even want to speak to her.

"I've missed you, so much," Kay whispered, looking up at Taylor, straight into her eyes. "It took me so long to get better, I'm sorry, so sorry I made you leave. The first thing I thought about when I found myself again was you, only you, I'm just sorry it took me so long, but I had to be away, my head was in such a bad place. I'm sorry for hurting you, for hurting Fran. I didn't mean to hurt anyone." Kay's eyes were still fixed on Taylor's.

"You don't need to apologise to me. God, you were lost, the assault, the terror you endured, no bloody wonder you couldn't cope for a while, but I never stopped loving you, and I hoped you would get well again." Taylor held her hand, a smile on her face. "You're stronger than even you know you are. It's me that should be saying sorry to you for not waiting for you," Taylor said with guilt in her eyes.

"No, I sent you away, I pushed you away. I made sure you left, and I would only have started to resent you if you had stayed. I never expected you to sit there waiting for me all alone. I didn't want you, I couldn't love, I didn't want to be loved, I wanted to be alone. I was empty, barely functioning. I had lost me, the very essence of me, but after all those months, it was your warmth that returned to my heart that reignited my senses, the will to live, not be beaten by that evil man! I thought of you, us, what we shared, happiness, love, anger, loss, disappointment, all of it. I just wanted to feel, feel everything.

That's what made me feel alive again!" Kay's eyes were filled with watery tears, her emotions visible, her words honest and from the heart.

Taylor put her arm around her and held her close, a comfort Kay had longed for, from the person she now knew she loved.

"What are you doing tonight?" Kay almost spat the words out, her nerves tingling with fear of rejection. "Do you want to come round to mine? I can make us something to eat, have a glass of wine, relax and catch up a little." She stopped talking and stroked her hand up Taylor's forearm. The sensation sent waves of thrilling expectation through her body, desire now burning inside, a sense of happiness consuming her, something she hadn't felt for a long time.

"I'd love too. What time were you thinking?" Taylor smiled, not hiding her willingness to rekindle their relationship.

"When you finish work, anytime. I just want to see you, have you there, be with you, alone, in private, not at work where we are constantly on edge, being watched." Kay's hand squeezed Taylor's, her finger slipping into Taylor's clenched hand, and her message was clear.

"Are you two still here?" Findlay's voice bellowed through the office, ignorance personified, rude and unprofessional as always, making Kay jump and pull away from Taylor, creating distance to avoid his jealous distaste. Taylor was angry again, with the quick ending to the intimate moment they were sharing.

Marcus smiled falsely, holding up the printouts towards Findlay as Taylor leant forward in full view of the Inspector and kissed Kay full on the lips, a lover's kiss.

Findlay was incensed at what he saw, his rage outwardly visible, almost green with envy. Taylor smiled at him, knowing he had wanted Kay for years, conceitedly thinking he had a chance.

Taylor looked right at him, smiled happily and said, "Just leaving, sir, had to get paper for the printer," which wasn't a lie. She turned and left the office, a little triumphantly. This battle she had won. Marcus and Taylor looked at each other, tittering when Findlay's office door slammed loudly as they left.

Marcus just shook his head. "Did that just happen? Poor Brooke. She must be devastated. How come that fat useless bastard hasn't been ousted out of his seat is beyond me. It's just so unfair."

Taylor too was still raging, angry that Findlay seemed to float under the radar, allowed to be the bigoted twat that he was.

"Brooke will be okay, you know. Just look at the statistics. Making mistakes helps you get up the ladder. There is a long and distinguished list before her that are sitting pretty at the top, with a trail of devastation left behind them," Marcus said trying to convince Taylor that the DCI would land on her feet, knowing that the good ones tended not to fare so well after a mistake.

"But she didn't actually do anything wrong, unlike the prestigious predecessors leading the trail before her. And they were all incompetent, rule-breaking twats that kept their mates close, that didn't have a clue," Taylor moaned, feeling bad for her boss, especially as she was partly to blame for the choice of personnel that ended up at the safe house that day.

"C'mon, there's nothing we can do but offer her support. We need to get on. Findlay will be gunning for us. Any little thing and we will be joining her up in Shetland. Let's do this. Which one first, vehicle accident with crushed body parts or bloated corpse?"

"Choices, choices!" Taylor finally smiled at her loyal friend and colleague.

They left smiling at each other, as they went off to yet another gruesome job, with its life-changing, far-reaching tentacles of sadness and heartbreak that would touch the lives of so many.

Chapter 52
Finally

Kay sat in her living room. She had chosen to redecorate. The room was different; she wanted everything in her life to be different now, changed from the last sad and lonely month she had endured, just existing. She wanted the evil of the past to leave her, so she could have a fresh new start. Being back home was where she wanted to be. She wanted to be able to carry on like before and feel comfortable in her home, live as much of a normal life as she could. Months in rehabilitation had allowed her to free herself from the controlling feelings she had once been imprisoned by. The time away had given her her strength back. She had relived and dealt with her memories and fears over and over in her head and now she could finally put them in a place where they could no longer have the power to harm her. It had only been just over six weeks since she had left the residential unit, but she was getting there. This was her home and she was not going to allow that vile creature John Brennan to ruin her future. His brutal crimes had already so nearly destroyed her.

She stood up and looked around, eagerly awaiting her visitor. She now longed for that forgotten pleasure, the warmth of affection, the physical delights that she couldn't face before. Desire had been ripped away from her, the brutality she endured etched forever in her physical scars, but now it was no longer in her heart and mind. She had beaten him at last. They had all beaten him.

Taylor looked in the mirror as she was about to leave, loose blouse, fitted jeans, boots and a scent Kay had mentioned she liked. She stared at her own face, tired and a little worn, her recent efforts taking their toll on her. She too was nervous, not sure how the evening would go, but her inner nerves and anticipation showed she cared.

***

Marcus was home and he and Maria had just got little David off to sleep. They stood at his bedroom door and sighed, hearts filled with so much love for their precious little boy. Marcus started to turn away when Maria gently took his arm. Her unexpected touch made him look at her more closely.

"What is it?" Marcus asked a little concerned.

"I've got something to tell you," she said quietly.

"What is it, are you alright, is everything okay? Tell me, Maria, you're starting to worry me," he said, reaching out to hold her.

"No, no, there's definitely nothing wrong, nothing to worry about anyway, everything's fine. Very fine in fact. Don't you just feel you could burst with love sometimes? Maria said as she stood lovingly in front of Marcus, holding both his hands, staring up at him. "That you couldn't love any more than you already do?"

"I do, I feel the same! I love him so much it hurts," Marcus said, his smile filled with adoration for his little lad.

"Well you're going to have to find some more of that love from somewhere else," Maria said grinning.

"Why would that be?" Marcus was confused. He had no idea what she was going on about.

"I'm pregnant, Marcus! We're going to have another baby!" Maria blurted out, her face flushed, her rosy cheeks beaming with the broadest smile on her face.

"When!, how long? We're barely in the house long enough to kiss, far less make a baby!" he said jokingly, as the realisation of the wonder of the situation hit home.

She smiled again. "Eight weeks, and you most certainly were there long enough. I remember it well, very well," she said, nudging him in the ribs.

He just smiled at her, kissed her and held her tight, tears in his eyes, happiness engulfing him. "I love you so much, so, so much. Wee David will be over the moon to have a little brother or sister." Marcus was elated at the news, the warmth of love now surrounding him. There had been so much sadness, pain and hurt in the last year but goodness had won through over evil.

Their shared happiness lifted them up, their bond even stronger than before. Maria smiled again and led Marcus towards their bedroom, the look of love for her husband beaming out of her eyes, along with a hint of naughtiness. "Gently now, please," she said as he kissed her deeply and reached for her waist as she pulled him into the bedroom.

**

The doorbell rang. Kay sat bolt upright, a habit she had not yet managed to get out of. Fear was always the first instinctual emotion she felt when someone came to her door, but she was working on it. The routine of peeking through the curtains, sweat beads on her forehead, nerves tingling, senses alive, anticipation creating waves of nausea, followed by the task of convincing herself it was okay and calming herself down to answer it was still a ritual that she needed to do, for now!

She carefully looked out, ensuring that there was no movement in the curtains. Her heart quickly changed from fear to excitement, but it did not stop racing, and she did not want it to calm down. She wanted to feel, feel what she was now feeling, desire, excitement and anticipation.

Kay too was wearing fitted jeans, low at the naval, a white linen blouse, smart boots calf-length, white gold jewellery, with the residue of last year's tan setting her ensemble off nicely. She combed her fingers through her wavy hair, very conscious of the thinner patches where her hair had not yet grown back.

She looked through the spy hole, another habit, checking that Taylor really was still Taylor and had not been swapped. She knew this was totally illogical, her mind still subconsciously untrusting and constantly on edge.

Taylor was about to ring the doorbell again when the door finally opened and both of them just stood there. No words passed from either of them, eyes just taking in one another, letting the silence of the moment last a little bit longer, neither of them wanting to make the first move.

Finally, it was Kay who came out and walked down the steps to where Taylor stood, not having moved. Taylor looked a little lost, not her usual confident self, unsure how she should be, what she should or should not do, not knowing what Kay wanted or needed. She feared she would get it wrong, and she really wanted this evening to go well and not ruin it.

"Are you coming in or are you just going to stand there staring all night?" Kay asked, smiling kindly as she slipped her hand into Taylor's and gripped it gently. Flutters swirled inside her, spiralling from top to toe, sending tingles of excitement everywhere imaginable. Her heightened senses could barely cope with the sensory overload as she kept trying to hold herself back a little.

Kay made it clear with her first deep and sensual kiss that holding back was not what she wanted. She didn't want to be treated like a broken vase. She wanted to be treated like a woman, the Kay of old, the vibrant, effervescent, vivacious lover she used to be and hoped to be once again.

Taylor smiled as this scintillating woman moved into her space, her breasts leaning deliberately into Taylor's, her arms reaching round her, her kisses now feverish, needy and exhilarating. Taylor responded, hesitantly at first, as Kay led her up the steps into her house, their mouths only pulling apart when Taylor nearly fell off the edge of the steps into the bush. They laughed into each other's mouths as Kay pulled her back in line.

Taylor hesitated as she entered. "I know what you're feeling," Kay said softly. "These walls have seen too much pain and hurt for you. This is where I lost myself and pushed you away, pushed you out and you didn't deserved that, I just couldn't get over what happened to me that night. I'm sorry I hurt you."

Taylor realised too that Kay would still have to endure more, whenever she was there alone, alone to fight her inner demons, the invisible memories that would sometimes resurface to haunt her.

Taylor was also very aware that Kay might never have been able to set foot back in her house after the atrocities that had taken place there, both their homes offering up very different issues and memories for Kay and Taylor to have to deal with in the future. They looked at each other sympathetically and then smiled, shrugging their shoulders, the old familiarity coming back as they started to relax a little.

Kay led Taylor through to the living room. The last time they had been there Kay had told Taylor it was over. Taylor's heart was still sore from the loss the had felt that day, the memory of Kay's words still vivid in her mind, the recurring vision of losing Kay. The emotional pain still twisted her insides cruelly and the fear of it happening again still circled uncomfortably in her mind.

Kay kissed her again, open-mouthed and sensual, her tenderness reassuring Taylor that everything was okay with her now and she should be too. Everything in the room was warm in colour, the soft textures and the faux fur covers making it a comforting safe place to be, freed from everything that had happened before.

Taylor sat back on the new sofa, its luxurious cushions helping her to relax as she stroked the velvety texture.

"I'll get some wine," Kay said, gesturing with her hand to her mouth. "Merlot!"

Taylor sat there for a few minutes as she waited, wondering what Kay was doing and was about to get up and see, when she came through in a lightweight silk dressing gown, loosely tied as the waist. Kay's long lithe legs were visible up to her thighs, the flesh of her breasts cleverly hidden, but her taught nipples revealed deliberately beneath the silky material, her figure breath taking .Taylor sat back down, her eyes fixed on Kay and her natural beauty and wonderfully sculpted body.

Taylor longed to touch her, to love her, as Kay moved towards her slowly, her heart now beating heavily, a little nervous about being touched once again and how she would react.

She came right up to Taylor and stood before her, offering herself to her. She pulled gently on the tie of her gown and it opened enough for Taylor to see her most intimate places.

Taylor sat still staring at her, desire inside overwhelming, as Kay moved closer, her body gently brushing against Taylor's mouth, and then again, tempting, teasing, wanting. Taylor looked up at her, hazel eyes fixed on Kay's as her hands moved up the back of Kay's thighs, stroking gently up and over her bottom, and down again as she pulled Kay gently towards her, her face leaning against her pleasure, her tongue subtly touching her, gently caressing her soft and glistening haven. Kay moaned ever so quietly, the sensation tender and thrilling, her desire to feel it again overwhelming. She moved closer once more to allow Taylor to do it again. This time Kay's slender fingers gripped gently at the back of Taylor's head, the slight touch of Taylor's tongue on her was too much, too sensitive for her to endure. She needed to feel her more physically, the intensity of the pleasure mounting was untenable. She could not fight it any longer. Taylor felt her need and pulled her towards her, her tongue pushing forward and taking her into her mouth, her grip now tight on Kay's bottom. Kay's moans became louder as she let her weight fall forward onto Taylor, her gown slipping off her shoulders as she carefully lifted her leg over Taylor and knelt onto Taylor's knees, a guttural sound of pleasure breaking free as Taylor pushed deep inside her, complementing the pleasures being offered by her tongue. Taylor's face and neck were crimson with desire with the need to make love to Kay. There was something so intense between them, the natural chemistry they shared, the passion and thrill of their love making immense, a sensory overload. Kay's back arched in a cat-like fashion as her hips rose and fell with the pressure from Taylor's mouth and fingers,. She could feel her orgasm building deep inside. Kay's body tensed as she curled up away from Taylor's mouth momentarily, the intensity and sensation almost too much to bare, only to drop back onto her fingers to allow her release, swirling and gripping, pulsing and twisting through her, months of denial finally freed. Kay's head was now in a euphoric state, dizzy with the exhilaration of her physical release. She shuffled down until she was at eye level with Taylor. Smiling deeply, she cupped her face and kissed her intimately.

"I LOVE YOU!" She kissed the words into Taylor's mouth.

Taylor reciprocated the word filled kiss, her voice soft and lusty, her heightened state of pleasure obvious, but her words came from deep within her heart. "I love you too!"

THE END

Book one in the Taylor Nicks and Marcus Black series:

Devil's Demise

A cruel and sinister killer is targeting Edinburgh's most powerful women. His twisted sense of superiority driving him, as he revels in the suffering he inflicts on his victims. A twist of fate, and the overwhelming will of one of his victims to survive, threaten to ruin his reign of terror. His tormented prey will now need all her courage to survive once more, as he focuses on hunting her down.

DS Nicks, a strong, intelligent and striking woman struggles to get a positive lead, while the unlikely monster wreaks havoc on the city. The pressure is mounting on Nicks, both at work and in her eventful private life.

A fast paced, nail biting thriller, that will have you on the edge of your seat. Not for the faint hearted.

Book Two in the Taylor Nicks and Marcus Black series:

Porcelain Flesh of Innocents

Detectives Nicks and Black are back in a brand new investigation trying to track down a sadistic vigilante, who has a penchant for identifying and torturing paedophiles in the City of Edinburgh.

High powered businessmen are being found seriously injured, after suffering at the hands of the perpetrator. One thing they all have in common is the sinister double life they lead.

Exposing their crimes, the hunt for justice in the vigilante's own depraved way, spirals out of control and officers are now hunting for a killer.

Nicks and Black are taken aback at the level of violence and cruel measures used, but when the victims' own deviances are exposed, it becomes even more alarming.

As enquiries continue, Black finds himself at the mercy of the Gods, when he learns first hand just how one single act can change your world. The race is on to stop these brutal crimes and save the most precious thing Black has.

Vivid, dark and deeply unsettling, this is the perfect next read for serious crime thriller fans.

Lee Cockburn is a serving officer with Police Scotland and has been for nearly 19 years. Currently a Sergeant/Acting Inspector working in the centre of Edinburgh, Lee has been on the front line for the majority of her service, with three years in the specialist public order unit, involving drug raids, large scale disorder and serious incidents with high levels of risk and violence.

As a six foot one, ex international rugby player, with 81 Caps for Scotland and the British Lionesses, she feels that her stature and physical ability are ideally suited to helping serve the public and preventing crime.

She has first-hand knowledge of police procedures, cop humour and the importance of teamwork and trust in your colleagues, which helps with her writing.

She is in a civil partnership with Emily, another serving officer and they met when they joined Lothian and Borders Police on the same day. They have two 9-year-old sons and enjoy their time together as a family, when not fighting crime, fighting each other or sleeping.

Lee only started writing in 2009, two weeks before she fell pregnant. Emily gave birth three months later. After the births, writing became a thing of the past, until the boys were two, when Lee picked up Devil's Demise again and finally completed it.

Her reason for writing her first novel was down to reading a dull book, the first ever she chose not to finish. With this, her decision to write one herself was made. She wanted to write books that were fast paced and gripping; crime thrillers that would make your hair stand on end, and books that would be filled with their fair share of passionate love scenes.

Lee herself enjoys a good sense of humour and making others laugh, physical activity/sport and most importantly her family. She is actually a big softy, with a strong sense of what's right and wrong, and good versus evil, whereby evil must be defeated in the end, even if it seems to take a while.

Her novels are based on hard hitting topics, the content graphic and brutal, which leaves very little to the imagination, but they're also filled with the good people that dedicate their lives to fighting against the evil ones that live hidden in plain sight among us.

Lee herself enjoys a good sense of humour and making others laugh, physical activity/sport and most importantly her family. She is actually a big softy, with a strong sense of what's right and wrong, good versus evil, whereby evil must be defeated in the end, even if it seems to take a while.

Her novels are based on hard hitting topics, the content graphic, brutal and leave very little to the imagination, but they're also filled with the good people that dedicate their lives to fighting against the evil ones that live hidden in plain sight among us.